THE HAVE NOT

BETH CROWLEY

THE HAVE NOT.

Copyright © 2024 by Elizabeth Crowley.

All rights reserved.

Printed in the United States of America.

This is a work of fiction. Names, characters, places, and incidents are products of the author's imagination or are used fictitiously and are not to be construed as real. Any resemblance to actual events, locales, organizations, or persons, living or dead, is entirely coincidental.

No part of this book may be used or reproduced in any manner whatsoever without written permission except in the case of brief quotations embodied in critical articles and reviews.

Published by Beth Crowley Music, LLC

Copy/Line Edits by Jennifer Rees

Cover Design by Steffani Christensen

Interior Design by Megan Duke

ISBN 979-8-218-41111-4 (paperback); 9798990850903 (ebook)

Printed in USA

www.bethcrowley.com

PRAISE FOR THE HAVE NOT

"A beautiful story of the things that break our hearts, and the people who put them back together again. With this debut, Beth Crowley proves herself as brilliant an author as she is a songwriter."

— CASEY L. BOND, AUTHOR OF *WHEN WISHES BLEED*

"Crowley's debut novel, *The Have Not*, is a moving YA Romantic Comedy that delivers poignant moments often interjected with humor, which keeps the story from weighing the reader down. It's the perfect balance of laughter and tears. The music added to the book is a wonderfully immersive experience and brought even more depth to the characters. Overall, it's a wonderful read and I eagerly wait to see what more Beth Crowley will write."

— QUINN LOFTIS, AUTHOR OF *THE GRAY WOLVES* SERIES

"Beth Crowley captures a heartfelt and true to life story of being young, being in love, and being unsure of what comes next. Her approach to grief, especially from a teenage perspective, is so real I have no doubt readers of all ages will be able to relate."

— MEG ALIVIEN, AUTHOR OF *OF MAGIC AND MEN*

The Have Not

BETH CROWLEY

For all of my readers who were my listeners first.

A Note From the Author:

As a singer-songwriter, it was important to me to incorporate music into this story. There is a 10-song companion soundtrack to *The Have Not* that is available to stream anywhere you listen to music whenever and however you wish, but you will find specific scenes throughout the book where you'll be directed to listen to a particular song that was specifically written for that moment. To make it easier, I've also included the QR code you can scan with your phone at each of those scenes that will take you to a landing page for the soundtrack. Happy listening!

ONE

"Are you hungry? We can stop and get something if you're hungry," my mother says timidly, attempting to make small talk with me for what feels like the zillionth time. I steadfastly ignore her and continue to scowl out the window of the car whose backseat we're both currently occupying.

"All of the registration paperwork has been submitted for you to start at Winston Academy in the fall," she tries again, changing topics. "Senior year. So exciting!"

Once again, I don't reply. She does not seem to grasp that I'm currently not speaking to her. Giving someone the silent treatment is a lot less gratifying when the person you're trying to give it to doesn't even recognize it's happening.

"It really is the most prestigious school in the area. Anyone who is anyone sends their kids there. And they won state in boys' water polo last year!"

I turn in my seat to shoot her a withering look I hope conveys exactly how much I care about boys' water polo. My mother breaks eye contact first, her gaze falling to the perfectly manicured hands folded in her lap for a moment before saying meekly, "Cam . . . I already told you I didn't know the press would be there."

"Ha," I bark a humorless laugh. "I'm sure, Mother."

"I didn't!" she repeats earnestly, looking back over at me with eyes the exact same shade of hazel as mine. "I only told a few people I was going to the service. I wasn't even sure that I'd be able to make it until the day before."

"And you getting on the front page of *E!Online* is just a happy coincidence, right?" I say bitterly. "*'Jackie Jenson Mourns Father of Her Teenage Daughter.'* I'm sure you were thrilled to see they put the photo of you looking like Funeral Barbie right next to this week's *Bachelor* contestant elimination interview."

"That's a terrible thing to say," my mother whispers.

I hadn't been aware there were paparazzi lurking around the cemetery during my father's memorial service until the next day when one of my friends texted after seeing the photos online. Despite being so angry I could barely form a complete sentence, I called my mother, incoherently screaming accusations that she used the funeral as another publicity grab. She vehemently denied it, saying her agent, Vic, must have mentioned it offhand to someone and the information was leaked. But she's done some pretty questionable things throughout the years trying to stay relevant, so I wouldn't put it past her to have tipped them off herself.

"Please believe me," my mother pleads now.

It never ceases to amaze me how I can be related to someone I relate so little to, even down to the way we're sitting: me, hugging one knee to my chest, my Doc Marten making a slight indentation on the leather of the car seat, her with one Jimmy Choo-adorned foot tucked behind the other at the ankle, not a single strand of blonde hair out of place.

After a moment, I shake my head a little, too tired to keep pressing the issue, and look back out the window, mumbling, "Whatever you say."

As we pull up to the entrance of my mother's beautiful hillside mansion and the gate slowly glides open, I feel a dull panic set in.

It's not like I haven't been here plenty of times before. The custody agreement between my parents required me to spend three weeks out of the summer with my mother, plus every other Christmas and Thanksgiving. But this time is different. This time is permanent.

The driver, a mustached man who looks to be in his seventies and who I realize too late must think I'm a total brat, gets out of the car to open the door on my mother's side first. She demurely slides out of her seat, smoothing down her figure-hugging pink dress. I take several deep, calming breaths as I wait for him to come around to my side. I found out a long time ago that car service drivers get cranky when you try to explain how you're an able-bodied female in the 21st Century and can open your own damn doors. By the time he reaches me, I've composed myself enough to say a breathless "thank you" before grabbing my backpack and following my mother into the house.

The click of her heels echoes as she leads me up the imperial staircase and down the hallway to the right, past my older brother Charlie's bedroom, his design studio, the billiards room, and the music room. I'm only half-listening as she prattles on about how she hired some designer who has a show on HGTV to redecorate my room, though I occasionally catch phrases like "combining classic and post-modern" and "elevated yet refined." When we finally reach my bedroom, she pauses at the closed door and turns around.

"Oooh, I can't wait for you to see it!" she purrs. She opens the door and gestures for me to follow her in. The layout of the space is the same as it's always been: a large room with a cathedral ceiling, a bed to one side, and a sitting area with a TV on the other. Giant bay windows look out onto Los Angeles, with a door in the middle leading to a balcony.

But instead of the fairly minimalistic decor I've always had since I never bothered putting much effort into a space I only occupied for a few weeks each year, now the room looks like something off of a sorority girl's Pinterest page. It has a rose gold and navy color scheme with a bed frame, dressers, and coffee table all made from the same distressed wood. My mother even had a fireplace installed, which seems ridiculous considering it never even gets that cold here. A bookshelf by the TV holds assorted knick-knacks, like an old ice skate with a dried hydrangea stem coming out of it (what?) and a white bust of an eagle (why?).

It is tasteful.

It is beautiful.

It is not me at all.

"Do you like it?" my mother says, looking satisfied.

"*What am I doing here?!*" I want to scream. "*Why couldn't you just let me go live with Aunt Margaret in Georgia like I wanted?*"

Instead, I force a smile.

"It's . . . lovely." I say, trying to ignore the pang of longing for the coziness of the tiny bedroom back in Arizona that isn't mine anymore.

Listen to Track One: "Trying"

I spend the next few hours unpacking boxes filled with all of my earthly possessions that two stoned-looking guys from the moving company brought up to my room. I'm just opening one of my many boxes of books when there's a soft knock on my door.

"Come in," I say, and the door cracks open a few inches, revealing my mother's face.

"I just figured I would let you know Jim got here," she says, opening the door wider to reveal my Great Dane standing beside her. I hadn't realized how badly I needed to see him until this moment.

Jim bounds over to where I'm sitting on the floor, nearly knocking me over as he tries to lick my face. He's been at a boarding facility for the last few weeks while the funeral arrangements were made and the house packed up, and they were nice enough to find us a pet transport service that could get him to L.A.

"Hey, pal!" I coo, taking care to avoid his tail, which swishes back and forth like a whip. I can feel tears prickling in the back of my eyes, but I fight them. "It's good to see you."

Jim starts walking around to explore the room, and I turn back to my mother. She's smiling at me.

"Was there something else you wanted?" I ask.

Her smile falters a bit.

"Oh," she says. "No, that was it. Unless you want something to eat now? Because if you do, I can make something up for you."

"No," I say hurriedly. "I'm pretty tired. I think I'm just going to watch some TV and go to bed."

"Okay," my mother says. I turn back around to Jim and hear her shut the door behind me. After petting him long enough to feel like I've made up for the time we've been apart, I collapse onto my new bed. It pains me to admit it, but it's the softest comforter I've ever felt in my life. Like getting hugged by a pile of baby bunnies made of clouds. I watch the blades of the ceiling fan above me rotate for a few minutes, feeling sorry for myself.

This time last year, I was just a sixteen-year-old girl living a pretty simple life with my dad in Preston, Arizona, and successfully avoiding drawing attention to the fact I have a famous mother. Because my mother is not famous for something awesome, like being an Olympic athlete or world-renowned humanitarian. Oh, no. I have the unique misfortune of being the daughter of someone who millions of people have seen have sex.

When my mother was twenty-two, she started dating a hotshot NFL quarterback. Just a few months later, a tape of the two of them in bed together was leaked to the public. He said the original VHS tape (because this was before smartphones) was stolen from his house, but my mother has always suspected he released it himself to fund the gambling addiction that caused them to break up shortly after the tape got out. But thanks to him being the highest-paid football player in the league at the time and her being a pretty young blonde, my mother went from bartender to socialite almost overnight.

More than twenty years later, she has still managed to keep herself anywhere from B-List to D-List status depending on what online publication you believe, having made a career out of creating and promoting everything from a fragrance collection to workout videos to a line of fur coats for dogs. That last one really backfired on her, though. There might not be anything sadder than seeing a group of PETA protesters throw a tiny cup of red paint on a chihuahua in a mink stole.

"Oh, Jim." I slide off the bed and onto the floor, clutching my knees to my chest. Jim stops studiously licking his own genitals and peers at me with droopy eyes. "What am I supposed to do now?"

He rests his head on his leg and continues to gaze at me. I look back at him thoughtfully.

"You have to poop, don't you?"

He instantly perks up and starts wagging his tail.

"Should have figured," I mutter, standing up. "Let's go outside."

I find Jim's leash in a box of his food and toys sitting outside of my room and take him downstairs and out the back door to the terrace. I navigate down the stucco stairs and around the pool and hot tub, which are glowing blue thanks to the sophisticated lighting system my mother had installed a few summers ago. The sun is just starting to disappear behind the outline of the stunning view of Beverly Hills the house has from where it's tucked into the side of a hill. I stand looking at it for another moment then start walking Jim around the yard.

"I wouldn't if I were you," a sing-song voice says from somewhere behind me. I whirl around to find that Charlie has emerged from the house, donning bright pink swim trunks and a towel draped around his neck. "Mom just had fresh Bermuda sod put down last week."

I roll my eyes at him.

"It's grass, Charlie," I say just as Jim finds the perfect spot. "And poop is biodegradable. Also, I have bags."

"Why is he staring at me?" Charlie says, squinting at Jim. "Doesn't he know making direct eye contact with someone while defecating makes them uncomfortable?"

"I'm sure he just wants you to feel included."

I clean up after Jim, and when I return from throwing the bag away, Charlie is just stepping into the hot tub.

"Hey, half-brother," I greet him.

"Hey, half-sister," he says, grinning back at me.

Despite coming from two completely different upbringings, Charlie and I have actually become pretty close over the years. When he was ten and I was seven, he moved to Los Angeles to live with our mother. He had just finished the fifth grade at a private boarding school in Vermont at his dad's insistence but was completely miserable, so after a lot of begging and pleading, his father let him move out to Beverly Hills.

Now twenty, Charlie has already started making a name for himself in the fashion industry. Personally, I would never be caught dead in most of the things I've seen him come up with. Then again, I doubt my standard uniform of t-shirts and jeans is going to put me on a best dressed list any time soon.

"So, Chamomile," he says, settling into the water. I glare at him. He never misses a chance to use my full first name, probably because he knows how much I hate it. My mother had me in her brief granola, tree-hugging hippie phase and, according to my father, was completely unyielding about her choice for my name: Chamomile Namaste Donovan. The compromise was calling me "Cam" for short. By contrast, Charlie was named after his father, an old-money New England lawyer my mother dated for a few years while living in New York City before they broke up and she moved to L.A., so he got to be Charles Thomas Cabot III. "I'm guessing you saw Mom's little room makeover project."

"Yeah," I grumble, kicking off my boots and socks and rolling up my jeans so I can dip my feet in the water. Jim plops down a few feet away, happily chewing on a stick that somehow infiltrated the precious Bermuda sod. "Thanks a lot for the heads-up."

"I tried to tell her it wasn't what you would want," he says, leaning his head back and closing his eyes. "But she meant well."

"That almost makes it worse."

"She really is trying."

"Not sure why she decided to start now," I mutter before I can stop myself.

Charlie opens his eyes, studying me for a second with a serious expression.

"How are you?"

I almost flinch at the sympathy in his voice.

"I sure wish people would stop asking me that," I say, trying to keep my tone light. Maybe it's just my dark sense of humor, but it's genuinely hilarious to me how many times in the last few months people have asked me that question when the answer should be glaringly obvious.

"I know I suck at this," he replies. "I have no idea what to even say to you. I'm sorry I had to leave right after the funeral service. I had a deadline I had to meet and—"

"Please," I hold up a hand to stop him. "It's really okay. It just means a lot that you came all the way to be there."

"I wouldn't have missed it. I liked your dad a lot."

Charlie and Dad really only ever saw each other in passing when he was dropping me off in L.A. until a few years ago. One of the first things Charlie did when he got his driver's license was make a trip to Preston for a long weekend. It must have been strange on some level for Dad, what with Charlie being his ex's kid with another guy. But if it was weird for him, Dad never showed it. He packed the itinerary, and by the end of the weekend I'm pretty sure Charlie was ready to ask Dad to adopt him.

"He liked you, too," I say quietly, eager to change the subject. I quickly learned that successfully avoiding having to talk about your feelings when your parent dies requires a certain artistry, and I've become the Van Gogh of the redirect. "So tell me, where does one go to hang out in this two-bit town?"

"Well, that depends," Charlie says with a wicked grin. "What kind of scene are you into?"

"Scene?" I scoff. "I'd say the kind of scene where people don't use the word 'scene.'"

"Fair enough," he says. "I'd say just get to know the neighborhood around here first. Then *'I can show you the world, shining, shimmering—'*"

"Okay, Aladdin," I cut him off before he can bust out a full musical number on me. Standing up, I collect my shoes and socks and pull Jim away from the stick he's been annihilating. "I'm beat. I think I'm going to call it a night."

"Let me know if you need anything," Charlie says. "I'm just down the hall."

. . .

By the time I wash my face, brush my teeth, and put on the extra-large sweatpants and t-shirt I sleep in, Jim has already settled into the oversized chair in the corner and is snoring loudly.

"Well, someone sure knows how to adjust quickly," I mumble. I walk around, lazily picking up and examining different decorative items that sit on various shelves around the room. A fake succulent. A miniature globe. Despite knowing this is my room, I keep expecting someone to jump out and tell me I'm not supposed to touch anything.

I come to a giant painting hanging on the wall next to my bed and study it. I'm sure my mother paid an absurd amount of money to some emerging artist making a huge splash in the art scene around Beverly Hills for it, but I hate modern art and always have.

And I swear, it's just a tan canvas with a single purple line going through it.

I tilt my head to the left and squint. Yep. Still just a purple line. All of the pretentious students in every art class I've ever taken would tell me I'm too closed-minded and pedestrian to really "get it," but I still think the thing is absurd. I guess I'm just a post-impressionism girl living in an abstract expressionism world.

It takes about three seconds for me to unhook the frame from the wall and replace it with a giant signed poster of one of my favorite fantasy author's book covers. A few years ago, Dad surprised me by driving us both to Salt Lake City where she was having a signing for the release of her final installment in the series. He even let me skip school since it was on a Tuesday. We drove all day to make it to the event, got a cheap hotel room for the night, and drove back the next morning. We were completely exhausted, but he still took me straight to the frame shop afterward. It's still one of my favorite possessions.

I step back to admire my handiwork. I'm right at eye level with the heroine of the story, who is looking fierce and wielding a saber in one hand and a whip in the other. Now *this* is art.

After settling into bed, I glance around. A remote control sits on the bedside table, so naturally I decide to fiddle around with it to see what it does. I press a green button and nearly shriek as what I thought was just a wooden storage bench at the foot of my bed opens up and a second TV rises out of it. I gawk as it comes to a stop at the perfect viewing height. Dad never let me have one TV in my room, let alone two.

Putting on a rerun of *The Office*, I burrow under the covers and fall asleep within minutes.

Two

Just like every morning since my dad died, there's a moment right before I open my eyes when I'm still half-asleep where I forget he's gone. As he got sicker, I woke up less and less often to the smell of him cooking bacon or him coming in my room belting one of his favorite 90s rock songs off-key. Instead, I would wake up to my alarm telling me it was time to drive him to one of his chemo treatments, or him shouting at me to get up for school using the bullhorn I got him as a joke when he wasn't able to get out of bed easily anymore.

Now, having to realize he isn't here anymore—every single day—almost feels like him dying all over again. As I clutch my chest and wait for my heartbeat to return to its normal rhythm, I wonder dejectedly how long this will last.

Trying to shake off the thought, I take a robe from my closet and open the door to go scrounge up some breakfast. I'm met with a tray sitting outside my room containing fresh fruit, a basket of pastries, a plate of bacon, and orange juice. I bend down to pick up a little note that has my name written on it in loopy handwriting. It's from my mother.

Cam,

I had to leave early this morning for a meeting in the valley. See you tonight!

Love,

Mom

I bring the tray out onto the balcony and examine its contents. Upon closer

inspection, something looks off about the bacon and pastries, but I can't quite put my finger on it. I tentatively break off a piece of bacon and pop it into my mouth.

"Uggh!" I exclaim, spitting it back out onto the plate. I look at the pastries suspiciously.

"I'm counting on you," I tell them somberly. I sample a piece of what looks like toast. Not terrible, but it definitely still tastes odd. Seizing up the tray, I march down the hall to Charlie's room. After a minute or so of me knocking (then banging) on the door, he opens it looking sleepy.

"What's up?" he asks, rubbing his eyes underneath his clear frame glasses. I thrust the offending breakfast tray at him.

"What in the name of our lord and savior Dolly Parton is this?"

"Is that a trick question?" he says through a yawn. "Because it looks like breakfast to me."

"But it tastes funny," I whine. He blinks at me for a second, then smirks.

"Don't tell me you've never had vegan bacon."

"Vegan . . . oh no," I protest. "No-no-no-no-NO. Bacon comes from pigs! You don't just get to be made of tofu or whatever and still call yourself bacon."

"I'm guessing you feel similarly about gluten-free breads?"

"Haven't I been through enough?" I plead to no one in particular.

"Well," Charlie says, taking the tray from me. "I happen to like vegan bacon, so your loss."

"Dibs on the fruit and O.J.," I reply, trailing behind him into his room. "I'm not going to starve and let that imposter that calls itself bacon win."

After a heated debate over the benefits and drawbacks of various health foods while we eat, I'm confident a breakfast consisting of a few pieces of cantaloupe is not going to do it for me. Charlie gives me the name of a diner nearby he describes as "quaint but kind of basic, just like you," so I take a shower and throw on a t-shirt, jeans, and Vans. I pull my wet hair into a bun on top of my head, grab my backpack, and start downstairs.

"I went ahead and called the car for you," Charlie says as I walk by his studio. I pause at the door to find him bent over a sketch table, still in his pajamas.

"I thought you said it was right down the road. I can't just like, bike it or something?"

"Um, hi," he says sarcastically. "It hasn't been that long since you've been here. Do you not remember how miserable that hill is?"

"Fair point," I concede.

I'm sitting on the front steps scrolling through Instagram when my phone begins blaring.

"Shit!" I yelp, jumping at the sudden noise and dropping it on the ground. I scramble to pick it up when I notice I accidentally already accepted the call.

"Well, that's no way to greet someone," my best friend, Annie, is saying on the other end of the line as I hold the phone up to my face. "Or is that a thing we're doing now? Just swearing instead of saying hello?"

"Har-har," I say sarcastically.

I hear the clink of what sounds like dishes from the other end of the line. Annie is probably in the middle of baking something. She's somewhat of a prodigy when it comes to making pies, cookies, and any other type of confection one could possibly imagine. I can almost picture her in the "Don't Mess with the Chef" apron I got her a few Christmases ago, powdered sugar dusting her red hair.

"So what's up?" I ask, watching a ladybug crawl up the stair railing. "You realize you calling me goes against everything our generation stands for, right? Actually talking on the phone? So passé."

"I just miss you already," Annie says ruefully. "Jenny Wise's birthday party is tonight. Who am I going to go with so we can make fun of all of the idiots at our school?"

The gates begin to open, and a black sedan slowly pulls through. It makes its way around the circular driveway with a giant fountain statue of Poseidon in its center—(my mother picked it out because she said the "detailing on his abs is fabulous")—and comes to a stop next to me.

"You can just Snapchat me all of the highlights," I suggest as the driver comes around the car to open my door and I slide into the backseat.

"Not the same," Annie says dolefully. A small crash sounds in the background.

"Whatcha making?" I ask, feeling my mouth water before I even hear the answer. After the bacon debacle this morning, I'm happy to vicariously live through my friend's carb-filled baking.

"I'm trying out a new apple crumble recipe," she replies. "I got the best Granny Smiths from the farmer's market this morning."

"It sounds amazing." I can hear the longing in my own voice.

"Oh, it will be," she says smugly.

"Where to?" The driver's voice interrupts the apple dessert

fantasies that have just started forming in my head. I cover the mouthpiece on my phone.

"Joe's Diner, please," I tell him. He nods and starts back toward the gate.

"Your mom is going to shit a brick when she finds out you pretty much live on pizza," Annie laughs.

"Not necessarily a brick," I muse. "A one-of-a-kind Italian vase, maybe."

I hear a shuffling noise on the other end of the phone.

"Oven's preheated!" Annie chirps. "I'm going to need two hands for this."

"Sure," I say, feeling disappointed at the conversation being cut short. "Next time, text me like a normal socially-stunted person our age, will ya?"

"Never! Bye!"

I look down at the phone, blinking back tears. I have *got* to get it together.

"Ms. Donovan, correct?" the driver asks, peering at me in his rearview mirror. I recognize him as the same driver who brought us home from the airport yesterday.

"You can just call me Cam," I reply, feeling bad that I was having such a rager of a self-pity party yesterday that I barely said two words to him.

"I'm Leo. I've been driving Ms. Jenson and Mr. Cabot for almost a year now." When he grins at me, there's something about the crinkle around his eyes that is calming, reminding me of my own grandfather. "It's nice to officially meet you, Cam."

"It's nice to meet you, too." I offer a small smile in return. "Are you from around here?"

"Lived here all my life," Leo answers. "Started out as a camera operator on film sets."

"That sounds awesome," I say, picking at a frayed spot at the bottom of my t-shirt.

"It was for a while, but the schedule just got to be too grueling.

I've been out of the game for sixteen years now and haven't regretted a single day." Leo continues chatting amiably until we arrive at a small stand-alone building with a giant sign that reads Joe's.

"This is your stop."

"So, uh, how does this work?" I ask as Leo opens my door. "What do I do when I'm ready to leave?"

"Here's my number," Leo says, pulling a card out of his coat pocket. "I'll be nearby. You can just text me."

"Okay, thanks," I reply awkwardly. I put my backpack on my shoulders and walk into the diner. A sign says to seat myself, so I find a little table in the corner and pluck one of the folded paper menus out from where it's sitting behind the salt and pepper shakers.

"Hey," a voice above me says. I look up to see a boy who appears to be a few years older than me holding a notepad and pencil. He has messy black hair and is donning a Red Hot Chili Peppers t-shirt and navy blue apron over tattered jeans. "I'm Milo. I'll be taking care of you today. What can I get started for you?"

I glance back down at the menu.

"A root beer and a stack of chocolate chip pancakes."

"Did you want the regular or gluten-free pancakes?"

"Oh, for the love of—" I huff. "Regular. In fact, if anything, I want my pancakes extra gluten-y."

"Don't think that's a thing, but I'll see what I can do," he says as he scribbles down my order. "That's it?"

"Better add an order of bacon."

"Got it," he says, making the additional note. "You're easy."

"That's what all the bathroom stalls say," I deadpan.

Milo freezes, mouth quirking up at the side, though he doesn't look up from his notepad. Still, for some reason just getting that little smile out of him is incredibly gratifying.

"Alright then," he says, turning around to head back to the server's station.

I look around the diner. The place has a cozy soda shop atmosphere but with modern touches. There's a long counter that runs the length of the restaurant with red stools, but the walls are all brick and Edison bulbs hang from the ceiling, giving off a soft glow.

A few minutes later, Milo comes back with a tall soda glass in hand. He sets it down and folds his arms, sizing me up with narrowed green eyes. I look back at him expectantly.

"I told the chef you wanted extra gluten in your pancakes."

"Sweet."

"He just stared at me."

"I see."

"He told me to stop being a smartass and get back to work."

"He is clearly lacking a sense of humor."

"Syrup?"

"Huh?" I say stupidly.

"Do you want syrup for your pancakes?" he replies, over-enunciating every word.

"What kind of question is that?"

"An interrogative one."

"Of course I want syrup for my pancakes," I scoff, rolling my eyes as I unfold my silverware and place the napkin on my lap. "I'm not a heathen."

Milo laughs, and it is such a nice sound that I instantly find myself trying to figure out how I can make him do it again.

"Yes, ma'am," he says, giving me a dramatic bow before walking away.

I settle back into my chair, put in my headphones, and scroll through Spotify until I find the Red Hot Chili Peppers.

As I watch the hustle and bustle of the diner, I can't help but think how much my dad would like the vibe of this place. He was always looking up new hole-in-the-wall restaurants for us to try, insistent that the shabbier the spot, the better the food would be. I grin a little to myself, imagining the tirade he would have launched into if he found out there was such a thing as vegan bacon.

My mother and father met when she got a flat tire as she was passing through Preston on her way to a wellness retreat, back when she actually drove herself and didn't hire private planes or car services to travel everywhere. She didn't know how to change a tire, so she called the nearest auto repair shop, which happened to be owned by my dad. She never did make it to the retreat. Somehow, she hit it off with my gruff father, and they wound up talking for hours. He had no idea who she was, though she was pretty recognizable at the time. Even when she revealed her past, my dad was undeterred.

As a result of their whirlwind romance, my mother got pregnant with me within the first two months of her and dad dating. Charlie was only three but was still primarily living in Connecticut, so she was free to travel back and forth between Los Angeles and Preston. But something changed when I was born, though my father insisted I had nothing to do with the end of their relationship. I think he asked her to move to Preston permanently and she refused, but I've never known that for sure. Either way, she went back to Los Angeles for good when I was two months old and gave my dad full custody with the agreement I visited in the summers and alternating holidays.

There were a lot of trips where I ended up spending more time with a babysitter or Charlie than with my mother because of how demanding her work schedule could be. But as a kid, it was hard for me to understand how stuff like red carpet events or TV show tapings could be "work" rather than fun things that she preferred doing instead of being with me. The older I got, the more I came to realize it really was her version of working. Regardless, I always preferred the privacy and quiet steadiness of living under the radar with my dad, helping out at the shop after school and having a predictable but comfortable life.

A plate of pancakes materializes in front of me. I look up to see Milo's mouth moving, though I can't hear what he's saying over "Under the Bridge" playing through my earbuds. I quickly pull them out of my ears and fumble to pause the song, though not before Milo glances down at my phone and sees what was playing.

He smirks. I blush.

"Great taste in music," he says lightly.

"I know." I avoid his eyes as I snag the container of syrup he set down next to the plate and start pouring liberally.

"Mmm-hmm," he replies. "Is there anything else I can get you right now?"

Just my pride back.

"Not a thing," I say. I watch him walk back to the kitchen as I vigorously cut my pancakes into little pieces. It's not that I have ever been especially smooth with the opposite sex, but this is such an amateur mistake. Note to self: stalkerishly look up the things a boy is interested in when you *aren't* in the same room with him and he can catch you red-handed.

I practically inhale my pancakes and am starting in on the bacon by the time Milo comes back to check on me a few minutes later.

"Damn," he says, eyebrows raised.

"What?" I say defensively, shrugging one shoulder. "I was hungry and they were good."

"It was probably the extra gluten," Milo observes.

"Obviously."

"Do you want anything else?"

"If I say 'no' does that mean you'll do that thing where the servers bring the check and say 'I'm just going to leave this here, but it's no hurry at all' but it's really their super passive-aggressive way of telling you to get the hell out?"

We stare at each other for a moment.

"No, I don't want anything else," I finally say. He doesn't move. "Dude, it's fine. You can leave the check."

"What's your name?" he asks, giving me an assessing look. My stomach gives a little flip, and I'm pretty sure it isn't only because I just bodied an entire stack of pancakes.

"Cam."

"Well, Cam," he says, ripping off the ticket from his notepad and setting it on the table next to me. "Will I be seeing you around here again?"

"That depends," I say, rifling through my backpack and pulling out the wad of cash my dad always insisted I keep with me because he hated credit cards. "How good are your waffles?"

"Oh, they're good," he confirms. "Best in town."

"Then you will definitely be seeing me again," I reply, unfolding enough bills to cover the check and a pretty generous tip and throwing it on top of the ticket. I stand up, stretch, and toss my backpack over my shoulder. "Bye."

He gives me a little nod as I walk out the door and into the parking lot. I text Leo that I'm all set to go home and find a bench nearby to wait on.

"How was breakfast?" Leo asks me a few minutes later as he pulls out of the parking lot.

"I think that place might be a new favorite."

THREE

I go back to Joe's the next morning, mostly because I need to get out of the house. My mother made multiple attempts to spend time with me yesterday afternoon and evening, but I'm just not ready.

The day my dad broke the news to me that I would be coming here, he had just gone into hospice care. I was sitting in the recliner we had set up for me next to his bed and we were working a cross-word puzzle together when out of nowhere he said, "I need to talk to you about something, kiddo."

I peered up from where I had just filled in twenty-six across, and something about the way he was looking at me made me set my pencil down.

"Your mother and I discussed it," he continued. "And we've both agreed that you'll go live with her until you graduate next year."

"Wh-what?" I stuttered, completely taken aback. "But . . . Dad, no. I thought I was going to live with Aunt Margaret. You know how I feel about L.A.—"

"Listen, Cam," my dad cut me off, his voice gentle but firm.

"This isn't up for debate. Legally speaking, your mother becomes your guardian if something happens to me—"

"You can change that!" I protested shrilly, feeling the blood start to rush to my head. "I mean, you can, right? Just sign me over to Aunt Margaret instead."

"It doesn't really work like that," my dad said patiently, a smile playing on his cracked lips. "You aren't the title to a car."

"She's making you do this, isn't she?" I accused through angry tears.

"No," he replied simply. "I know you and your mother have never been close, and I'm partly to blame for that. I should have encouraged it more. But you have one more year until you are out on your own, and I think it will be good for you to spend it with her."

I wanted to scream and cry and argue until he backed down, but looking into his gaunt face, so different from the robust, scruffy one I had known all my life, I made a decision. I knew how little time he had left, and I wasn't going to waste a second of it fighting with him.

"Okay," I said quietly, shoving all of that anger and bitterness down as deep as I could. And that was that. We went back to our crossword puzzle and never brought it up again.

"You look surly today," Milo observes as he brings me the root beer, blueberry muffin, and side of bacon I ordered.

"Well, aren't you just the sweet talker," I say grumpily, breaking my muffin into halves. "For your information, my mother tried to get me to go do a face peel with her this morning. Have you ever heard of anything more horrifying than the idea of paying someone money to remove a layer of your face as if you're in *Poltergeist*?"

"It definitely sounds unap-PEEL-ing," he says with a straight face.

"I can't believe you just did that." I shake my head and grab a piece of bacon.

"So I guess you two don't really get along?" he says, twirling a straw in his fingers.

"Me and my face? It's kind of a love-hate situation. We have our good days, we have our bad days—"

"Oh my god," Milo interrupts, looking exasperated. "You and your *mom*."

I consider how to answer this for a moment before saying, "Honestly? Same answer."

He waits for me to say more, and I have an internal debate about much I should tell him. Finally, for reasons I myself don't even fully understand, I decide to say screw it.

"Have you heard of Jackie Jenson?"

"Like the Jackie Jenson from the celebrity dancing show?" Milo asks.

"Among other things, yes. That would be the one. She's my mother. I moved here because my dad died, and now I have to live with her even though we barely know each other and have absolutely nothing in common. Boom."

"Boom?"

"Boom. As in short for 'kaboom.'"

"Why kaboom?" Milo looks at me inquisitively.

"That's some heavy shit right there," I explain. "'Kaboom' seemed appropriate."

"I'm sorry—" he starts.

"Please don't." I wave a hand at him. "People keep saying that as if they were the ones who gave my dad cancer."

Milo glances at a nearby table where a couple just sat down. "I need to go get their drink order." He looks back at me hesitantly. "Are you good?"

"If you're asking me because you're afraid that when you walk away I'm going to have an emotional breakdown in the middle of this restaurant, don't worry," I say reassuringly. "I promise I'm a quiet crier and the napkins are well-stocked and seem fairly absorbent, so I'll be able to clean up after myself."

Seeing the wide-eyed, vaguely panicked look on Milo's face, I quickly say, "I'm kidding. Go make those dolla dolla bills."

"You are kind of exhausting," Milo says, though he is smiling.

"That's me. Surly and exhausting."

"You met a boy?" Charlie exclaims that evening as we're taking a break from binge-watching a show on Netflix.

"You just came dangerously close to squealing," I say, examining my split ends. "It wasn't that big of a deal."

"Except that it is!" he replies. "You've been here all of, what, two days?"

I roll my eyes. "It was just a few conversations. Were they starting to stray into flirtation territory? Maybe. But I'm . . . I don't even know what I am right now. Definitely not trying to add anything else complicated to my life, that's for sure."

When I don't meet Charlie's eyes, he says in a lighter tone, "Ugh, do you have any idea how hard it is to find a nice guy in this town? I should know. I've been trying to for years."

"Wait, so what happened to Patrick?" I ask, eager to shift the focus off of myself. Charlie had been dating a personal trainer named Patrick for a while in the spring, but I realize now I haven't seen any trace of him on Charlie's social media accounts lately.

"Oh, Patrick," Charlie frowns. "Things went very south with Patrick, and not in the fun way."

"Okay, gross," I say, scrunching my nose.

"Hey, what are you up to tonight? A friend of mine is having a party out in the valley. You should come."

"I don't know, Charlie . . ."

"Oh, come on," he needles. "It's your first Saturday night here. What else are you going to do?"

I start to protest again, but then mull over the prospect of a night in this giant house alone, or worse, with my mother.

"Fine," I relent.

"Yay!" Charlie claps his hands together. "What are you going to wear?"

I look pointedly down at my t-shirt and jeans.

"No, no, no," Charlie protests, looking affronted. "You can't go to your first L.A. party in that."

"I'm certainly not going out in public in some skintight dress you would put me in," I argue.

"I'm sure we can find some middle ground," Charlie says with a mischievous grin.

Half an hour later, Charlie and I are in my bedroom standing in front of the full-length mirror. After a few moments, I break the silence.

"I have to say, Charlie, I've read a lot of Young Adult novels where the girl gets a makeover and that's all it takes to bring out the beauty and confidence that was within her all along."

Charlie nods, not taking his eyes off of my reflection in the mirror.

"This is not one of those moments," I conclude.

I indulged Charlie when he dragged me to a closet where he keeps samples of designs he's pitching to stores. In theory, the orange romper with wide leg pants he held up for me to try on didn't look so terrible. But with it on, I look like a deranged but highly fashionable pumpkin from the 1970s.

"Yeah, it's terrible," Charlie agrees.

"Well, don't spare my feelings or anything," I sulk.

"Back to the drawing board," he says, whisking me away to his collection of clothes.

We land on a simple black babydoll dress with cap sleeves and fishnet tights. I put on my black combat boots, even though they don't quite go with the vibe of the dress. But when badasses are heading straight into battle, badasses don't wear ballet flats. They wear combat boots.

"All black?" Charlie laments when I emerge from the bathroom. "I was hoping you would do a heel or a statement necklace to add a pop of color."

"There is no way I'm wearing heels," I say matter-of-factly. "Plus, I'm in mourning, remember? My dad just died."

Charlie looks mortified. "Cam, I am SO sorry—"

"I'm just messing with you," I say quickly. "But I'm also not changing my shoes."

Rather than calling Leo, Charlie opts to drive us out to the party. As he whips us around a tight turn in his fancy little sports car, I say through clenched teeth, "Dear God, Char. This car is way too expensive for you to be driving like such a maniac."

"Oh, don't be so squeamish," he says, though he does slow down enough that I'm able to stop fearing for my life for a few minutes.

We eventually pull up to a white stucco house where cars are already lining the street in either direction. As we park and get out, I can hear people laughing and what sounds like a live band coming from the back. The panic must be showing on my face because Charlie puts his arm around me, steering me to a gate in the fence leading into the backyard.

"This will be fun," he promises me.

"Who are these people again?" I ask, an edge creeping into my voice.

"Some friends from design school," Charlie says as he pulls the gate open. "They are a hoot and a half."

"'Hoot and a half?'" I echo, trailing along behind him. "Who even says that?"

What we walk into is unlike any party I've ever seen. Granted, back in Preston most of my friends and I opted to spend hours playing Cards Against Humanity or Catan rather than go to the parties the football players and cheerleaders threw when their parents weren't home, and they could bribe an older sibling to buy them a keg of beer. Though the few times I found myself at one of those parties, it was child's play compared to this.

Strands of lights are hanging everywhere, creating a bright halo above a giant pool in the middle of the yard. A stage has been set up to the side, where a band is playing to a flock of people bobbing up and down in the water, holding solo cups and plastic wine glasses in the air. A crowded makeshift bar adorns the other side of the yard, where several dozen more people are gathered around high-top tables.

"Do you want anything?" Charlie shouts over the noise.

"Water!"

"Still or sparkling?"

I just look at him.

"Whatever," he says. "I'll be right back!"

I watch Charlie make his way to the bar, then look around for a corner I can duck into. I take a deep breath and lean back against the fence, feeling slightly stupid for letting Charlie talk me into this. I hate crowded places.

A few minutes later I see a hand above the crowd holding up a bottle of water coming my direction.

"Just so you know," Charlie shouts in my ear when he reaches me. "I'm not having anything to drink tonight."

"How saintly of you," I say back. "Considering that you are the one who convinced me to come and also drove me here."

Charlie rolls his eyes. I watch him scan the party and wave at a group of people standing near the stage.

"Come on," he says, taking my hand. "I want to introduce you to some of my friends."

We duck and dodge our way over to where Charlie's friends are standing. Thankfully, the band has taken a set break, and we can actually hear each other over the house music that now plays.

A pretty girl with dozens of rows of braids cascading down her back smiles at me and extends a hand.

"Alexis," she says. "You must be Cam."

"That's me," I confirm, shaking her hand.

"I'm Ivan." A tall blond guy gives me a little wave.

"Jeremy," the other guy with shortly-cropped black hair says, lifting his glass up with one tattooed arm and nodding at me.

"It's nice to meet you all," I say, attempting a smile.

"How are you liking L.A. so far?" Alexis asks kindly.

"It's, uh, definitely different than what I'm used to," I tell her. "I haven't spent a lot of time here before now—mostly just a few weeks each summer."

"I know it can be overwhelming, but you'll get used to it," Alexis says soothingly, and I feel myself relax a little.

"I'm starting to think you're stalking me," a familiar voice says behind me. I whirl around to find Milo standing next to me, hands in his jeans pockets. He's got on a t-shirt with a sloth wearing headphones that says "The Vibes Are Impeccable" and black Converse sneakers, his black hair looking as ruffled as ever.

"What are you doing here?" I ask, feeling my pulse quicken a little.

"My band is playing."

"You're in the band?" I can't help but be impressed.

"Yeah, The Discount Curses," he affirms. "I play keys."

"My, aren't you fancy?"

"The fanciest," Milo grins at me.

"I don't believe we've met." Charlie materializes next to me. "But I just know Cam was about to introduce us."

"Of course," I say. "Milo, this is my brother Charlie. Charlie, this is Milo. He works at Joe's Diner."

"*The* Milo?" Charlie blurts. I elbow him in the ribs.

"I didn't know I was *the* Milo," Milo says, the light from the pool making his green eyes dance as he looks at me. "What are my powers and privileges?"

"Babe, I'm thirsty," says a whiny, high-pitched voice. A

gorgeous blonde girl in a short mini-skirt and crop top sidles up next to Milo. She trains her gaze on me and narrows her eyes.

"I was just heading to the bar," Milo assures her. "Leighton, this is Cam. She's been to the diner a few times. Cam, this is my girlfriend, Leighton."

"Hi," Leighton says in a dismissive tone, giving me an assessing look before turning her attention back to Milo and tugging on his shirt. "Seriously, babe."

"Okay, okay." Milo seems irritated. I try to keep my face neutral as he gives me an apologetic look before heading in the direction of the bar. Leighton turns and strides back to a group of equally attractive girls without so much as a second glance in my direction.

"Well, then," Charlie says nonchalantly.

"That's all you have to say?" I ask incredulously, then lower my voice so that only Charlie can hear me. "Who does that prissy twat think she is?"

"Welcome to L.A., sis," Charlie says apologetically. "Though I will say, it did seem like there was a definite spark between you and Milo."

I watch as Milo walks up to Leighton and hands her a glass. She takes it, wrapping an arm around his waist as she whispers something in his ear.

I thought there was, too.

The rest of the party is relatively uneventful. Shortly after my unfortunate encounter with Leighton, Milo's band starts back up again. They are actually really good, with their indie rock songs being catchy enough that I find my head nodding along to the music. My eyes can't seem to stop drifting to Milo as he stands at his keyboard, skillfully playing and occasionally singing backup vocals.

After a few hours of hanging out by the pool with Charlie's

friends, Charlie catches me yawning and asks, "Are you ready to go?"

"I can call Leo if you want to stay longer," I say.

"Nah," says Charlie. "Let's get out of here."

As we reach the gate, I look back and find Milo's eyes on me, though he doesn't miss a beat as his fingers move across his keyboard. I give him a half-smile and follow Charlie to the car.

"Where have you two been?" my mother says as we walk into the kitchen for a snack when we return home. She is perched on a bar stool at the kitchen island, a glass of wine in hand as she closes the magazine she's reading.

"Party," Charlie says, opening the fridge door and scanning the shelves.

"You didn't tell me you were going to a party."

I look up from where I'm texting a recap of the evening to Annie to see my mother looking directly at me.

"Oh," I say, taken aback. "Um . . ."

"I'm your mother, and you need to at least ask me before you go out and I have no idea where you are."

Charlie, walking over to hand me a bottle of water, starts to laugh before seeing the look on my mother's face. "Oh, you're serious."

"Of course I'm serious!" she exclaims heatedly. She sets her glass down and stands up, readjusting the belt of her pink silk bathrobe. Charlie edges his way over to the door slowly before making a mad dash up to his room. Traitor. "We need to establish some ground rules here."

"Okay," I say reasonably.

My mother pauses, her index finger pointing in mid-air from where she was obviously anticipating my objections.

"That seems fair," I continue when she doesn't immediately say anything.

"Well, good." She obviously doesn't know what to do with this victory. "If you're going to go out at night, I need to know where you are. And no going out on school nights. And you probably need to have a curfew."

"Probably," I say, stifling a yawn as I unscrew the cap of my water bottle.

"You have to be home by midnight."

"Midnight it is." I'm eager to put an end to this conversation so I can go to my room to change into more comfortable clothes before I take Jim out. I get up and start toward the stairs.

"One last thing," my mother says, and I detect a hint of self-satisfaction in her voice. I turn back around.

"I made us a reservation at the spa tomorrow morning. Non-negotiable."

I'm too exhausted to protest so I just say "fine" before heading quickly to my room. After changing into pajamas, I pat my leg so Jim, who is laying on the chair with all four legs hanging off the side, will follow me.

"Chop chop, Jim."

He instantly reacts to the phrase for "let's go" that my dad and I taught him when he was a puppy. We thought it would be funny to get him to respond to weird commands, like 'that's not for you' when he's getting into something he shouldn't, 'park it' for when we want him to sit, and 'tuck in' for when we feed him.

"Well, this should be a good time," I mutter a few minutes later as I walk Jim back into my room and let him off his leash. Jim just busies himself with sniffing the dress I had been wearing, which is now balled up on the floor. I get a milk-bone out of a plastic tub on my shelf and hold it out to him.

"There's more where this came from if you can give me some solid advice on how to get through a spa day with Mommy Dearest tomorrow," I offer, but Jim just eyes me for a second before taking the treat and heading straight to his bed to settle in for the night.

FOUR

I'm having the most wonderful, lifelike dream involving Milo serenading me on his keyboard when a much different voice jolts me awake.

"Good morning, sunshine!"

"Ohhhhhh my God, what is happening?" I groan, yanking the covers up over my face.

"Time to go," my mother's chipper voice says.

"Go?" I say, pulling the covers back down enough to peek at her from beneath them. She has turned on a floor lamp in the corner, but otherwise the room is still almost completely dark.

"To the spa," she replies as she bustles around my room, fluffing throw pillows and straightening items on the shelves.

"What time is it?" I peer over at Jim in his corner. If dogs could have murderous looks on their faces, that is how he's looking at my mother.

"Five o'clock," she replies.

"*Five o'clock?*" I squeal incredulously. "In the *morning*?"

"It's a sunrise treatment," she says, as if this were the most obvious thing in the world. She comes to stand above me at the side of my bed, arms folded primly. I notice that even this early in the morning, she still has her hair pulled back into a perfectly shaped bun and the kind of makeup a person puts on when they're trying to make it look like they aren't wearing any. I close my eyes and exhale through my nose. If my mother knew even the most basic facts about me, she would know that while I'm certainly not a late sleeper, my ideal wake-up time on a weekend is in the neighborhood of eight or nine o'clock. But one look at my mother and it's clear she is not going to relent.

"Five minutes," I say in resignation. "Just give me five minutes."

I throw on a loose-fitting tank top, a pair of leggings, and sneakers, sweep my hair into a messy ponytail, and quickly brush my teeth. After scrawling a note to Charlie asking him to take Jim for a walk when he wakes up, I find my mother waiting for me in the foyer.

"We need to get going," she says, ushering me out to where Leo is standing next to the car. I spare one last longing look at the direction of my bedroom before sluggishly crawling into the backseat.

We sit in silence as we ride, looking out of our respective windows at a still-dark Los Angeles. Finally, the car pulls into a driveway leading up to a large stucco building. We get out and walk up the lighted path to where two women in white button-up tunics and black pants stand, each holding a glass of water.

"Ah, Ms. Jenson," one of them says in an airy voice, stepping forward and handing my mother a glass. "We're so pleased you could join us this morning."

"Thank you, Talia," my mother purrs, then gestures toward me. "This is my daughter, Cam."

"So nice to meet you, Cam," Talia says. "This is Miriam. She will be your masseuse today."

Miriam steps forward and gives me a small smile, holding out the water glass.

"You wouldn't let me trade that in for some coffee, would you?" I whisper hopefully.

"It's crucial that you hydrate before your treatment," Talia informs me.

I try not to show my disappointment as I accept the glass from Miriam. I take a sip, then promptly spit it back into the cup in surprise. My mother, Talia, and Miriam all stare at me.

"It, uh, tastes a little funny," I say sheepishly.

"It's a detox blend," Talia explains. "Cucumber, lemon, and mint. I could see how it would startle you if you weren't expecting it."

"I'll get you a fresh one," Miriam says, a hint of laughter in her voice.

"Thanks," I mumble.

We step inside, and Talia leads us through the dimly lit atrium to a door on the right.

"You can leave your clothes here," she says as we enter a small room with a double vanity and a cushioned bench in the center where two neatly-folded bathrobes are sitting. "We'll be outside when you're ready."

"Thank you," my mother says. I watch as Talia closes the door, then turn around to find my mother already peeling off her shirt.

"Oh my God, Mother!" I say, looking away quickly as she reaches around to unfasten her bra.

"What?" she says, tossing it onto the bench.

"I'm going to the bathroom to change," I say in as dignified of a voice as I can manage.

My mother just gives me a little "hmm" before stepping out of her leggings. I snatch up a robe and duck into the small stall on the far side of the room, changing as quickly as I can.

"Okay, let's do this," I say, reemerging to find my mother sitting at the vanity applying lip gloss.

Miriam is waiting outside for me with a new glass of water in hand.

"No cucumber this time," she says with a wink.

We follow Miriam and Talia down the hallway to a set of double doors. Talia opens them and gestures to two massage tables set up on a covered private balcony overlooking a small pool. The skyline is just starting to take on a dark orange hue as we each settle onto a table, disrobing underneath a thin sheet and turning so we are face-down.

"Isn't this nice?" my mother's muffled voice comes floating from somewhere to my right.

"Sure," I reply as Miriam starts kneading my back.

I hate to say it, but the massage is actually pretty relaxing. Or at least it could be if my mother would stop trying to talk to me every five seconds. Why she thinks the perfect bonding time is when I'm stark naked with a stranger trying to work seventeen years' worth of stress knots out of my back is beyond me.

But she doesn't give up. She relentlessly chats my ear off about everything from her latest makeup collection to an offer she got to be on *Ice Skating with the Stars* all through the facial, volcanic ash mud bath, pedicure, and sauna steam. By the time the sun is fully up, I'm in desperate need of caffeine and sustenance.

"Mother," I say, slightly panicking when she picks up the spa menu with the clear intention of ordering yet another service. "I'm as detoxed, exfoliated, and moisturized as a person could ever possibly hope to be. But I'm also *starving*."

My mother glances back at the menu longingly for another moment, but after a pleading look from me she agrees we can call it a morning.

We end up at a small brunch place a few miles from the spa. My mother orders an egg wrap, and I get the waffles.

"Can I get a side of peanut butter with that?" I ask the waitress. As she walks away, I look across the table and catch my mother smiling to herself. "What?"

"That's how your dad liked his waffles," she replies affectionately. "You two are the only people I know that eat waffles with maple syrup and peanut butter."

I can feel myself tense at the unexpected mention of my dad.

"I guess I picked it up from him," I say with false indifference, pulling out my phone and scrolling through Instagram just for something else to do.

My mother continues to reminisce. "He was always a little quirky when it came to food." She chuckles a little. "Did he ever make you try watermelon with hot sauce?"

"Listen, Mother—"

"Will you stop that?" my mother interrupts abruptly, suddenly looking irritated.

"Stop what?"

"Calling me 'Mother,'" she says. "It's so . . . formal."

"Would you rather I call you Jackie?"

"I would prefer you call me 'Mom.' You always used to call me 'Mom.'"

"Yeah, when I was like, five. At this point I don't think you've clocked enough parenting hours for me to think of you as 'Mom' and not 'Mother.'" She's looking like a wounded animal, and I know I should ease off, but my temper is starting to rise. "And we're not doing this, chatting about my dad like we were all some kind of happy family. Dad and I were a family. The two of us. Don't pretend like you were part of it."

My mother's face reddens a bit as her mouth opens and closes a few times. I can tell I've hurt her, but at this moment I don't care. The silence seems to stretch on forever before I say, "Let's just eat and go home."

After we finish our breakfast, she goes to the bathroom, and I pick my phone back up. I'm mindlessly scanning through a gossip account I follow, *Chick About Town,* when I nearly choke on my orange juice. *"Jackie Jenson's Daughter Partying Her Grief Away?"* is written in thick text above a picture clearly taken on a cell phone that shows me standing with Charlie at the party we went to last night. I have my head thrown back laughing and am holding a wine glass. The caption below reads:

"Jackie Jenson's daughter, Cam Donovan, who recently moved to L.A. after her father's death last month, was spotted at a party in Beverly Hills Saturday night. Sources say the 17-year-old seemed to be enjoying herself, drinking and joking around with her friends, including brother and fashion designer, Charlie Cabot. Looks like the new socialite is already making herself at home here in the Hills."

"I'm going to have Leo drop you off at the house before I run to a meeting." My mother is sliding back into her chair and appears to have regained her composure. I vaguely wonder if the whole pretending-your-problems-don't-exist-so-you-don't-have-to-deal-with-them thing might be genetic. When she sees the look on my face, she says, "What is it?"

Wordlessly, I hand her the phone and watch her read through the *Chick About Town* post. She just sighs and hands the phone back to me.

"Well," she says, pulling out her pink wallet and placing her credit card on top of the check that I hadn't noticed the server set on the table. "I figured this might happen. Luckily this one is pretty harmless. The underage drinking doesn't look great though—"

"Pretty harmless?!" I sputter, finally finding my voice again. "I wasn't drinking! Alexis went to the bathroom, and I was holding her glass of wine for her!"

My mother just gives me a skeptical look as the server comes to pick up our bill.

"I wasn't!" I persist. "Who even are these people? Why do they care what I do?"

"This is my fault," she says, pulling out a lipstick and applying it using her reflection in a knife. "I should have prepared you better, but it's not like there was a lot of time."

"Prepared me better for what?" I say, still totally nonplussed.

"For the attention," my mother explains, smiling at the server who has just brought her credit card back. "You're fresh blood in the water, and people are curious. You've always been somewhat of a mystery—Jackie Jenson's off-the-grid daughter."

"Just because someone lives somewhere other than L.A. doesn't mean they're off the grid," I protest weakly.

"Look, hon," my mother says, leaning in sympathetically and reaching to hold my hands across the table. "It's going to come with the territory for a while, but they will move on to the next thing pretty quickly. At least, if that's what you want."

"What do you mean '*if* that's what I want?'" I can feel my waffles churning in my stomach. Then I picture the headline *"Jackie Jenson's Daughter Hurls Up Her Breakfast: Does She Have an Eating Disorder?"* and tell myself for the 107th time in the last 48 hours to keep it together. "Why would I *want* to have people creepily taking my picture and then writing lies about me?"

"I'm just saying there's an opportunity here if you want to take it," my mother explains, as if all of this is painfully obvious. I can only sit here and gawk at her stupidly with my mouth hanging open. Any semblance of decompression I had experienced at the spa has completely vanished. I am definitely compressed again. What a waste of essential oils. "You can capitalize on this—how would you describe your brand? Charlie and I can show you how to build up your social media accounts, get some sponsorships, enter the influencer space . . ."

My mother trails off as our plates and silverware rattle from where I've banged my head down onto the table. The laminate feels cool against my forehead, which immediately starts to throb a little. *"Jackie Jenson's Daughter Suffers Self-Inflicted Concussion at Local Eatery."* Awesome.

"Cam?" I hear my mother say from somewhere above me. I respond with a muffled grunt.

"Is everything okay?" The server must have come to check on us. She sounds genuinely concerned.

"Oh, we're good," I can hear my mother trying to sound casual, but her voice is strained. I snicker a little to myself before lifting my head back up and smiling at the server, who looks downright alarmed now.

"Just perfect," I say sweetly.

The server hurries away, and I grab my bag and walk outside, not bothering to wait for my mother.

When we get home, I go straight up to my room. There's a note on my door from Charlie that says, *"Took Jim to the dog park."* Selfishly, I'm bummed that neither of them are here. I'm still reeling from the conversation at breakfast with my mother. And I'm kicking myself a little, too. How did I not see this coming? It's not like I've never been photographed before when I've been in L.A. visiting my mother. There was certainly more than one occasion where we had gone out to lunch or shopping, and our picture wound up in some celebrity magazine.

But the idea of this being a regular part of my life now? I was so focused on having to move here it never occurred to me that the world might be watching to see if Jackie Jenson's daughter would be following in her mother's footsteps.

I hear a gentle knock on my door, but I don't answer. There is absolutely no way I'm going to listen to my mother give me more reasons to lean into this insanity. Instead, I glance over to an unopened box in the corner of my room labeled "Art Supplies." After hesitating for a moment, I get a pair of scissors from the drawer of my nightstand and walk over to it. The containers of colored pencils and sketchbooks are haphazardly packed in the box from where I hurriedly threw them in a few weeks ago. I pick up a sketchbook and run my fingers over it.

My dad noticed when I was really young that I was super fidgety, so he bought me my first sketchpad and a set of colored pencils to help keep my hands busy. I took them with me everywhere, and pretty soon it became clear I actually had a knack for it. I think Dad had secretly hoped I would take interest in some kind of sport, like baseball or basketball, but he was fully on board when he saw art was going to be more than just a hobby for me. He let me sign up for every art class I could take both at my school and a few galleries in the area that offered them. In the beginning, I mainly stuck to realism and photorealism, wanting to capture every aspect of a place or subject exactly as it was.

But a few years ago, I started creating comics. At first it was short strips, but eventually I fleshed out some of my ideas into a full comic book series about a teenage vigilante who's a quiet book nerd by day but a badass crimefighter by night. I had even decided I was going to major in illustration and graphic design in college with Dad's full support.

I thumb through the pages of the last comic book I was working on when Dad died. It's a story arc where my heroine, Scarlet, is trying to put the police onto a local money laundering scheme. In the time Dad has been gone, I must have sat down to try and draw a hundred times but I just . . . can't. I'm sure a therapist would say it is some sort of manifestation of my grief or whatever, but I am not about to try to peel back the layers of that psychological onion.

Tossing the sketchbook back in its box, I grab a paperback book from my shelf and snuggle up in bed, happy to lose myself in fictional people's problems.

Five

I don't leave the house again until Thursday. It's partly because I have genuinely been busy unpacking, then meticulously arranging and rearranging my room, but mostly I've just been avoiding going out in public and potentially being photographed again. My mother tried to talk to me about it again the other night, but I told her it was fine to placate her. I thought Charlie would be sympathetic, but I grossly underestimated his need for the love and adoration of the public.

"A photo of us at the party?" he said when I recounted the breakfast disaster after he arrived back home with an exhausted but happy Jim. "Was I in it? How did I look?" I must have given him an especially murderous glare because he quickly said, "Never mind. Doesn't matter. Not important."

"The craziest thing is our mother started going into how I could take advantage of the attention and become an 'influencer' or whatever."

"I mean," Charlie said carefully. "She isn't wrong, you know."

"You have to be freaking kidding me," I moaned.

"I don't know why you're acting so shocked that people are paying attention to you," Charlie countered matter-of-factly.

"Come on, Char," I said, exasperated. "The world is divided into two categories: the 'haves' and the 'have nots.' I am decidedly a 'have not,' so why does anyone care what I do?"

Charlie just put the pencil he had been twirling in his fingers back down on the large design table and swiveled his chair around to face me where I was sitting next to him. He brought his fingertips to touch and rested his chin on them, considering me thoughtfully.

"I hate to break it to you, sis," he said finally. "But you're a 'have' now. I'm not telling you what to do, but you're in a unique position here. You're already at an advantage over most people if you decide you want to try to make something out of it."

"All I'm trying to do right now is function on the most basic level," I admitted, unable to stop the tiniest amount of the emotion I have been forcing down recently from coming to the surface. "Almost every aspect of my entire life has changed in the last month, and honestly, most of my focus is going into reminding myself to breathe half the time."

Through the tears that were suddenly swimming in my eyes, I saw the blur that was Charlie reach out and pull me toward him. We collided awkwardly given that both of us were in desk chairs with wheels, and he wrapped me into a firm hug.

"I'm sorry," he said gently, stroking my hair as I actually let myself cry for the first time in weeks. "You're right. This is the last thing you need to be thinking about right now."

"That's the thing," I said, pulling myself up enough to look at him. "I don't even know what I'm supposed to be thinking about or how I'm supposed to be feeling. Every time I smile or laugh or feel happy for even a second, I feel so guilty because it's like I've forgotten about Dad. But then I know Dad wouldn't want me to be sad, so I feel guilty for feeling guilty."

"I'm sorry," Charlie said again as I put my head back against his chest. I could hear the waver in his voice and could tell he was fighting back tears of his own. "Have . . . have you tried talking to Mom about it?"

I let out a harsh laugh. "Absolutely not."

"I think . . . maybe you should," he said tentatively.

"I'm fine," I said, standing up quickly and swiping at my eyes. "I'll be fine."

"Cam—" Charlie began, but I was already walking out of the room.

So after four days of avoiding the topic of anything having to do with me and my "brand" with my mother and repeatedly trying to convince Charlie that I'm okay after my mini-meltdown, I decide it's time to get over myself and quit being a hermit. I text Leo (I've got to see if my mother will get me my own car) and have him drop me off at Joe's. Charlie reminds me as I'm leaving that there are hundreds of other places to eat in Beverly Hills, but I tell him I'm a creature of habit and it reminds me of the cafe back in Preston where my dad and I used to always go for breakfast, which shuts him up.

There are plenty of free tables, so I pick a small booth by the window and settle in. I check my phone and see Annie has texted me.

"WHERE. In. The. HELL. Have. You. BEEN????"

"been a weird week. tell you all about it tonight. phone date?"

The reply comes back almost immediately.

"phone date. and you better verbally wine and dine the shit out of me."

I text a laughing/crying face emoji just as a familiar voice says, "Well, hello there."

I look up to see Milo grinning down at me.

"Hey," I smile back, my heartbeat picking up a little as I set my phone on the table. *Nope,* I silently chide myself. *You are not doing this. Whatever little crush you may or may not have been developing doesn't matter anymore because he has a girlfriend.*

"I was wondering when I was going to see you again."

"Were you now?"

"Well, yeah," he says, using the pen he's holding to scratch his eyebrow. "I don't know if I've ever met anyone as enthusiastic about breakfast food as you are."

"Oh, I get it." I sit back against the booth and fold my arms. "You see someone thrice in the span of two days and you think, 'Am I lucky enough for this to be the new normal?'"

"'Thrice?'" he repeats mockingly.

"Thrice. You know. Once more than twice."

"Mmm-hmm," he says. Just then, a pretty Asian girl with thick-rimmed red glasses and hair pulled into two twin buns on top of her head appears at his shoulder.

"Milo," she says imploringly. "Seriously. My glass has been empty for like, two hours now. Hi, I'm Mei."

I start a little when I realize she has abruptly turned her attention on me.

"Oh. Hey. I'm Cam."

She beams warmly at me before focusing back on Milo.

"Seriously, I'm parched."

"Oh my God, woman," Milo says, pocketing his pen and notepad. "You can't harass me like this at work in front of customers."

Mei cocks her head a little, giving me an appraising look.

"She seems cool to me."

"Totally beside the point," says an exasperated-looking Milo. "Cam, I'm sorry. I'll be right back."

He starts to walk back to the kitchen, stopping at a booth a few down from mine to pick up an empty glass, shake it dramatically at Mei, and roll his eyes.

"So," Mei says, taking a seat across from me. "How do you know my brother?"

"Your brother?" I repeat stupidly.

"Yep," she says, folding her hands in front of her.

"Just from here," I answer. "That is to say, I don't really *know* him, know him."

"Ah," she says. "I thought for a minute you might be another groupie hanging around the diner. So pathetic."

"Wait, really?" I forget to be awkward for a second, intrigued. "Does he really get groupies?"

Mei laughs.

"Not as many as he would if he played a cool instrument instead of the keyboard, but he gets his share of desperate teenage girls fawning over him," she says, shaking her head. "Discount Curses is pretty well known in this area."

"So I've heard," I reply.

"From Milo I'm sure," she giggles. I laugh too just as Milo comes back up to the table with two glasses.

"I brought you root beer," he says to me, setting the glasses down. "What's so funny?"

"Definitely nothing having to do with you," Mei says with a serious face.

"We absolutely weren't talking about you or your questionable choice of musical instrument," I affirm, looking innocently up at him.

"Has anyone ever told you that subtlety is not your strong suit?" Milo asks me, the corner of his mouth tugging up as he pulls his notepad and pen back out.

"Subtlety is overrated," I answer. His eyes linger on mine for a moment longer before he glances over at Mei.

"You realize your stuff is going to get stolen if you leave it sitting over there much longer," he tells her. She looks at me.

"Mind if I join you?" she asks a little tentatively. "I was trying to find a monologue for my drama class but I am so over it."

"Sure," I say, attempting to not be too obvious with how pleased I am to have some company. As she goes over to her booth and starts gathering up various books and her laptop, I quirk an eyebrow up at Milo.

"She's a character." He wears an easy smile as he watches her.

"She seems great." I fiddle with a string coming out of the hem of my *Doctor Who* t-shirt.

"So what can I get for you today?" Milo inquires, making a little flourish with his hand as he poises it over his notepad.

"Double bacon cheeseburger," I say without hesitation.

"What is it with you and bacon?"

"Bacon is proof that God loves us and wants us to be happy."

"Pretty sure that's beer."

"Oh, it's bacon. Beer is sad bread water. Bacon is the Lord's food."

"Well, Benjamin Franklin said it's beer."

"He must not have ever tried bacon."

At this point Mei has sat back down at my booth and is watching our conversation, head popping back and forth between me and Milo like she's watching a ping pong match.

"I would also like onion rings," I announce grandly.

"You need a vegetable."

"Onions are vegetables."

"A non-fried vegetable."

"The burger comes with lettuce."

"Let me guess—God's garnish?"

"Cheese is God's garnish, you blaspheme."

"Okay, coming right up."

I watch Milo walk to the kitchen and turn to see Mei looking at me, an amused expression on her face.

"So," I say, taking a sip of root beer. "Milo is your brother?"

"Yep," Mei confirms. "He's adopted."

"He's . . . wait, *he's* adopted?" I say, reacting too quickly to suppress my surprise.

"Yep," she quips. "God, I love the look on people's faces when I tell them that. Priceless."

"Hmm," I hedge, not knowing the proper thing to say.

"It's a fascinating story." Mei sits back in her booth. "Honestly, it's wild that no one has optioned the rights to it yet because it's a Netflix movie waiting to happen if I've ever seen one. Our dad is a trauma surgeon at St. Agnes Hospital, and one night this teenage couple comes through that was in a head-on car crash with an eighteen-wheeler. The girl, she was like nineteen or something, is eight and a half months pregnant, and the doctors are able to deliver the baby, but the guy and the girl don't make it."

So far, I would qualify this story as more horrifying than fascinating, but I don't interrupt.

"Neither of them have any next of kin. Her parents were both in jail for drugs or whatever and his parents were already dead. So my mom and dad end up adopting the baby, Milo, because they had been told the chances of them being able to get pregnant were really slim. But then that turned out not to be true because a few years later I came along!" Mei concludes dramatically.

"So Milo's last name is—"

"Chen," Mei says.

"Your burger," Milo reappears, setting a plate containing a gigantic burger and heap of onion rings in front of me. I regard it reverently for a moment.

"It's . . . so beautiful."

"I had them put extra lettuce on it."

"Did you now?"

"I'm concerned about your arteries."

"You barely even know my arteries."

"I can't be complicit in helping you destroy them."

"And you think an extra piece of lettuce is going to fix that?"

"Baby steps. Extra lettuce today, maybe a slice of tomato tomorrow."

"Tomatoes are a fruit."

"Something tells me you could stand to eat some fruit as well."

"Do you intervene in all of your customers' food choices like this?"

"It's a thankless job."

"You're a true humanitarian if I've ever met one."

Mei is studying us again, her eyes narrowed.

"Are you two always like this?" she asks me suspiciously. "I feel like I'm in an episode of *Gilmore Girls* or something."

"I've only been here a few times," I say through a mouthful of burger.

"Thrice, actually," Milo says, echoing our earlier conversation. He is looking at me, an expression on his face I can't quite decipher.

"You need to go," I urge Milo as I swallow and turn my attention to my onion rings. "Mei is telling me your life story, and it's less uncomfortable if you aren't standing here."

"Fantastic," he says sarcastically. "I'll leave you to it then."

"Interesting," Mei says as soon as he is out of earshot, crossing her arms and sizing me up.

"What is?"

"Oh, nothing," she says lightly. "So what about you? What's your deal?"

I feel my insides lurch at the prospect of having to talk about myself.

"Um," I say eloquently. "I don't really have a deal. I just moved here to live with my mother."

"Oh? Is she anyone I would know?" Mei asks with interest.

"Uh, maybe," I say, squirming a little in my seat. "She's Jackie Jenson."

"Your mom is Jackie Jenson? Wasn't she on a season of *Athletes' Ex-Girlfriends of Beverly Hills* a few years ago?"

"That she was." I can feel myself turning red. A look of recognition comes over Mei's face.

"That means . . . oh. I'm sorry about your dad," she says quietly.

"Thanks," I say quickly. "So where do you go to school?"

Mei looks a little relieved I initiated a change in subject.

"Winston Academy," she says, snatching an onion ring off my plate. "I'm going to be a junior."

"Yeah? I'm going to be starting there in the fall. I'll be a senior."

"Nice," she says. "It's not a bad place. A lot of celebrities' kids go there, which always keeps things interesting."

"Ugh," I say, unable to help myself. "I hate that I fall into that category."

"There are plenty of non-celebrities' kids there too," she assures me. "It's a mixed bag."

Mei starts to tell me about the drama program she's in at Winston, and pretty soon she's launched into a full rundown of all of the clubs I should join and teachers I should avoid. I mostly let her talk because truthfully, I'm completely dreading the prospect of spending my senior year anywhere other than Northside High School in Preston with all of the kids I've known since elementary school. I have successfully avoided thinking about it the same way I have avoided thinking about all of the other painful reminders of my current lot in life—stubbornly opting to deal with it later.

Milo strides purposefully to our table, frowning at Mei.

"Don't you have your drama class today?"

Mei checks the time on her phone and swears.

"Give me your phone," she says as she stuffs her laptop back in her messenger bag. I hand it to her, and she hurriedly puts in her number. "Text me!"

I watch her practically fly out the door and send her a quick waving hand emoji so she has my number, too. I look up to see Milo still standing there, eyebrows raised.

"I'm pretty sure your sister and I are like, best friends now," I say cheerily.

"Looks like it," he says. "So what did she say about me?"

"Oh, all kinds of things," I say, examining my cuticles. "All kinds of horribly embarrassing things."

"Well, this is a fun development," he says, trying to sound grumpy, but he's smiling.

"So hey," I say, attempting to sound nonchalant. "The other night. Your band was really great. And your girlfriend seems . . ." I trail off, not knowing exactly where I was going with that. I fight the urge to end the sentence with "like a total shrew" and instead hear myself say, ". . . well-groomed."

I silently chastise myself for my incredibly poor attempt at easing the subject into finding out more about Leighton.

"Well-groomed?" Milo repeats, looking puzzled.

"Yeah, you know," I continue despite every fiber of my being silently pleading for me to shut my mouth. "Like she watches a lot of YouTube tutorials on hair and makeup, but unlike some people who are definitely not me who follow the instructions exactly how the person says but somehow still end up looking like a clown who got caught in a wind tunnel, she actually gets it on the first try."

We look at each other for a beat.

"Is that even a compliment?" asks Milo, still looking bemused.

"It's not *not* a compliment," I offer.

Milo continues to study me.

"So I'm gonna go," I say, hastily pulling out some cash, tossing it on the table and grabbing my backpack.

"Wait, Cam—"

"See ya!" I practically run out the door. A few seconds later, I hear footsteps behind me. I whirl around to see Milo has followed me outside. I feel my face flush as he walks right up to me. We stand facing each other for a few seconds before he holds up a fifty-dollar bill.

"You left this on the table," he says.

"I . . . wha—?"

"I just figured you didn't mean to leave this much money. Your bill was only, like, eighteen bucks."

"Oh," I say weakly. I definitely did not mean to leave that

much money, but I'm not going to go back on it now. "Well. You did give me extra lettuce."

"Not thirty-dollar lettuce."

"Just keep it," I say, starting to walk down the path outside the diner that leads to the parking lot. "Consider me an investor for the next Discount Curses album."

I pull my phone out of my back pocket to text Leo that I'm ready to go home when I hear Milo's voice behind me say quietly, "She's cool once you get to know her."

I freeze for a moment before turning back around to find Milo standing about a foot away from me, his hands in his pockets.

"What?" I say, my breath catching a little.

"Leighton," he clarifies. "I know she can seem kind of . . . but she's been through a lot. Her dad is a real asshole, and she left home when she was sixteen. . . . Anyway, she can be guarded when you first meet her, but she's a great girl."

"Why are you telling me this?"

"Honestly . . . I don't know." Milo pulls a hand out of his pocket and runs it through his hair, looking uncomfortable. "I guess because she was a little rude to you the other night."

"Well, I've also 'been through a lot' recently," I say using exaggerated air quotes, starting to feel irrationally irritated. "I don't use it as an excuse to be shitty to people."

"Except your mom, from what it sounds like," Milo mutters, and it feels like a slap in the face. His eyes widen as he realizes what he just said, but I've already started backing away from him.

"You don't owe me any kind of explanation of why you like your absolute delight of a girlfriend," I say with a calmness I don't feel. "Honestly, it sounds like you're trying to justify it more to yourself than to me, but whatever. The important thing is that you and I met each other, what, like, five minutes ago? We're strangers. So don't act like you know the first thing about me or my mother."

I turn on my heels and storm through the parking lot, ignoring Milo calling after me.

Listen to Track Three: "Villain or Hero"

SIX

"So let me get this straight," Annie says on the phone later that night when I finally get around to telling her about Milo. "You met a guy."

"I did," I confirm, trying to balance the phone between my shoulder and ear as I finish painting my toenails a dark shade of purple to match my mood.

"But he has a girlfriend."

"He does."

"And you chewed him out in the middle of a parking lot?"

"Also correct."

"Man, L.A. has already changed you," she says, and I can tell she is trying not to laugh.

"Not helpful."

"But seriously, Cam." I hear the tone in Annie's voice shift. "Are you okay?"

"I'm fine."

I say it so often now that it's almost automatic, but Annie doesn't back down. My phone beeps, and I see she is requesting to FaceTime me. I groan as I put the bottle of nail polish down and accept the call. Her face pops up on the screen, eyebrows furrowed with concern.

"You are not fine," she says, not missing a beat. "Your dad just died and your whole life got uprooted—"

"Thank you for reminding me," I snap before I can stop myself. "I had completely forgotten about that."

"Don't bite my head off," she says calmly. "Just talk to me."

I hop off the counter and carefully walk over to the empty garden bathtub in the corner. Climbing in, I sit down and lean my back against the porcelain of the tub, letting my elbows rest on either side as I hold my phone. Annie is watching me, patiently waiting.

"It's been . . . hard." I close my eyes for a second. "You know what? No. This is so much harder than hard."

"Oh, Cam," Annie says sadly. "Have you talked to your Aunt Margaret?"

"No," I confess. "I just don't want to worry her or make her feel guilty that I'm here and not with her."

"She didn't get much choice in the matter," Annie reminds me. "Your dad was pretty insistent that you go to Los Angeles with your mom."

"I'm sure that was my mother's doing," I say crossly. "But I'll call her. Really."

"Okay," Annie nods, seemingly satisfied. "I have to go. My mom is bugging me to watch a movie with her tonight. But let's start trying to plan a weekend for you to come visit. I know everyone would love to see you."

"That sounds nice," I agree. "Have fun with your mom."

"And you should try spending a little more time with yours," she replies.

"After our little spa day I think I've fulfilled my mother-daughter time quota for, oh, I don't know, the next two years."

"Ha," Annie says, unamused. "Alright, I'll talk to you later."

I end the call and examine my toenails, which seem to be dry, so I decide to see what I can scrounge up for dinner. As I walk past Charlie's design studio, I see he's hovering over his work table.

"Hey," I say, poking my head in. "I think I might order a pizza. You want in?"

"Pizza?" he says with disgust, pushing a strand of his blonde hair out of his face. "Just hearing the word 'pizza' has made me gain five pounds."

"You don't have to be so dramatic," I scoff as I start to leave.

"Seriously though, half-sis," he says, getting up and following me downstairs. "You've been eating like a truck driver ever since you got here, which is especially impressive considering how people in this city really only eat to live. But it can't be good for your overall health."

"I know," I grudgingly acknowledge, opening the fridge to pull out a Diet Coke. "I was actually thinking of trying to find a yoga studio. Or maybe someplace that has kickboxing. I kind of got into kickboxing before . . . well, a few months ago."

"I think that's a great idea," Charlie says, opening the pantry as I pull out my phone to search for a pizza place nearby that delivers.

"Yeah, I can tell I need . . . What the hell is that?"

I finally get a good look at what Charlie is holding as he rummages around for a spoon.

"Sweet potato puree," he says, avoiding my eyes.

"Char," I say slowly. "That looks like baby food."

His shoulders slump a little as he admits, "I'm on a diet."

"What diet?" I ask, mortified.

"The Baby Food Diet, obviously."

"Please be joking." I can hardly keep the disgust out of my voice. "You're insane. Just have some pizza with me."

"Can I just, like, sit and watch you eat it?" Charlie says longingly as I dial the phone number for a place a few miles away called Luigi's.

"Don't make it weird, dude."

After ordering a large veggie pizza and giving the guy on the phone instructions for how to operate the call system on our gate, I sit at the kitchen island and watch Charlie prepare his "dinner" of pureed peas and sweet potatoes.

"You're making me lose my appetite," I say, wrinkling my nose as he spoons a glob of congealed green goo onto a plate.

"You have to make sacrifices when you're in The Industry," he says haughtily.

"Do you want me to help?" I ask him, scooping a spoonful of peas and holding it up. "I can pretend it's an airplane if you think that would make it easier."

Charlie just glares at me.

"Come on, Charlie! Who's a big boy?" I say in my best baby talk voice.

"You are such a brat." Charlie snatches his spoon back, though he is grinning.

I hear the buzz of the call box by the front door, so I leap up to answer. As I walk into the foyer, I hear Charlie mutter "ugh, screw this" before shouting to me, "I hope you got extra cheese!"

Thirty minutes and an entire pizza later, Charlie and I are sprawled out on the living room sectional couch taking turns tossing bits of pizza crust for Jim to catch.

Trying to sound laid-back, I say, "So I had a bit of a moment today."

"What kind of 'moment'?" Charlie asks suspiciously.

"I went to the diner and kind of had a fight with Milo."

"Whaaaaat?"

"I know, I know," I say, fiddling with a loose thread on one of the many throw pillows decorating the couch. "He just made me so mad."

"What in the world did the cute waiter who you have known for all of a week do to make you mad enough to blow up at him at his place of employment?" Charlie is looking at me incredulously.

"Okay," I say, starting to feel defensive. "Well, first off, you met his girlfriend. She's heinous, right?"

"Compared to some of the women I've met here she's downright pleasant," Charlie says.

"Whatever." I wave a hand dismissively. "She sucks."

"I think I know what's happening here," Charlie says knowingly. "This is because you have a thing for him. His girlfriend could have been the nicest person in the history of humanity and you still would have hated her."

"So maybe I thought there could have been something there," I concede. "But clearly I was wrong about the type of guy he is if girls like Leighton are what he wants."

"Maybe," Charlie answers. "But you still didn't need to yell at him about it."

To bolster my case, I start to tell him what Milo said about me and our mother, but I don't feel like getting into a whole discussion about it with Charlie, so I just say, "Okay, okay."

"At his job."

"Okay."

"In front of people, I'm guessing—"

"OKAY!" I shout, throwing the pillow at Charlie. "Anyways, I'm going to have to smooth things over with him because I met his sister today and she's pretty cool."

"My little Cammy made a friend today?" Charlie squeals, reaching over to wrap me into a hug.

"Oh, my God," I say, as he gives my head a noogie.

At that moment, my mother walks in the door and stops short at the sight of the two of us wrestling on the couch.

"What's going on in here?" she says, setting down an armful of shopping bags and walking over to sit on the opposite end of the sectional as Charlie and I straighten up.

"Cam was just telling me about how she met a girl today who could be a potential new friend." Charlie sticks out his tongue at me when I shoot him a look.

"Really?" my mother says, sounding genuinely pleased. "That's wonderful! Who is she?"

I decide to fight my natural urge to not tell my mother anything about anything ever. I've already been unpleasant enough today. So I launch into explaining all about Mei and her family and how they adopted Milo as a baby. Pretty soon Charlie is recounting a meeting he had today with a huge diva of a client, and my mother is talking about some photoshoot she has in a few days. As the three of us sit and talk, it's almost easy to imagine this could be my life now: eating pizza on the couch, chatting about how our day was.

But then the image of my dad flashes in my mind.

"I'm tired," I say abruptly, interrupting my mother mid-sentence. "I think I'm going to hit the hay. Chop chop, Jim."

Ignoring the startled looks from Charlie and my mother, I jog upstairs with Jim following closely behind me.

I put on my pajamas, but as I pull my t-shirt over my head, I find Jim looking at me pleadingly.

"Damn it all," I say crossly. "I forgot to take you out."

At the word "out," Jim bounds over to my closed door and looks back as if to say, "What are you waiting for, human?"

I hook on his leash, take him downstairs, and try to go through the back door as quietly as possible in the hope that Charlie and my mother don't hear me. But a few minutes later, the door opens, and my mother emerges in her pink bathrobe.

"I thought I heard you out here."

She walks over to a small patio table, taking care not to get dirt on her slippers. After perching herself in one of the chairs, she watches me as I finish up with Jim. Resigning myself to the inevitability of being unable to go straight back up to my room, I take a seat opposite my mother. Jim, blissfully unaware of how gigantic he is as per usual, manages to wriggle under the table and lay down, though his entire back half is still sticking out. I pet him with my foot and look up to see my mother gazing at me, an oddly sad expression on her face.

"What?" I ask uncomfortably.

"Oh, nothing," she says wistfully. "It's just . . . you look so much like Luke."

"I'm sure I look the same as I did when you saw me last summer," I say a little too sharply, caught off guard.

"No, there's something different about you."

I look back at my mother. She has taken off her makeup and swept her blonde hair in a loose knot on top of her head. I'm struck by how much younger she looks like this. She has surprisingly never had much major plastic surgery done on her face. Of course, I know for a fact she gets Botox regularly, and I suspect she's had some kind of filler put into her lips, but it's honestly pretty subtle. I try not to smile at the irony that all of the makeup she cakes on every day to try and look younger isn't as effective as how she looks right now, bare-skinned.

"Maybe it's just the whole newly-dead-parent vibe," I answer blandly after a moment.

"Cam!" My mother looks horrified.

"I'm sorry," I say quickly, feeling guilty when I see her eyes have filled with tears. "I shouldn't have said that. It was a stupid joke."

"Tell me what to do," she whispers, a slight waver in her voice. "How can I make this easier for you?"

"There is no making it easier for me," I say bluntly. "If you had wanted to make it easier for me you would have let me go live with Aunt Margaret."

My mother looks down at her lap. I see several tears have fallen onto the satin of her robe, leaving blotches that are slowly growing larger as they spread.

"This has been hard for me too, you know," she says quietly. "But I thought maybe the silver lining could be getting the chance for us to get closer."

"You've had seventeen years to get close to me." I hear the cold-ness in my voice as I try to silently coax back the familiar anger that has started roiling around in my stomach. My mother is still looking down at her hands, and they shake as she reaches up to tuck a few loose strands of hair behind her ear. Finally, her eyes lift up to meet mine, her face tear-streaked and looking so pained that my anger instantly evaporates, and I suddenly feel overwhelmingly tired.

"I need time," I say, standing up and tugging lightly on Jim's leash to wake him up. "Just give me more time."

My mother nods, and I take Jim back up to my room and collapse onto my bed. I can see from the soft glow of the deck lights through the sheer curtains of my balcony door that my mother hasn't gone inside yet. I wait for them to go off, but they are still on when I eventually fall asleep.

Listen to Track Four: "You Should've Been Better"

On Tuesday, I get a text from Mei asking if I want to meet at the diner for dinner and then go to an art show a few of her friends from Winston are in. My mother is currently in New York City doing a photoshoot, and Charlie has been working nonstop on some new collection, so I've been watching A LOT of Netflix the last few days. The curiosity of wanting to see what some of the art kids at Winston are like outweighs the dread I feel at the prospect of facing Milo after my little tantrum, so I tell her yes.

"How have your first few weeks been?" Leo asks as we drive the now-familiar way to the diner.

"A little overwhelming," I admit.

"I understand," Leo says, smiling in his rearview mirror at me. "My wife passed away three years ago, and I still have days out of nowhere that it hits me just as hard as it did when it first happened. It doesn't get easier necessarily, but it does get more bearable."

"Thank you," I say, my throat tight. I've discovered when someone you care about dies, lots of people tell you about their own loved ones who have also died as if they are doing you a favor by offering you a glimpse into what it's like when more time has passed and apparently the pain stops being so sharp. But Leo is just so authentically kind that I don't mind hearing it from him.

We pull up to the diner and I let him know about my plans with Mei, who had followed up her initial invitation with the offer to drive us to the art show and drop me off at home afterward. After getting out of the car, I stand outside of the diner for a moment and try to get my heart to stop beating so fast. I can see my reflection in the glass of the door. I had no idea what to wear to an L.A. art exhibit, so Charlie helped me put together an outfit consisting of a black crop top, leopard print mid-length skirt, and my Converse sneakers. I hope I don't look like I'm trying too hard. Or not trying hard enough.

Clutching the strap of the new crossbody bag Charlie insisted on getting me so I would stop taking my backpack everywhere, I take one more deep breath and walk into the diner. I quickly scan the room for Mei but don't see her, so I slide into a booth in the corner facing away from the kitchen in the hopes Milo didn't see me come in.

"Hello," a familiar voice says.

Damn.

"Hey," I reply, my voice shaking slightly. Milo has his arms crossed over a Discount Curses t-shirt and is looking at me consideringly. He doesn't say anything for a moment, so I gesture at the shirt.

"Doing some self-promo today?"

"It's laundry day," he says before we start talking at the same time.

"Look—"

"I need to—"

We both stop and start a few more times before I finally find myself shouting "ME!" loudly enough that people from several nearby tables turn to look at us.

"Jackie Jenson's Daughter Suffering from Random, Self-Aggrandizing Vocal Outbursts."

Fantastic.

But it's effective, because I seem to have stunned Milo into silence.

I clear my throat and sit up straighter with my chin in the air, trying to pretend like I'm a person who isn't barely grasping onto the last shred of their dignity. "What I mean to say is, me first, please." I seize the pepper shaker and start spinning it around on the table. "I'm sorry I was such a dick the other day. I shouldn't have ripped you a new one like that. Though I'm realizing I did shout at you just now, so I guess you can include that under the umbrella of this apology. It's just been a weird few days. Well, few months actually, and I don't think I am handling everything great, and SHIT!"

I knock the pepper shaker over in surprise. I'd been spinning it faster and faster as I was talking, and Milo abruptly reached out and stilled my hand with his. His hand is warm and soft, and we both stare at it for a moment before he quickly pulls it away.

"No," he says, and I can almost swear there is a little color on his cheeks that wasn't there before. "I'm the one who should be sorry. What I said about your mom . . . that was totally uncalled for."

Just as I open my mouth to reply, Mei bounds over to our booth. She's wearing a yellow floral print maxi dress and sandals, with her hair in loose space buns on top of her head again. Her lipstick is the same bright red color as her glasses, and she definitely looks the part of an art show attendee better than I do.

"Sorry I'm late!" she apologizes and slides into the booth. "Traffic was a freaking nightmare. What'd I miss?"

SEVEN

Mei orders a ham and cheese sandwich, and I opt for a grilled chicken wrap, which Milo, who thankfully seems to be back to his normal self, commends me for.

"It's a small miracle. I must be getting through to your arteries."

"I eat healthy things from time to time, thankyouverymuch."

"Your track record here says otherwise."

"Categorically false. My extra lettuce from the other day is highly offended."

"Don't you dare try to take credit for that," Milo says, pointing his index finger at me accusingly.

"Okay, you two," Mei cuts in, tapping her watch. "We're on a schedule here."

"Sorry," Milo and I say in unison, and he heads toward the kitchen to get our drinks.

"So how often do you come here?" I ask Mei.

"Way too much," Milo calls behind his shoulder.

"Only because I can always count on you to cover the bill." Mei sticks her tongue out at his back.

"Yeah, which comes out of MY paycheck," he retorts, shaking his head but not turning around. Mei just shrugs.

"So," she leans in. "The exhibit tonight is at this gallery and coffee shop in West Hollywood. A few people I know who paint sets for the theatre program at Winston took a class there, and this is their final showcase. I honestly don't know how good they are outside of painting fake living rooms. We may be looking at a lot of baskets of fruit. Or nudes."

"Or nude models holding baskets of fruit," I offer just as Milo reappears. He gives us a quizzical look as he sets our glasses down.

"Do I need to be concerned about what you two are getting up to tonight?" he asks, sounding like a big brother in a way that makes my heart sink a little. Not that it makes any difference, of course, but the thought of him viewing me as a little sister makes me want to throw up.

"Oh, please," Mei says, plunging a straw into her Diet Coke.

"I don't know though," I say, thoughtfully tapping my chin. "What if we see some drawings of boobs tonight and it makes us want to see some actual boobs? Milo, what do you know about the strip clubs around here?"

Mei practically does a spit take of the huge gulp of her drink she has just taken, which then leads her to start choking a little as she tries to swallow through her laughter. Milo glares at me as he thumps her on the back a few times.

"Oh, come on," I needle him. "Not even going to crack a smile?"

"About the suggestion that you may take my baby sister to a strip club?" he asks grumpily.

"Chill out," I say as Mei's coughing fit finally subsides. "She wouldn't be able to get in anyway. I haven't had enough time to get a fake I.D. made for her."

"You're hilarious," Milo says dryly as Mei starts giggling again. "Absolutely hysterical."

I give him a cheesy grin and double thumbs up before he huffs back to the kitchen.

"Do you really know someone that makes fake I.D.s?" Mei asks.

"Hell, no," I laugh.

"Oh," she says, sounding disappointed before brightening up a little. "You probably can get in anywhere you want without one."

"Yeah, right," I say. Milo brings out our food, and I grab the ketchup bottle, pouring a generous helping onto my plate before dunking one of my fries into it.

"I'm serious!" Mei says earnestly, picking up half of her sandwich. "You're Jackie Jenson's daughter."

"Don't remind me," I moan.

"So I bet you would have no problem getting into all kinds of clubs and bars and—"

"Whoa there," I put a hand up to stop her. "I hate to disappoint you, but my idea of fun is more of the dinner-and-a-movie kind than the awkwardly-stand-there-as-a-lot-of-drunk-people-grind-on-each-other kind."

"I can respect that," Mei says, nodding solemnly.

We spend the rest of the meal talking about books. It turns out we've read a lot of the same series, so we take turns ranking our favorite male characters and debating whether or not broodiness has any direct correlation to hotness.

Milo comes back to the table, and I hand him some cash, insisting I pay for Mei's meal since she is driving tonight.

"You're such a good date," Mei says jokingly, batting her eyelashes at me. "What is your type, anyway?"

"Uh," I say, a little taken aback at the bluntness of this question. "I don't think I have one, really."

"Well, I'm sort of talking to this guy in the show tonight, Eric," she explains. "His friend Cassidy who goes to St. Thomas is, like, offensively good-looking and happens to be single."

"Offensively good-looking, huh?" I ask, my eyes unwittingly

darting over to where Milo is standing and taking an order at another table.

"Oh yes," Mei says, not appearing to notice. "Maybe we can all go do something afterwards."

"Sure," I agree distractedly as Milo comes over to hand me my change.

"Don't get home too late," he tells Mei as we collect our stuff to head out.

"So strict," Mei says, making a pouty face at him.

As we start to walk to the door, I tell her, "You go ahead. I'll be right out."

She gives me a quizzical look, but just nods before heading out the door. I gather up my resolve as I turn around and walk back up to the table to where Milo has started collecting our dishes. Whatever I thought might have been between us at the beginning doesn't matter because he is taken. Plus, there has to be some kind of waiting period after something traumatic happens to you where you're not allowed to make any big life decisions, like dating someone new.

"Hey," I say, a little louder than I intended to. He straightens up, looking surprised.

"Hey," he replies, his tone questioning.

"I just wanted to make sure we're cool," I say, the words tumbling out of my mouth. "I know we exchanged apologies already, but I really don't want things to be weird because I like Mei and I like this diner and I'll probably be seeing you around and it would be cool if we could be friend . . . ly."

I stumble over the last part, having intended to say "friends" but realizing it's an awfully big leap to assume Milo and I are friends based off of several conversations in a diner where, let's face it, it's his job to talk to me. His eyes search mine for a moment, and I do my best to keep my face neutral.

"Yeah," he says slowly, scratching the back of his neck, then nodding resolutely. "We're good."

"Great!"

There is an obnoxious note of false enthusiasm in my voice that makes me internally cringe. I reach up and punch Milo lightly in the shoulder, then head outside before he can see the resulting look of mortification on my face. Mei has pulled up to the front of the diner and is waiting for me in a bright green Volkswagon Beetle. I let out a breath and climb in, not bothering to look back as we drive away.

The parking lot is mostly full when we pull up to the art show, but we find a spot toward the back and head inside. The coffee bar is set up in the corner, and a decently long line has already formed. We join it as I look around the space. The walls are painted a burnt orange color, and the room is adorned with mismatched couches and chairs gathered around several coffee tables. A large arched entryway to the side opens up to what must be the gallery.

"They have the best cappuccinos here," Mei tells me. "And they have open mic nights we like to go to sometimes on Friday nights that can be really fun."

Just then two guys and a girl come running up to hug Mei. I stand awkwardly as they greet each other, though Mei quickly introduces me.

"This is Cam," Mei says. "She just moved here from Arizona. Cam, this is Toby, Claire, and Aaron. We're in the theatre program together at Winston."

Toby and Aaron both look effortlessly put-together, with Toby in dark jeans and a purple paisley button-down shirt and Aaron in slim-fitting khaki pants with a white t-shirt and navy scarf.

"Are you a theatre kid, too?" Toby asks, putting his arm around Aaron's waist. Claire rolls her eyes at them. She is a good foot shorter than I am, with bright blue hair falling almost to the waist of her black shift dress.

"You'll have to forgive them," she says, lovingly elbowing Toby in the side. "They just got together after what has felt like years of 'will they, won't they,' and now their mission is to constantly make me feel like the third wheel."

"You know you love us," Aaron says, winking at her.

"Congratulations," I laugh. "And to answer your question, no. I don't do theatre."

We continue to make small talk until we get to the front of the line. Finally, with coffees and sodas in hand, we head into the area where the art is set up. A fair number of people are milling around the room which, in addition to having art hung up on every wall, has several temporary displays set up in the center. From the looks of it, each artist has five to six pieces.

"This is awesome," I say, genuinely impressed.

"Shall we?" Mei says, and the five of us start wandering around. Pretty soon we find Eric, a cute boy in cuffed chino pants and a short sleeve, button-down shirt who leans down to give Mei a quick hug before reaching out to shake my hand.

"Your stuff is great," I say as I look around at the pieces in his exhibit. All of his paintings are portraits of different people, each one done in bright, swirling colors.

"Thanks," he grins. We continue making our way through the room, stopping at several displays so Mei and her friends can say hi to the people they know from Winston. At one point they all start talking about a party at some football player's house that got busted up by the cops the previous weekend, so I say I'm going to find a bathroom and duck away. I hope I'm not coming across as too anti-social, but I can feel my chest starting to tighten in the way it does sometimes when I meet a lot of new people all at once. I walk slowly along the room, studying the paintings and drawings filling the walls. It makes my heart ache a little to watch the artists enthusiastically explain their work to the people who approach their display, remembering how I used to be just like them.

I stop at a cluster of pen and ink drawings. A mermaid sitting and brushing her hair. A broken light bulb with shards of glass fanned around it. A feather quill dipping into an inkwell.

"Hey," a deep voice says from over my shoulder. I whirl around and find a blond boy wearing skinny jeans, white Vans, and a blue striped shirt standing there holding a cup of coffee.

"Hi," I say. "Did you draw these?"

He blows into his steaming coffee cup and studies the artwork behind me.

"I did," he says.

"Nice."

I turn back around to glance over the drawings again. I feel the boy come up to stand beside me.

"Thanks," he says.

"Hey, have you ever thought about being a tattoo artist?"

He laughs. "Drawing and tattooing are very different."

"I am aware of that," I reply, trying not to roll my eyes. "I'm just saying your linework is good."

"Thanks," he says again.

"You've met!" Mei comes flouncing up to us, Eric close behind her.

"What?" I ask.

"This is Cassidy!" Mei says, gesturing at the blond boy.

"Aaaah," I say, nodding with understanding. Cassidy frowns, looking back and forth between me and Mei questioningly.

"Cassidy, this is Cam," Mei explains. "I was telling her at dinner that we should go to that juice bar a few blocks over after this."

"I never say no to a good cold-pressed," Cassidy says, flashing me a grin. I can see what Mei means about him being offensively good-looking.

"I think everything is wrapping up," Eric says, looking around at the room, which has thinned out considerably. "We can probably leave any time."

We agree to meet at the juicery in fifteen minutes, which gives

Eric and Cassidy enough time to check out with their art teacher while Mei and I take the chance to say a quick goodbye to Toby, Aaron, and Claire.

"Sooooo," Mei says in a sing-song voice once we get in the car. "What did you think?"

"It was great," I say earnestly. "Did you see the one woman who does the 3D art with spoons? That was—"

"I meant about Eric," Mei interrupts as if she is unable to hold back a second longer.

"Ah," I say. "I didn't get much of a chance to talk to him, but he seems nice."

"He is incredible. Kind of shy at first, but so sweet. And he wants to be a veterinarian," she concludes, as if someone wanting to take care of animals for a living is all the proof I would need that she should start getting her dowry in order now.

"How long have you two been dating?" I ask, checking my phone and seeing a text from my mother that her plane landed at LAX.

"Oh, we haven't actually gone on a date."

"Wait, what?"

"Yeah," Mei says sheepishly. "We do text sometimes, and I've been dropping hints like crazy, but he is either completely clueless or isn't interested."

"Clueless, definitely," I say encouragingly. "You should have seen how he looked at you tonight. He obviously has a thing for you."

"You really think so?" Mei asks as we pull into the parking lot of a small shop with a bright sign over it that says Juicy Details.

"I do."

Eric and Cassidy are already inside reading a large display board with a list of various fruit and vegetable concoctions.

"What sounds good?" Cassidy leans over to ask me as I survey the menu. "It's on me."

"A milkshake?" I offer. Cassidy laughs.

"Not really into health foods?"

"Let's just say I prefer my celery covered with ranch and accompanied by wings."

"There are a lot of benefits to juicing," Cassidy says knowledgeably. "It's full of vitamins and minerals, not to mention all of the antioxidants—"

"Okay, you're starting to sound like a fitness influencer," I interject. "Just get me whatever you're having. I'm going to get us a table."

I wander outside to where several small tables and chairs are set up and plop down. Closing my eyes, I lean my head back and take a moment to enjoy the warm breeze that reminds me of being back home. Do I even get to call Preston home anymore?

"Here you go," a voice says from above me. I open my eyes to find Cassidy holding a plastic cup out to me. I take it and examine it as he sits next to me, Mei and Eric still chatting away animatedly inside.

"It's green," I point out.

"That's the kale," he says, taking a sip from his own cup as he drapes an elbow across the back of his chair.

"Cool," I say, wrinkling my nose. "Cool, cool, cool."

"It's good for you," he beams at me. "It's also got spinach, apples, and lemon."

"Like a party in a glass." I frown at it. The door chimes as Mei and Eric walk out to join us.

"Just try it already," Cassidy coaxes.

I heave an exaggerated sigh and take a tentative sip. Cassidy is looking at me expectantly.

"Well?" he says.

"It's delicious," I admit irritably.

"I have never heard someone sound so cranky about liking something," Cassidy observes. I just raise my eyebrows at him as I sip through my straw. "It's all about the hydraulic press. It's more time-consuming, but sometimes you have to take your time to do it right." Cassidy says this last part suggestively, winking at me.

"Ah, is that a sex metaphor?" I ask him sweetly. "Was that your way of letting me know that you are a gentle but thorough lover?"

"Cam," Eric interjects as Cassidy practically chokes on his juice. "Mei said you moved from Arizona?"

"I did," I say slowly, instantly wary of going into too much detail about my present circumstance. "I moved down here to live with my mother."

"I knew I recognized you!" Cassidy says in a strained voice, his eyes watering slightly. "You're Jackie Jenson's daughter."

"That's me," I say, my stomach starting to sink.

"I saw a post about you on *Chick About Town* yesterday."

I can feel my face turning red. I have been purposefully avoiding *Chick About Town*, but apparently, I must still be a hot topic.

"Oh?" I say, trying to sound unbothered.

"Yeah," Cassidy nods. "It was all about how you were on some shopping spree, something about 'adjusting to your new LA life-style with retail therapy.'"

"Okay, shopping spree my ass," I say angrily. "There was no 'spree.' I was buying new sports bras. They have excellent bounce control and a chafe-resistant band, and I regret nothing."

There is a moment of silence in which Mei, Eric, and Cassidy just look wide-eyed at me as I fume.

"Eric is going to be a senior at Winston, too," Mei says suddenly.

"It's true!" Eric says a little over-enthusiastically before asking me about what classes I'm planning on taking. I can tell he's trying to keep things light, and it makes me see why Mei likes him so much. We stay and talk for a while longer before going our separate ways.

"I'm sorry," Mei says as we drive. "Cassidy is a bit of a prick sometimes . . ."

"It's fine," I say dully, staring out the window.

"Hey, it's still pretty early," Mei says, glancing down at the clock in her car, which reads 9:37 p.m. "Do you want to come over to my place for a bit?"

I check my phone and see my mother has texted me.

Just got home. Where are you?

I type a quick reply letting her know I'm with a friend and will be home by my midnight curfew before smiling over at Mei.

"Let's do it."

EIGHT

I still have a very tenuous grasp of the layout of Los Angeles by day, so at night it's impossible for me to know where we are when we drive up to the gated neighborhood where Mei lives. She rolls down her window and punches in a code, which causes the gate to slide open. We drive in and pass about a dozen modern-looking houses before pulling into the driveway of a large brown and white Spanish-style home.

"Dad's not home," Mei says as we get out of the car and walk around to the back of the house through a latched gate. We pass by a pool and small pool house before reaching her back door. "He's got the night shift at the hospital. But mom should be home by now."

Mei pulls out a key and opens the door to a beautiful open kitchen, all decorated in white and gray with a large granite-topped island in the center. She begins scrounging around in the fridge, pulling out a jar of salsa and two bottles of water. After getting a bag of tortilla chips from the pantry, we each sit in a stool at the kitchen island.

"I thought that might be you." A pretty woman with long black hair wearing a slim t-shirt and black leggings appears, holding a glass of white wine. She comes over to sit in a stool across from us, sets her glass down, and reaches over to get a chip.

"Mom, this is Cam," Mei says through a mouthful of salsa.

"Hi, Mrs. Chen," I say, smiling at her. She looks like some kind of beautiful porcelain-skinned doll.

"I've heard a lot about you, Cam," she says warmly.

"You have?" I reply, my heart leaping with the unwitting thought that Milo might have told her about me.

"Mei tells me you have taken a liking to Joe's Diner," Mrs. Chen says, taking a sip from her wine glass.

"I have," I say, silently chiding myself. Of course she would have heard about me from Mei.

"I'm so sorry about the circumstances around you moving here," says Mrs. Chen kindly. "But I know Mei will be happy to introduce you to some people, try to make you feel welcome."

"She already has," I assure her. "I'm lucky to have met her."

"I am loving this conversation," Mei says, looking self-satisfied as she dunks another chip into the jar of salsa. "Please, keep going on about how wonderful I am."

Mei, Mrs. Chen, and I sit for a while just talking, and it's impossible to not be a little jealous that Mei's mom is exactly how I pictured a normal mother would be who doesn't have a sex tape floating around on the internet for the rest of eternity. Actually, she is way more badass than that. Even though I would imagine Dr. Chen makes enough money that she wouldn't have to work if she didn't want to, she's a top marketing consultant at a huge advertising agency. I'm aware that I'm biased, but that seems like way more important work than getting paid to promote press-on nail stickers on your Instagram like my mother did the other night.

Before we know it, it's almost 11:30, and Mei can't stop yawning. I insist to both Mei and Mrs. Chen that I'm perfectly fine to wait outside for Leo, who I had texted earlier that I needed a ride home after all. So I say my goodbyes and go outside to curl up in a pool chair, letting my eyes go unfocused as I gaze out at the water and think about how wonderful it will feel to get out of this outfit and into some pajama pants.

"Yams," a soft voice says behind me. I practically jump out of my skin but manage to keep from shrieking. I look up to see Milo standing next to me.

"You—holy sh— What?" I splutter.

"I didn't want to startle you but it seemed unavoidable, so I figured I would say the least threatening thing I could think of."

"And you went with 'yams'?" I ask incredulously, my heart still racing. Milo shrugs and walks around to sit in the chair next to mine. We sit for a second in silence before I say, "What are you doing here?"

"I live here," he replies simply. "Well, technically I live there." He points at the pool house.

"Oh," I say stupidly. "I just figured—"

"That the nineteen-year-old who is not in college and waits tables has some kind of penthouse apartment? Not so much."

"Who wants a penthouse anyway?" I say, glancing sideways at him. The light from the pool makes it look like his dark hair is shimmering. "What if the elevator breaks? Then you're just the jackass with the twentieth-floor walk-up. No, thank you."

He laughs.

"So," I continue, stretching my legs out and crossing my ankles. "Your parents are cool with you not going to college?"

"They weren't at first," he confides. "But things were really picking up with the band so they let me defer my acceptance to USC for a year."

"You got into USC?" I ask, quirking an eyebrow up at him.

"What, I don't strike you as being smart?" he says, crossing his arms.

"Yep, you got me. That's exactly what I meant. I've just been biding my time waiting to tell you how dumb I think you are."

"The timing does feel right, I have to admit."

"Thank you for the opportunity."

"You are so welcome."

We sit in silence for a minute.

"So USC, huh?" I prod. Milo blows out a breath and turns to sit so he is facing me, propping his elbows on his knees.

"Yeah. The only thing is the band hasn't had the momentum I thought we would over the last year, and now the deadline is coming up for letting USC know if I'm going to attend in the fall or not."

I swing my legs around so I'm directly across from him and smooth my skirt down over my thighs. Our knees are only a few inches from each other, and I look up to see he's watching me. I give him a small smile and ignore the flutter in my stomach.

"So what are you going to do?" I ask him.

"I have no idea." He runs his hands over his face and groans.

"Can you do both?"

"I guess, in theory," he replies contemplatively. "I just know I wouldn't be able to give one hundred percent to either one of them if I try to do both."

I pick at a hangnail on my thumb for a moment before I say, "I would love to pretend like I'm full of some sage wisdom I could throw at you, like 'everything happens for a reason' or 'follow your bliss' or whatever, but I am in no position to be dispensing advice right now."

I look at him and see his expression is sympathetic.

"Don't look at me like that," I say a little harsher than I intended. Milo looks startled.

"Like what?"

"I can tell you think I'm making some allusion to my own situation." I point at him accusingly. "Like me saying I don't have any wisdom or whatever is some vague implication that I'm having a hard time or something—"

"Cam—"

"But I'm fine. I just don't want to give you some cheesy clichéd adage about how you never know how long you have, so you've got to 'live for today because tomorrow isn't promised' or whatever dumb shit they say—"

"Cam—"

"For no reason other than crap like that is completely unhelpful—"

"YAMS!" Milo shouts, immediately silencing me. We stare at each other for a beat.

"Wh—why are you yelling about yams?" I stammer.

"It seemed like an effective way to get you to stop talking," he says calmly. I start to protest, but he continues. "Just for a minute. So I can get a word in edgewise."

I consider this.

"What does that phrase even mean, 'get a word in edgewise'?" I ask him after a moment. He sighs dramatically.

"Will you focus for a minute?" Milo chastises me, looking amused.

"Sorry."

"Why does it make you so upset to think that people feel sad for you?" he says gently. I start to feel the heat of anger rising up in my chest.

"Because I don't want anyone feeling sorry for me—"

"I didn't say 'sorry' for you," Milo interrupts, his eyes still calmly focused on me. "I said 'sad' for you. There's a difference."

"And how is it different?" I counter. I can feel the sting of tears behind my eyes, but I absolutely refuse to cry in front of him.

"I've always thought that when people feel sorry for you there's something almost patronizing about it," he says slowly. "As if they are somehow above whatever situation you're in. Being sad for someone is more like the two of you are equals, and it causes them pain to know that you're in pain. More of an empathy thing."

I swallow against the lump forming in my throat.

"So why does it make you so upset to think that people feel sad for you?" he asks again. I look at him for a few seconds.

"Six months," I say, my voice shaking a little. "My dad was diagnosed with pancreatic cancer, and then six months later he was gone."

I think I see Milo's hand twitch a little almost as if he is going to reach out and take mine, but he doesn't.

"Here's the kicker," I barrel on before he can say anything. "Finding out how bad his prognosis was, watching him go through the treatments and not get better, losing him—that was all hard enough to try and deal with. But I never anticipated that all of the sudden the things that defined who I was as a person before it happened would be overshadowed by this one huge new thing. So now instead of being 'Cam, the girl who loves books and drawing and sour gummy worms and nineties rom-coms,' I'm 'Cam, the girl whose dad died,' or 'Cam, Jackie Jenson's daughter who just moved to L.A.' I just don't know how I'll ever get back to being me again."

I start to chew on my bottom lip, tasting salt and realizing my face is wet. Dammit.

"I know Mei told you about how I came to be part of this family," Milo says softly. "She loves telling that story, but I would be happy if I never had to tell it again. My mom and dad, the Chens, have been my parents practically from the day I was born. I honestly don't think about it most of the time because I've never known anything else. But I think 'Milo, the white guy adopted by a Chinese American family' and "Milo, the guy with the dramatic backstory' are always going to be part of what defines me whether I like it or not."

I hastily swipe at my face as I mull this over.

"What I'm trying to say," Milo continues, leaning forward so I'm forced to look him in the eye. "Is that I can't say I understand what you're going through with losing your dad. But I do kind of get how it feels to be put in categories you didn't have any control over."

I can feel tears clinging to my lashes, but I don't move to wipe them away. There's a heat building in my stomach as Milo looks back at me, the corner of his mouth crooked up in a tender smile. God, his eyes are such a beautiful shade of green. I'm wondering what combination of paint colors I would have to mix up to create his exact hue when he suddenly stands up and gestures toward the parked car in the driveway just beyond the fence.

"I think your ride is here," he says. I take a moment to collect myself before standing up and following him to the gate. Before he can reach to open the latch, I hear my own timid voice say, "Milo?"

He turns around to face me, and we stand there for a while longer looking at each other.

"Thank you," I whisper, and reach out to wrap my arms around his waist. After a brief hesitation he hugs me back. With my ear pressed to his chest I can almost swear it sounds like his heart is beating as fast as mine.

He steps away too soon and pulls the gate open to where Leo is waiting.

"Goodnight," he says a little roughly as Leo gets out of the car to open the passenger door. I give him a small wave and hurriedly climb in the car.

"How was your night?" Leo asks as he backs out of the driveway.

"It was good," I say softly. I can still make out Milo's silhouette in the dark, standing with his hands in his pockets per usual as he watches the car pull away.

I head up the stairs when I get home and see the light is still on in my mother's room down the hallway to the left. I instinctively start to go straight to my room before pausing, sighing, and walking to her door.

"Come in," I hear her say after I knock, so I open the door a crack to poke my head in. She's sitting in bed reading a magazine, her entire face covered in a seaweed green face mask.

"Just wanted to let you know I'm home," I say, trying not to laugh at how ridiculous she looks.

"Wonderful!" She appears to be attempting to smile, but the mask has rendered her face immobile. "Did you have a fun night with your new friend? What is her name again?"

"Mei," I tell her. "And yeah, it was nice. How was your trip?"

"Oh, I love New York," she gushes. "And the photoshoot was just phenomenal."

"That's great, Mother," I try and fail to stifle a yawn. "Well, I'm going to bed. Goodnight."

"'Night!"

I groggily shuffle to my room. There's a note on my door from Charlie saying that Jim has already gone out, and I silently make a vow to myself that I will buy my brother all the baby food he can handle tomorrow to repay him. Jim barely raises his head as I stumble in, quickly replace my top and skirt with a t-shirt and pajama pants, wash my face, and fall asleep almost the instant my head hits the pillow.

Over the next few weeks, I start to establish somewhat of a routine. My mother has continued to be relentless in her attempts at doing mother-daughter bonding activities, and so far, we've gone pottery-making, seen a musical, and attended what turned out to be a very awkward couples' cooking class focused on foods that are aphrodisiacs. Charlie practically hyperventilated from laughing when we got home, but I couldn't help but notice he had a lot of questions regarding what we learned about.

I usually call Annie or my Aunt Margaret right afterwards to complain, but it honestly hasn't been that bad. The biggest down-side is that despite my best efforts to be utterly uninteresting, *Chick*

About Town has still been posting regularly about me. The cooking class got twisted into the headline *"Jackie Jenson and Daughter Attend Sex Workshop Together"* and my mother dragging me to her aesthetician for her chemical peel turned into *"Cam Donovan Looking to Get Plastic Surgery?"*

I finally broke down and bought some cereal for the house so I'm only going to the diner for breakfast once or twice a week, but Mei and I have started meeting up after her drama class on Tuesday and Thursday afternoons and even though we've tried out a few other places, we still usually wind up there.

"You have to come," Mei whines to me on a Thursday afternoon over a plate of fries.

"You really should," Milo agrees. We're his only table, so he's sitting next to Mei in the booth across from me.

"Only if I get to be on the list," I say. Discount Curses is playing a show at an all-ages music venue tomorrow night, and Mei is trying to persuade me to go with her, Eric, and Cassidy.

"What kind of list?" Mei asks.

"You know, *the* list," I explain. "The kind where I walk up to the front of the line and the door guy is like 'we're full' and I'm all 'I'm on the list' and he checks his clipboard or whatever and begrudgingly waves me in while all the rest of the peasants in line give me the stink eye."

Mei and Milo just gape at me.

"Those are my terms," I say, plucking a fry off the pile. "I'll go, but I want to be on the list."

"I don't think there is even going to be a list," Milo says, shaking his head. "It's a decent-sized venue, and we don't anticipate being sold out or . . ." He trails off at my look of consternation.

"I want," I say slowly, carefully enunciating every word, "to be on the list."

"Whatever," Milo groans.

"The top of the list," I amend.

"Fine," he affirms. "You will be at the top of the list."

"I'm your sister!" Mei protests. "If anyone is at the top of the list it should be me."

"There isn't even going to be a list!" Milo says in exasperation.

"I'm willing to share top billing with you," I tell Mei, ignoring Milo.

"I'm listening," Mei says.

"Together, at the top of the list, we will be unstoppable," I reply solemnly.

"You two are insane," Milo says, getting out of the booth and stretching.

"I have an insatiable hunger for power," I say. "Also a hunger for pie. Do you still have blueberry?"

NINE

The following night I find myself next to Cassidy in the back seat of Eric's Range Rover as we head to Milo's show.

"So what are you working on now that the art show is over?" I ask Cassidy conversationally as Eric and Mei chat in the front seat.

"I actually won't have much time the rest of the summer to work on anything new," he answers, pocketing his phone from where he had been scrolling through TikTok. "I'm interning at my dad's tech company for the rest of the summer. He only agreed to let me do the art class to build up my college resume."

"Really?" I ask, taken aback. "But you're so good."

"Drawing is just a hobby," Cassidy says dismissively. "Like playing football. Just something fun to do in my free time."

"Wow," I say, shaking my head.

"That surprises you?"

"Well, yeah," I frown. "I just thought . . . you don't want to do something with it for a living?"

"Even if I did, my dad would never let me. He fully expects me to come work for him after I get my business degree. That's always been the plan."

"Wow," I say again. I always took it for granted that my dad never blinked an eye at my plan to major in art in college. "You didn't really strike me as the tech bro type."

"Oh?" Cassidy eyes me curiously. "And what type did I strike you as?"

"The type who has a very strong and kind of weird love of juice?" I suggest.

"The human body is a temple," Cassidy says with what I hope is a fake seriousness, but I bite the inside of my cheeks to keep from laughing just in case. "Where are you planning to go to college?"

"Oh," I say, wishing I had never brought the subject up. "I don't really know."

"You have to have some idea," Cassidy presses.

"Well, I actually was thinking about majoring in art," I explain hesitantly. "Graphic design at Savannah College of Art and Design in Georgia. My aunt lives there, so I could get in-state tuition after a year. But I don't know if I'm doing that anymore."

Cassidy considers this for a moment. Just as he opens his mouth to say something else, I see we've pulled into the venue and blurt, "Oh look! We made it! And there's a parking spot!"

This is hardly a revelation seeing as how the parking lot is only about half full, so there are plenty of open spots, but at least it gets us off the topic of our stupid futures. We pull into a space and make our way to the entrance of the venue. There are three bands playing tonight, and the first one doesn't go on for another twenty minutes; so, much to my dismay, there is no line for us to make our way to the front of. I still throw my chin up as I stride up to the bouncer and say, "Cam Donovan and Mei Chen. We're on the list."

"There isn't really a list . . ." the guy at the door starts to say, shuffling through his papers. "Oh, do you mean this?"

He holds out a piece of paper that has "The List" written at the top in Milo's slanted handwriting. Underneath, Mei's name and mine are in all caps, with "everyone else" written in minuscule text below it.

"That's us," I say importantly.

"And these are our guests," Mei says, gesturing to Eric and Cassidy.

"Go on in," the door guy says, looking slightly confused as he puts on our wristbands that indicate we're under twenty-one.

"Nice touch," I whisper to Mei as we walk in.

"I thought so," she says as we walk up to the bar. We each get a soda and head to sit at one of the tables lining the balconies on either side of the room. Mei and Eric start talking about a new album that just came out by an artist I've never heard of, so I sit back and scan the room. There are several clusters of people standing in front of the stage area, and most of the tables seem to already be filled or reserved. Despite what Milo said, it looks like it's going to be a pretty full show.

"Hey," Cassidy says sheepishly, leaning in to me. "I meant to say this earlier . . . I got the sense that I upset you that night I brought up the whole *Chick About Town* thing. And then again tonight when I was talking about how I'm majoring in business instead of art. If it's more than just a hobby for you, I think it's great that you are thinking about going to college for art—"

"It's all good, really," I stop him.

"Okay, cool," Cassidy says, looking relieved. "Can we maybe just . . . I don't know, start over?"

"Of course," I reply.

Cassidy lets out an exhale.

"So, Cassidy . . ." I trail off.

"Slaton," he supplies.

"Cassidy Slaton," I say. "It's nice to re-meet you."

I offer a hand, which he shakes. He starts to say something else, but there's a cheer from the crowd as the first band walks on stage. Cassidy and I smile at each other and settle in. They are about three songs in when I happen to glance over to where a group of people is standing off to the side of the stage. I recognize the members of Discount Curses watching the show and see Milo is there, too . . . with an arm wrapped around Leighton's shoulders. I can't look away as she leans in to say something in his ear, which makes him laugh. My stomach gives a little lurch as he bends down to kiss her.

"I'm going to get a refill," I shout over the music, hoping the tightness in my voice isn't too noticeable. I take my purse and weave my way through the crowd, which has filled in significantly since we first got here. I push through the front door, tripping slightly in my hurry to get outside. The door guy reaches out and grabs my elbow to help steady me, eying me suspiciously.

"I'm not drunk, I swear," I say breathlessly to him, which is probably the exact kind of thing a drunk person would say, but whatever. He just shakes his head and turns back to the line of people now trailing into the parking lot waiting to get in.

I go around the other side of the building and find a spot to sit that doesn't look too dirty. I'm not wearing anything fancy—just a cropped vintage t-shirt, black jeans, and my Docs. But that doesn't mean I don't want to look at least somewhat put-together, even if I don't particularly feel that way right now. Sinking down, I stretch my legs out in front of me and lean my head back against the bricks of the building.

"You okay?" a voice says from above me. I look up to find Mei looming over me, her face scrunched up in concern.

"Yeah, I'm fine," I say as she takes a seat next to me. "I just get a little overwhelmed in crowds sometimes."

She nods, plucking a blade of grass up and twirling it in between her fingers. "Do you . . . want to talk about it?"

"Can we maybe just sit here for a minute?" I ask. She nods again, and the silence stretches out for a few moments while I wage an internal debate with myself. Finally, I blurt out, "Mei, I think I might kind of have a thing for your brother."

"I know," she says simply.

"You—wait, you do?" I ask, startled. Mei just rolls her eyes.

"You both are so obvious it's a little hard to watch, honestly."

"Us . . . both?" I say. "You mean, you think he—"

"I don't know for sure," Mei says, holding her hand up to silence me. "He hasn't said anything to me about it."

"What about Leighton?"

Mei makes a disgusted face. "She's the worst. But they have been together a long time, and for whatever reason he seems to like her."

I nod, untying and retying my shoelaces just to have something to do. "You should go back in. I just need one more minute."

"Are you sure?" she says, frowning slightly.

"Absolutely," I insist, giving her a half-hearted thumbs-up. I watch her stand up and head back around to the door. I close my eyes and imagine what my dad would say to me. For someone who probably went on fewer than ten dates my entire childhood, he dispensed some pretty great wisdom when I came to him about problems I was having with boys I liked. I conjure up the image of him sitting in his armchair, resting his chin on his hand, and listening intently while I pour my heart out to him.

"Cam, you aren't the kind of girl to go after someone else's boyfriend," I can almost hear him say while he scratches his beard thoughtfully. "You just have to ride this out. If you and this boy are supposed to get together, you will."

I smile to myself and whisper, "Thanks, Dad." The crunch of gravel jolts me out of my daydream. My eyes fly open to see several guys standing a few feet away in front of what must be the backstage door, holding vape pens and looking at me like I'm a lunatic. I scramble up, dusting off my pants, and give them a stern look.

"It's impolite to eavesdrop on people who are talking to themselves," I say haughtily before turning on my heel and walking away.

When I walk in, Discount Curses is just getting their gear set up on stage. I order another soda from the bar and rejoin Mei, Eric, and

Cassidy. Thankfully, Cassidy doesn't ask about my absence, and I don't offer up an explanation.

I survey the room, which is almost completely full now. I can't help but notice Leighton sitting with a group of equally beautiful girls at a table near the stage. Determined to ignore them, I turn to Cassidy and start to say something but am drowned out by sudden cheers.

"What's up, Los Angeles?" the singer asks the crowd. "I'm Chris and we are Discount Curses. Let's make some noise tonight!"

He launches into a guitar lick that I recognize from the pool party. I'm impressed that the crowd toward the front of the stage, which seems to be comprised of the most enthusiastic fans, knows every word to every song.

Roughly an hour later, Discount Curses finishes their final song, and Mei and I wander over to where they have a table set up to sell t-shirts, CDs, and vinyl albums. We stand in the line for a few minutes before the band members appear, ready to meet their modest but adoring fanbase.

"Things seem to be going well with you and Eric," I say quietly to Mei, glancing over to where the boys are still sitting at our table. Mei's eyes light up as she lets out a breath.

"Oh my God, I didn't want to say anything earlier because you were sad, and I didn't want to flaunt my love life in your face seeing as how you are pining for my brother—"

"Mei," I hiss, peering around to make sure Milo is out of earshot.

"Sorry! But yes, Eric asked me if I want to get dinner with him tomorrow night."

Mei is practically bouncing with excitement. I smile, genuinely happy for her. She starts rattling off the pros and cons of potential restaurant options, and pretty soon we've made it to the front of the line.

"Well, look who it is," Milo says, grinning at us. "I take it you didn't have any trouble getting in?"

"Please," I scoff. "Two high-ranking list occupants like ourselves? Of course not."

"You liked that, huh?" Milo chuckles.

"I almost thought about asking to keep it so I could get you all to sign it, but I didn't want it to look like this was my first time. Being on a list, I mean."

I see Mei smirking at me from the corner of my eye, so I clear my throat and continue, "I would like to buy one of the red t-shirts, please. Size medium."

"You don't have to buy anything," Milo protests. "We have plenty—just take one."

"Absolutely not," I say, pulling my wallet out of my bag.

Milo looks like he's about to argue, but at that moment Leighton materializes out of nowhere to drape herself around him. I hurriedly fish out a twenty-dollar bill as she kisses him on the cheek.

"Hello, Leighton," Mei says with obvious dislike.

"Hi, Mei," Leighton replies loftily, then looks at me. "Hi, Mei's friend."

"It's Cam," I say. "We've met actually . . ."

But Leighton has already refocused her attention on Milo. I find a shirt in my size on the table and lay my money down. Milo is too busy whispering to a pouty-looking Leighton to notice us leave to go sit back down.

"She really is the worst," Mei shakes her head as we rejoin Eric and Cassidy. I glance back to where Milo and Leighton seem to still be having a heated conversation, and I make a decision. I have too much going on in my life to worry about this guy who: 1) already has a girlfriend; and, 2) has a type that is nothing like me if said girlfriend is any indication. So I peel my eyes away and vow to ignore whatever feelings I have for Milo from this point forward.

We stay and listen to the last band, then head to a late-night pizza place nearby. Cassidy and Eric somehow end up going back and forth doing terrible celebrity impressions that have me and Mei practically rolling on the floor giggling. I reach for another slice of pizza, dabbing my face with a napkin from where Eric's attempt at a Christopher Walken impersonation has me laughing so hard my eyes are watering. In this moment, it really does seem possible to start figuring out how to move forward with my life.

I wake up the next morning feeling energized by my new resolve to make the best out of the shitty hand the universe has dealt me. After a quick shower, I put on yoga pants and a tank top and head to the kitchen. Ignoring my craving for pancakes and bacon from Joe's, I elect instead to make a smoothie from an assortment of fruits and vegetables I find in the fridge. I even take a picture of my smoothie, which is dark green thanks to the frozen spinach I added, and text it to Cassidy with the caption, *"aren't you proud of me?"*

Charlie jogs down the stairs in his pajamas, eying me warily as he walks in the kitchen.

"Whatcha doin'?" he asks, removing the pitcher from the blender and examining the contents.

"I'm going to a yoga class this morning," I inform him as I scroll through my phone looking at the schedules of various studios nearby. "Then maybe I'll go to the park and read, or do a little shopping. Today is all about me."

"We love a good self-care day," Charlie says excitedly, pouring himself a glass of smoothie. "Want some company?"

I feed Jim and take him out to pee, promising him that we'll have some epic play time this afternoon. According to Charlie, our mother had an early meeting this morning with a company that is interested in collaborating on a line of shoes, so we leave her a note letting her know our plans and head out. Charlie drives, and as we head to the yoga studio where he takes classes, I remark that I'm going to bring up the idea of getting a car to our mother.

"Whatever happened to that station wagon you had the last time I came to visit?"

"She finally croaked for good a few months ago," I say nostalgically. Bernie, my station wagon, was already in pretty rough shape when my dad and I had salvaged it from a junkyard and fixed it up enough to get me to and from school. "We were going to go car shopping but never got around to it."

"Well, I'm sure we can go out and find you something nice and boring that doesn't go too fast."

"So supportive," I joke, flicking him on the arm.

I thought any very rudimentary yoga skills I had picked up from the classes Annie convinced me to go to with her would be rusty seeing as how I hadn't been since my dad first got sick, but I'm impressed by how much I remember. After class, I sign up for a summer special they're offering students, and Charlie and I decide to ditch my original park idea and get lunch before we go shopping.

Shopping with Charlie turns out to be highly entertaining as he provides an almost constant stream-of-consciousness commentary on what he deems "fresh" or "stale." We spend the next several hours driving all around Los Angeles to his favorite clothing boutiques and home goods stores. I even convince him to stop at a used bookstore, which he has to practically drag me out of, though not before I'm able to purchase an armload of new books and comics.

When we finally pull into our driveway, it's mid-afternoon, and we're both exhausted. We haul our considerable amount of bags into the house and each immediately peel off to our respective rooms with the intention of taking a nap. When I walk into my room, however, I find my bed is already being occupied by a forlorn-looking Jim.

"Aw, crap," I say, looking into his pitiful face. "I promised you playtime. Alright, chop chop."

Jim launches off the bed, tail wagging furiously as I snag a tennis ball from a basket of his toys in the corner. I decide to just take him to the backyard since it's fenced in, even if my mother gets cranky when I let Jim run around off-leash. We play fetch until Jim seems exhausted and happy, and I head inside to get a glass of water. My mother is standing in front of the open oven, holding a casserole dish carefully in between two pink oven mitts. She gingerly pushes it into the oven and sets the timer. The woman may be totally helpless when it comes to most household tasks, but she is a damn good cook.

"What are you making?" I ask, getting a cup from the cupboard.

"It's a spaghetti squash bake," she replies as she starts putting away containers of various spices and herbs. "It's like eating pasta."

"Cool," I say, deciding not to point out that to me the only thing that is like eating pasta is eating actual pasta.

Just as I'm starting to lead Jim back upstairs, I notice a series of large photo printouts sitting on the kitchen table. I do a double-take, practically spitting out my mouthful of water as I try to come to terms with what I'm seeing.

"Mother," I manage to utter. She glances over to where I'm looking.

"Oh!" she says cheerily, wiping her hands on a dish towel and striding over to the photos. "Those are the proofs from that shoot I went to New York for a few weeks ago."

"Mother," I repeat. "Why are you naked?"

Indeed, each of the photographs features my mother completely nude and seductively clutching a sheet that barely covers the parts no daughter should ever have to see of her mother's past infancy.

"It's for *Touch Magazine*," she says, clearly unable to see how uncomfortable I am as she proudly looks down at the pictures.

"They wanted to do a 'stripped down' kind of thing for their September issue."

"But you're so . . . naked," I reply intelligently.

"Yes, honey," my mother says, giving me a concerned look. "That's kind of the point."

"Mother," I continue, unable to look at the photos anymore. "Did it ever occur to you that maybe your teenage daughter who is so desperately trying to keep a low profile might not love having your picture plastered right on the cover of a magazine looking so . . . exposed?"

My mother looks dumbfounded.

"Honey," she finally says. "It's not like I haven't done tasteful nudity before."

"Okay," I argue reasonably, trying to regain my composure. "But that was before I lived here when nobody cared who I was, and I wasn't being stalked by a gossip site."

"I could see about getting out of it," she starts, shifting on her feet uncomfortably. "Though the photos did turn out so lovely—"

"It's fine," I stop her, feeling resigned. "Just, I don't know, at least give me a heads-up next time."

"Of course," she says, looking relieved.

I inadvertently glance down at the photos again.

"You do look pretty hot though," I concede, which makes her beam. "Just please don't put me in a position where those words come out of my mouth in that order about my mother ever, *ever* again."

TEN

A few days after "Boobiegate," as Charlie has come to call it despite my threats to never talk to him again, I'm folding some of my laundry when my mother knocks on my bedroom door.

"Cam," she says after I tell her to come in. "I got an invitation today to attend the St. Agnes Hospital fundraising gala on Saturday. You should come with me!"

"I don't know—" I start to say as I search the laundry basket for the sock that matches the one I'm holding, but my mother cuts me off.

"Come on," she says plaintively. "Charlie is coming, and I would love to go as a family. It will be fun!"

"Ugh . . . okay." After my mother squeals with delight and bustles off to make some phone calls, I realize why the name St. Agnes Hospital sounds so familiar—that's where Mei told me her father works. I text her to ask if she'll be there and try not to wonder what the chances are that Milo will be, too.

. . .

My mother takes my consent to go to the gala as a green light to book what she feels are all of the necessary appointments we need in preparation for the event. She keeps me on a tight schedule every day leading up to Saturday, continually texting me reminders about my facial, manicure, and haircut. Finally on Thursday when I find her stylist Marcel waiting outside my yoga class to ask me what kind of "aesthetic" I had envisioned for myself, I text her, threatening not to come if she keeps bombarding me with these kinds of antics. Charlie is equally as offended, but I suspect it's only because he wanted to be the one to pick out a gown for me. He has had no issue pampering himself by tagging along to all of the appointments my mother has scheduled for us.

Chick About Town has managed to continue photographing what seems like every public outing I make, though I have no idea how. I've never noticed anyone who obviously had a camera and was taking our picture, but somehow, they have still posted photos of us all week: me and Charlie through the window of the nail salon, me and my mother as we left the spa after our facials. I had started to think the buzz around me was dying down a little, but ever since someone snapped a picture of me sitting on the ground outside of the Discount Curses show last weekend with my head in my hands, and the site posted it with the title *"Cam Donovan on the Verge of a Breakdown?"*, there apparently has been a renewed interest.

To my great relief, Mei confirms she will also be at the gala with Milo and their parents. Eric is out of town, so he isn't able to be her date, but she does warn me that Leighton is coming with Milo.

"It's really fine," I tell her when we see each other on Friday afternoon. I managed to slip out of the house for a few hours so we could get some frozen yogurt and I could take a break from the frenzy that comes with my mother getting ready for an event. Mei looks at me skeptically. "I decided I don't have the time or energy to be interested in someone right now."

"That's too bad," she laments, her spoon hovering over her cup. "I was kind of hoping you and Cassidy would start something up so the four of us can go on double dates together."

"Just because I don't want to date right now doesn't mean we can't all hang out," I point out. "But enough about my dating life or lack thereof—I need to know what you're wearing to this thing."

"I got the most beautiful gown," Mei sighs happily. "It makes me feel like I'm floating and should travel everywhere exclusively by bubble like Glinda from *The Wizard of Oz*. What about you?"

"I don't actually know yet," I say with a shrug. "Maybe my old prom dress if I have any say in it, which I probably won't."

"I hope it's nice enough," Mei frowns.

"Oh, relax. It's not like it's the Met Gala."

"I'm just saying," Mei says.

Despite my genuine lack of interest in fashion, I'm starting to second-guess myself by the time I get home a few hours later. I open my closet and fish out the garment bag containing my prom dress from sophomore year. Even though prom was only for juniors and seniors, I got to go because one of my senior friends in the art program wasn't out of the closet to his parents yet but didn't want to miss it. I was all too happy to be what he called his "one night only beard" for the chance to hang out in a limo with our friends.

I hook the bag on my closet door and unzip it, revealing the bright red taffeta dress. Annie had also gotten asked to prom by her junior boyfriend at the time, so we went dress shopping together. Whereas she was determined to get a ballgown that would make her look like a Disney princess, I opted for a simple red dress on the clearance rack that caught my eye. Once she saw it on me, Annie wholeheartedly approved. On the night of prom, she insisted on doing my hair and makeup, giving me a pinup hairstyle and a red lip. It was probably the prettiest I have ever felt. Dad took about a thousand pictures before we all piled into a limo and proceeded to have the quintessential perfect prom night. I mean, aside from my date being secretly gay. Though, honestly, I think that made the night that much better. There was no pressure to have sex, and he could tell me I had lipstick on my teeth without me feeling mortified.

Shaking myself out of my nostalgia, I zip the dress back into its bag before hastily hanging it up in the back of the closet. The idea of wearing that dress again knowing there is no way my memories of the night I first wore it could be topped is making me feel weird and sad. Plus, it serves as a painful reminder that I didn't get to go to my own junior year prom a few months ago because I was trying to spend as much time with Dad as possible.

I wait until my throat feels less tight before striding into Charlie's room, where I find him lounging on the burgundy chaise in front of his window.

"I have a problem," I say, throwing myself onto his bed. He looks up from the smutty romance book he's reading.

"Hello to you, too."

"You have to promise me that you won't be smug."

"Oh, Cammy," he purrs. "You know I can't do that."

He tosses his book on the floor and turns to face me, looking so much like Kate Winslet in Titanic that I almost ask him if he wants me to paint him like one of my French girls. But I refrain. I'm on a mission.

"I don't have anything to wear tomorrow," I admit reluctantly.

"I thought Mom had Marcel taking care of that," he says, frowning.

"About that," I reply lightly, not looking Charlie in the eye as I run my fingers through one of the fluffy throw pillows on his bed. "I may or may not have told him to screw off because I am a competent almost-adult who can dress herself. Though I may or may not have used some slightly more colorful language."

There's a brief silence in which Charlie just stares at me disapprovingly.

"In my defense, he completely ruined any semblance of inner peace I had found during my savasana."

"I'm going to help you," Charlie says as he grabs his phone and starts manically texting. "Because I'm a benevolent person and because if you look like a hot mess, that is a poor reflection on me."

"How altruistic of you."

"Do you want my help or not?"

"I am already regretting this . . . but yes, please."

Within half an hour, two of Charlie's interns are at the front door, each wielding a giant rack of long dresses.

"Don't get too excited," he says, mistaking my wide-eyed look as anticipation rather than apprehension. "Most of these are sample sizes, which run small. But I'm sure we can find something."

We help the interns wheel the racks into the living room, and I covertly slip each of them a twenty-dollar bill as they leave. I know for a fact Charlie pays his interns a small hourly wage in addition to the college credit they receive, but they still had to come all the way here just because I was kind of an asshat to my mother's stylist.

"Okay, so here's what I'm thinking," Charlie says as we both stand with our arms crossed, surveying the racks of dresses. "We divide and conquer. I take this rack, you take that one. We'll go through the dresses, pick out the ones we think are good candidates—"

"That one," I say, pointing to a long emerald green dress at the end of one of the racks.

"But—"

"That one," I repeat, pointing more emphatically. Charlie looks slightly grief-stricken.

"You haven't even looked . . ." he trails off as I ignore him, pluck the green gown off the rack, and march upstairs to try it on.

"At least let me help you," Charlie whines as he jogs after me.

"Charlie," I say solemnly after he zips me into the dress and we examine my reflection in the mirror. "I'm not going to bullshit you. I think a lot of the stuff you've designed is kind of weird. But this dress is really beautiful."

"I'm going to ignore the backhanded part of that compliment and just say that yes, it is. I outdid myself on this one."

"Your humility continues to be your best quality," I retort, rolling my eyes at him before turning back to look at myself again.

Miraculously, the dress fits me like a glove. I normally wouldn't be caught dead in a neckline this low, but the delicate beading and sequins are elegant enough that it doesn't make me feel scandalous. Plus, it has straps, so with a little dress tape I feel pretty confident I won't be in danger of having a nip slip, even though I'm sure *Chick About Town* would love to have some salacious story about me flashing a bunch of doctors and nurses.

"As disappointed as I am that I won't get to play dress-up with you like you're my own little real-life mannequin, I don't think we're going to do better than this," Charlie says as he unzips me. "I am going to absolutely insist you let Mom's glam team work on you tomorrow though."

"Fine," I consent. "I'm just ready for this whole ordeal to be over with."

When I come downstairs the next morning around nine o'clock, my mother is sitting in the kitchen drinking a cup of coffee. She looks me up and down as I open the fridge to pull out a container of orange juice.

"You look well-rested," she says. "Excellent."

"Thank you, I guess?" I respond, pouring myself a glass.

"The hair and makeup artists will be here at noon," she says, checking her phone. "And we will need to leave by five."

I choke down my mouthful of orange juice to keep from spitting it all over her. "It's going to take *five hours* to get ready?"

"You're right." My mother starts furiously typing into her phone. "I don't know what I was thinking. I'll tell them to get here at eleven."

"Mother," I say disbelievingly. "Don't you think that is a bit excessive?"

"Dear," she replies in a tone that sounds like she's trying to explain something very complicated to someone very stupid. "You haven't been to your first big event yet so you don't know how this all works. But it takes time to get red carpet ready."

"I thought this was a fundraiser. Is there even going to be a red carpet?"

"It's an expression," my mother says as she waves a hand dismissively.

"Whatever," I grumble. "I'm taking Jim to the park."

"Be back by eleven!" she calls after me as I head upstairs scowling.

The entire downstairs is a flurry of activity when I return home. The living room furniture has been moved to make space for three chairs, half a dozen portable lights, and several tables covered in curling irons, makeup, and jewelry. Charlie and our mother are already seated and wearing matching face masks.

"You're late," my mother says, not bothering to open her eyes underneath her white paper mask.

"Traffic was bad," I say as I let Jim off his leash and watch him lope upstairs, presumably to take a nap.

"Traffic is always bad," Charlie counters. He's sitting with his feet in a bubbling portable foot spa, flanked by two people who are each manicuring one of his hands.

"It's hard to take either of you seriously when you both look like serial killers," I point out. My mother and Charlie both raise their heads and give me matching dirty looks. "I'm going to go take a shower."

When I reemerge, I'm immediately whisked into a chair, and one of the many people clad in black who my mother refers to as her "team" starts blow drying my hair.

"You look thrilled," Charlie says with a smirk. He now has both of his feet wrapped in towels and is eating a salad.

"Do I really have much of a choice other than to just give myself over to the process?" I ask as someone else carefully fits a mask onto my face. Charlie pulls out his phone and snaps a picture.

"For posterity," he says when I glare at him. He picks his salad back up and holds it out to me. "Want a bite? It's broccoli and brussels."

I just wrinkle my nose in response.

"Whatever, your loss."

A few hours later, my nails are painted, my eyebrows are plucked, my hair has been swept back into a chignon at the nape of my neck, and I'm pleasantly surprised that despite how long it took to get my makeup done, it actually doesn't feel too heavy. The only thing left to do is put my dress on, though I refuse to let a bunch of strangers see me naked. I make Charlie come behind the temporary changing curtain someone put up to help zip me in. After we've gotten me securely into the gown, he gestures toward a table where at least a dozen pairs of heels are sitting.

"Ugh," I wrinkle my nose. "Do I have to?"

"What did you think, that you were going to wear your Keds?" he says patronizingly. When I don't reply, he continues, "Look, I have a pair of flats ready for you for when the dancing starts. But you have to at least start with the heels."

This seems like a fair compromise, so I pick out the least menacing-looking pair of heels and let someone strap them to my feet. My mother has emerged from behind her own changing curtain, where she had zero qualms with having no less than four people help her get dressed. She actually looks really beautiful in a sapphire one-shoulder gown with her blonde hair straight and swept to one side. She notices me and beams, gesturing me over to where she's standing in front of a giant full-length mirror. I walk over carefully, trying not to trip in my shoes.

"You look gorgeous," she gushes. I gaze into the mirror and gawk as I examine my reflection. The person staring back at me is almost unrecognizable. First of all, the dress is showing off a figure I didn't know I had and could probably not achieve showing off again if I tried. Second, it turns out that people who actually know how to do makeup and hair can make someone as plain-looking as me appear like they belong on a red carpet.

"Wow," Charlie exclaims, eyebrows raised as he walks out in his velvet purple suit and looks me over. "Check you out. It seems you got that rom-com movie makeover, after all."

I scowl. "You're doing that thing people do when someone who normally doesn't wear makeup gets all done up, and then you act really shocked that they're capable of looking good. It's a little insulting, you know."

"All you have to do is give them the crabby look that's on your face right now, and it will remind them that you'll turn back into a pumpkin at midnight," Charlie says in a falsely sweet voice. I punch him lightly in the shoulder.

"The car is here," my mother says, ushering us out the door. I can feel my eyes widen as I step outside and behold the black limousine waiting for us.

"Did you get an upgrade for the evening?" I ask Leo after he gets my mother and Charlie situated and comes over to the other side of the limo to open the door for me.

"Something like that," he says with a smile.

Even though the fancy hotel where the gala is being held isn't that far from where we live, it still takes forty-five minutes to get there because of traffic. By the time we arrive, it's almost six o'clock and I'm ravenous.

"Bet you're wishing you had some of my salad now," Charlie says smugly.

I give him a dirty look as we pull up to the bustling valet parking stand. Even though there isn't a red carpet, there is still a photographer posted up at the hotel entrance taking pictures as people walk in. I humor my mother and Charlie by posing for several photos with them before having to drag them into the building so I can search for some hors d'oeuvres. The ballroom where the event is being held is not hard to find, and I practically tackle the first waiter I see carrying a tray of food.

"Slow down," Charlie says through clenched teeth as I pluck up six meatballs on toothpicks.

"Don't be jealous of my balls," I say with a wink as I pop a meatball into my mouth. Satisfied to have at least a little something in my stomach, I look around the ballroom. It's beautifully decorated to resemble a garden at sunset. Between the soft blue and orange lighting, the real trees covered in twinkling lights that line the room, and the giant floral centerpieces on each table, it really does feel like we could be outside right now.

"Let's find our table," Charlie says. "Mom saw someone she was on *Baking with B-Listers* with, so she'll be a while."

"One sec." I've just spotted someone with a tray of spring rolls and make a beeline over. I shift my toothpicks of meatballs to one hand, holding them in between my fingers like I'm Wolverine, and start piling spring rolls onto a cocktail napkin.

"Someone's hungry."

I look up to see Milo and Leighton standing on the other side of the waiter. Leighton is wearing a shimmery pastel purple gown with a low-cut bodice. Her hair and makeup are flawless, of course, and she looks like a runway model. But my eyes are instantly drawn to Milo. He's wearing a simple tailored black tuxedo that seems like it was made for him. I can't even make fun of his bowtie because he looks like the love interest in every rom-com I've ever read. I snap myself out of it and peer down at my appetizer haul.

"Some girls like bouquets of flowers. I much prefer bouquets of meat."

Milo laughs, a sound I have inadvertently grown to love, and I can't stifle a grin.

"I'm Leighton, by the way," Leighton chimes in, giving me a simpering smile and extending a hand toward me.

"You . . . wait, are you serious?" I reply, frowning at her as I try to juggle all of my food so I can shake her hand. "I'm Cam. We've met like, several times now."

"Sorry, can't place you," she says dismissively.

"I think they're about to start," Milo says hurriedly, and I swear he looks annoyed. It does seem that everyone is moving toward their seats. I tell Milo I'll catch up with him later and do a quick scan for my mother and Charlie. I spot them seated at a table on the other side of the room, so I make my way over, careful not to trip in my heels. As I settle into my chair, I can see where Milo is sitting with Leighton, Mei, and Dr. and Mrs. Chen several tables in front of us. And I'm keenly aware of the fact that Milo and Leighton look like they are arguing.

Eleven

Thankfully, dinner is served while speakers from different divisions of the hospital get up to talk about the research their department is doing, and several major donors are recognized. There's a silent auction following dinner that I only half pay attention to as I eat my chocolate mousse dessert, then someone gets up to introduce the band that will be the entertainment for the rest of the evening. People start migrating toward the dance floor as the band, complete with both a male and female singer and a small horn section, begins playing their first song.

My mother gets up and starts circulating around the room, and almost immediately Mei is in her empty chair.

"Finally," she says, reaching for my mother's untouched dessert. "I swear these things get longer every year."

"Aw, you look pretty," I tell her as I admire her dress. She's wearing an elegant chiffon dress with cap sleeves in a tangerine orange color that only she could pull off. She touches a hand to her fishtail side braid as she preens a little.

"Why, thank you," she says. "You do, too! That dress is simply marvelous, darling."

"Thank you," Charlie says, leaning over from where he is sitting on my other side.

"Charlie, this is my friend Mei." I make the introduction as Charlie and Mei shake hands. "Mei, my brother, Charlie. He designed the dress, which is why he is so humbly taking all of the credit for how I look tonight."

"It's a great dress," Mei admires.

"I like her," Charlie says approvingly. "Now, enough with the talking. Let's dance."

Charlie stands up and extends a hand dramatically to each of us. The three of us start to walk arm in arm to the dance floor, but I stop them so I can unstrap my heels and toss them underneath my chair. Shaking his head, Charlie pulls out a pair of flat sandals from one of his jacket pockets.

"Ohhhhhh, my God, I love you so much," I moan in relief as I put them on.

The band has just started playing "Sweet Caroline," and Charlie, Mei, and I start jumping around like maniacs as we sing along. This band knows what they're doing, because every time one of us says we're going to take a break, they play yet another song we can't resist sticking around for. I don't mind though. For the first time in such a long time, I'm not feeling guilty about having fun. Dad was always the first one on the dance floor at a wedding reception, so I know he would be all about this.

After a while, I tell Charlie and Mei I'll be back in a few minutes, though they don't seem to care as they're too busy concentrating on doing the right moves to "Wobble." I head in search of a bathroom, which I find down the hall. After washing my hands, dabbing on some powder foundation that the makeup artist absolutely insisted I keep in my clutch, and re-pinning a few strands of hair I managed to dance loose from my bun, I head back into the ballroom and stop by the bar to get a Coke.

As I turn around, I notice I'm standing pretty close to Milo's table, where he is leaning back in his chair clutching a glass of red wine as he watches everyone on the dance floor. I hesitate briefly, then walk over to sit in the chair next to him.

"Hey," I say before taking a sip of my Coke. Milo looks over at me, eyes slightly unfocused. I search the room before continuing, "Where's Leighton?"

"She left," he says bitterly, looking down at his wine glass as he swirls it around. "She got a last-minute offer to do a paid Instagram post at some event, so she went even though she knows how important this is to my family..."

He shakes his head as he trails off.

"That sucks," I say gently. "I'm really sorry."

He looks up at me and shrugs before downing the rest of his wine in one gulp.

"Whoa, there," I say as he reaches for the half-empty bottle sitting on the table. "Aren't you afraid your parents will see?"

He just shrugs again and pours himself another glass. I watch him for a moment before standing up and snatching the glass away from him.

"Hey!" he objects.

"Come on," I demand, grabbing his bicep and pulling him up. I can feel his muscles tense beneath his tuxedo coat.

"Come where?" he replies, slurring little.

"You're going to come dance it out with us. Duh."

"Cam—"

"Nope," I say, holding a hand up to silence him. "I'm not going to sit here and let you pout and get drunk at your dad's big work event. Let's go."

I drag him over to where Charlie and Mei are still dancing, arms thrown up in the air as they sing along to "Mr. Brightside."

"Milo," I shout over the noise as the last chorus finishes. I cross my arms and give him a stern look. "Ask me if I ever."

Milo stares blankly back at me, his hands shoved into his pockets.

"I need you to ask me if I ever," I say with more urgency.

"I don't get—"

"I SAID ASK ME IF I EVER!" I bellow.

"Do you ever?" he asks flatly, looking uncomfortable.

"I NEVERRRRRR!" I belt in unison with the band and everyone on the dance floor as they reach the outro of the song. "Ask me again if I ever!"

"Do you ever?" Milo repeats, shaking his head at me as he catches on to what I'm doing.

"I NEVERRRRRR!" This time Charlie and Mei zealously sing with me, zeroing their attention in on Milo as well. Milo reluctantly cracks a smile and joins in so that we all finish the song together. We cajole him into sticking around, and within a few songs he seems to have loosened up, though I'm not sure how much of that can be attributed to the wine. The four of us continue like that for a while, dancing and laughing, until Charlie and Mei both say they are tapping out and go in search of some bottles of water. No sooner do they exit then of course the band starts playing a slow song. Milo and I stand awkwardly, looking at each other as people around us start to pair off. We both begin speaking at the same time.

Milo: "Should we dance—"

Me: "Want to get some fresh air—"

"Fresh air sounds great," Milo says, and I try not to look too taken aback that he just asked me to dance. "I think the outdoor lounge is this way."

I pick up my purse and follow him as he exits the ballroom. He pushes through a door leading to an outside area where numerous couches and chairs are situated around tables with fire pits built in.

"Pick a spot," he says, and I choose a comfy-looking couch in the corner. To my surprise, he settles in next to me on the couch rather than taking one of the adjacent chairs. My heartbeat picks up a little being this close to him, even though there are several other groups of people out here, so it isn't like we're alone.

I steal a look over at him to find he's gazing at the fire.

"You look nice tonight," he says, not taking his eyes off the flames. "I meant to tell you that earlier."

"Oh." I'm glad that it's pretty dark out here so he can't see me blush. "Thanks. I mean, maybe I did earlier before all the dancing. My mother's going to kill me if I'm in any pictures looking like a sweaty mess. I think if she had it her way, I would have sat in my chair the entire time to not ruin the hours' worth of work on my hair and makeup . . . and I'm rambling. I'm so sorry."

My phone vibrates, and I look down to see Charlie has texted me saying he and my mom are ready to leave. I glance up at Milo, whose eyes are still trained on the fire, and, after a moment's hesitation, text back to say I'll just call Leo to take me home.

"Can I ask you something?" I say tentatively. Milo turns his focus to me as he unclips his bowtie to let it dangle around his neck and starts undoing the top buttons of his dress shirt. "Wait, why are you undressing?"

"That's what you wanted to ask me?"

"No, but all of the sudden you started taking off your clothes, so that seemed like it needed to be addressed first. Pun intended."

"I am not 'taking off my clothes.' Have you ever worn a tie? It feels like a tiny noose around your neck."

"You were unbuttoning your shirt," I observe.

"I was loosening my shirt, you weirdo," he laughs, running a hand through his hair. "Are you going to ask me your question or not?"

"I was going to ask you about Leighton, but the timing feels a little inappropriate considering you just tried to give me a striptease." Despite my joke, I see Milo's face darken. "Never mind, it's none of my business."

"It's fine," he says tensely. "What do you want to know?"

"Okay," I say, searching for the right words as I play with a thread of beading on my dress. "I guess I want to understand what it's like between the two of you because . . . I don't get it."

"Why do you care?" he asks, and my eyes snap up to his. My

first instinctual reaction to his question is to be defensive, but he is just looking back at me expectantly. I'm pretty sure his question is coming from genuine curiosity and isn't an accusation. As I'm wrestling with how to answer, a shadow falls over us. I look up to see Leighton herself, still in her purple gown, arms crossed and glaring at Milo. Milo jumps up and says, "What are you doing here?"

"Your parents said you were out here," she says coldly. "I came back after making an appearance at that lipstick launch party because I felt bad for leaving. Looks like you had plenty of company though."

She turns and storms back into the hotel, leaving Milo looking as stunned as I feel. He gives me an apologetic look, and I answer with a little grimace.

"You should clear things up with her," I say in a remarkably steady voice. He looks like he might say something else, but just nods and dashes off after her. I feel the threat of tears prickling the back of my eyes and try to tell myself I didn't do anything wrong. Nothing happened. In fact, that's probably what Milo is telling Leighton at this very instant. That nothing happened. I'm just his sister's friend. Or maybe he would even be bold enough to say I'm his friend. But that's it.

"Hey," Mei appears from around the corner and comes to occupy Milo's vacated seat on the couch next to me. "What's going on? Milo rushed past us and said to come out here to find you and tell you he's sorry? Sorry for what?"

I briefly explain what Leighton probably thought she had walked in on, but Mei just dismisses it.

"She gets jealous all the time," Mei says comfortingly. "Don't worry too much about it."

I must look pathetic because Mei insists that I come stay over at her house for the night.

"I have clothes you can wear, plus we have a ton of brand new toothbrushes we got from the dentist that we never use because we all have electric ones."

"Mei, why are you still trying to sell me on this?" I laugh as we walk back into the ballroom. "I already said yes."

We find Dr. and Mrs. Chen, who let us know that Milo and Leighton already left. The four of us pile into Dr. Chen's BMW (apparently, unlike my mother, he drives himself around), and I text my mother to tell her my plans. We get back to the Chens' house, and Mei graciously lets me have the first shower so I can wash off all of the sweat and makeup from the night. Afterward, I put on a pair of sweatpants and a tank top that Mei lets me borrow and secure my wet hair on top of my head. When I go back downstairs to get a drink of water while Mei showers, I find Dr. Chen sitting in the kitchen eating from a big bag of sour gummy worms.

"I'm a late-night snacker," he admits when he sees me standing awkwardly by the stairs. "Don't mind me."

"I was going to get a glass of water," I explain, and he points to the cabinet where the cups are.

"Help yourself," he says kindly. "By the way, I hate that I didn't get a chance to speak with your mother tonight."

"My mother?" I frown, confused.

"Yes," he continues, popping another gummy worm in his mouth. "I know she didn't want to be formally recognized, but I had at least hoped to thank her in person."

"For what?" I ask, totally baffled.

"Oh," Dr. Chen replies, looking a little startled. "I thought you would have known . . . she made a very generous donation to our cancer center last month. I believe it was right after your father's passing."

I'm completely dumbfounded but try to cover quickly by saying, "Oh, the donation! Of course. I thought maybe you were talking about, uh, something else."

He doesn't seem totally convinced, but before he can say anything else I tell him I'm going to sit by the pool for a moment while Mei finishes up. I duck outside and take up my same pool chair from the last time I was here so I can try to process this unexpected new information.

I hadn't actually thought about how random it was for my mother to receive an invitation to the hospital's gala. It makes more sense knowing she made a donation, and a large one from the sound of it. What baffles me is why my mother, who does everything so publicly and works so hard to keep her place in the spotlight, would want to keep it quiet.

A light comes on in the pool house, and I realize Milo must be home. But instead, it's Leighton who walks past the glass sliding door of what I assume is his living room. She's wearing nothing but a men's button-up dress shirt as she rifles through a purse on the side table and gets out a lipgloss. I watch as she applies it, then walks out of sight again. A few seconds later, the lights cut off and the pool house is dark again.

They made up, I think to myself bitterly. Good for them.

Mei is already in her pajamas when I walk back into her room. She takes one look at my face and says, "Whoa, what's up?"

I shrug and sit on the rollaway bed the Chens set up for me.

"Seriously," Mei coaxes, sitting on her bed to face me.

"I'm fine," I say too harshly. Mei looks wounded, and the anger and jealousy that have been swirling around in my gut since I saw Leighton downstairs instantly evaporate, leaving me feeling guilty and exhausted. "Mei, I'm sorry. It's just been such a long day. Well, a long series of days. Months, actually."

"It's okay," Mei says.

"No, it's not," I counter, rubbing a spot on my forehead where I'm starting to get a headache. "I'm being such a hypocrite, questioning why Milo would be with someone as bitchy as Leighton when here I am being just as bitchy to the only friend I have in this stupid place."

Mei gets up to come sit next to me on my cot, and I half-laugh, half-sob as she wraps me up in a big hug. When she pulls away, I say, "I know we haven't been friends that long, so you can still cut and run if you want. In case you haven't noticed, I'm kind of a shitshow."

"You can't get rid of me that easily."

We talk until we both fall asleep, and I wake up the next morning to the heavenly smell of bacon. When we go downstairs, we find Dr. and Mrs. Chen cooking breakfast together in the kitchen.

"My hero," Mei coos, swiping a piece of toast and kissing her dad on the cheek.

It is so reminiscent of when I used to cook with my dad that I feel my stomach tighten, but I manage to say, "This looks amazing."

"Why, thank you," Mrs. Chen says from where she is flipping pancakes on a griddle. "Would you like blueberries or chocolate chips in your pancakes?"

Mei snorts and says, "You have a lot to learn about Cam's eating habits if you're asking that question."

A little while later, the four of us are sitting lazily at the kitchen table in front of our empty plates recapping the highlights from last night.

"I hate to be the first to bow out, but I have a mountain of paperwork waiting for me that I can't put off any longer," Mrs. Chen says, standing up.

"I should probably get home," I say. We all disperse from the table, and I text Leo to see if he's available to pick me up as Mei and I head back upstairs to her room.

"Do you and Eric have plans today?" I ask her after I brush my teeth and gather up my discarded dress and shoes from last night.

"He's supposed to call when he gets back in town," she says, barely able to suppress a grin.

"You two are so cute it's honestly kind of gross."

"Hey, we should pick a night for the three of us and Cassidy to go to dinner. Look, I know you like Milo and you said you didn't want to date anyone. But you have to admit we had fun that night after the concert. Maybe give it a try and see where it goes."

"Yeah, okay," I say, mostly just to placate her. Leo texts back and says he's almost here, so I give Mei a hug and head downstairs to wait for him. When I walk into the kitchen, I find Milo, still in pajama pants and a t-shirt, piling leftover pancakes and bacon onto a plate. He looks up when he hears me.

"Hey," he says tentatively. "Just grabbing some breakfast."

"For you and Leighton, sure," I say lightly, not looking him in the eye. "I saw her in the pool house last night."

"Cam—"

"I'm happy you got things straightened out," I continue. "You told her she has absolutely nothing to worry about, right?"

Milo just stands there studying my face, his plate of food sitting forgotten on the kitchen counter. I nod slowly, his silence being all the confirmation I need.

"Cool," I say, and start to walk past him to the back door.

"Wait." He reaches out and takes hold of my arm. I look down at his hand, which is firm but gentle, then up at his face.

"What?" My voice breaks on the word, and I'm painfully aware of how close his face is to mine. When he doesn't say anything, I shake him off. "That's what I thought."

Listen to Track Five: "What Will It Take?"

Twelve

I spend the entire ride home venting to poor, unsuspecting Leo.

"Does that make any sense to you?" I say exasperatedly after I finish telling him all about the situation. "Why do guys like girls that are so heinous?"

"Well," Leo says slowly. "In my experience having two daughters, girls can act very differently towards other girls than they do with boys. It sounds like this girl might feel threatened by you and acting catty is a defense mechanism."

"That's not . . . I mean . . . that's just absurd!" I sputter. "Why would she feel threatened by me? She is gorgeous, she's super successful, and she's got the guy. I'm, like, super average with a lot of baggage."

Leo simply shrugs. "It's only one old man's opinion."

We come to a stop in front of the house.

"Thank you for letting me rant," I say to Leo as he opens the door to let me out.

He lingers for a moment before saying, "You're far too hard on yourself, you know. Even if this Lilac girl—"

"Leighton."

"Lilac, Leighton, whatever her name is. Even if she is all that you say she is, don't you think for a second that she is any better than you."

Not trusting myself to say anything for fear that I'll start bawling, I step forward and hug Leo, breathing in his scent of old books and pine. When I finally let go, he squeezes my shoulder once before turning and getting back into the car.

When I walk into the house, I hear music coming from somewhere on the first floor. I wander down the hall until I find the source. My mother is in her home gym jogging on the treadmill. I give a small wave, and she taps her phone to pause the music playing from a portable speaker.

"Just wanted to let you know I'm home," I say, leaning against the door frame.

"Wonderful," she says a little breathlessly as she slows the treadmill down to a brisk walking pace. "Do you have plans for this evening? I was going to cook, but a friend of mine invited us to the opening of her new restaurant tonight."

"Does it require a hair and makeup team to get ready?" I ask skeptically.

"Nothing like that," my mother assures me. It really is unfair that despite being in the middle of a workout, she still looks beautiful. "Business casual dress, I would say."

"Okay, sure," I say, making a mental note to ask Charlie what exactly "business casual" entails. Then, remembering what Dr. Chen had said about her donation to the hospital, I come farther into the room and take a seat on the stationary bike next to the treadmill. "Hey . . . Mom?"

Her head snaps up from her phone at the word.

"I, uh, I heard about what you did," I continue. "I mean, about the money you gave to the hospital."

"How did you—"

"It's not important," I say, running my fingers over the buttons on the bike. "Did . . . did you do that because of Dad?"

She presses a button that stops the treadmill completely and turns to me. I feel her looking at me, but I can't meet her eyes.

"Yes," she says in a tight voice. "As you probably know, I didn't find out about his diagnosis until he was in the late stages."

I shift uncomfortably. She isn't wrong—my dad wanted to keep the news quiet from everyone, but especially from my mother. We talked about it and decided chemotherapy and radiation would be hard enough without the possibility that my mother would leak the news to the press and reporters might come snooping around. It was pretty unlikely that it would have been of much interest to any media outlet, but even though my parents hadn't been together since I was little, my dad would still periodically get calls from magazines or television shows that wanted more information about my mother's past. So, in the end, we didn't tell her until four months after his cancer diagnosis, when it was pretty clear his treatments weren't working.

"We just . . . didn't want to worry about it being some kind of tabloid story," I mumble.

"Would it really have mattered?" my mother says, and the hurt and bitterness in her voice make me look up. She takes a shaky breath as several tears roll down her cheeks. "If I had known earlier, I could have made arrangements to get him into the best treatment centers in L.A. Maybe it wouldn't have made a difference, but at least I could have done something. And who cares if the media found out as long as he was getting the best medical care? But no, neither of you thought I was important enough to tell until it was too late for me to be able to do anything to help."

I'm speechless, my mouth gaping open like a fish. This is such a stark contrast to her normal perky demeanor that it's jarring.

"So, when I found out that he . . ." she trails off, and I watch her jaw clench as she squeezes her eyes shut, clearly trying to hold back another wave of tears. After a few moments of tense silence, she continues, "I figured if I couldn't put that money toward your father's treatment, maybe I could at least help some other people who are going through the same thing."

I reach up, hastily wipe my own eyes with the bottom of Mei's tank top, and say, "Why didn't you tell me?"

"I don't know," she sniffles. "I just . . . didn't."

"It was a really nice thing to do," I say shakily. "Thank you, Mom."

I start toward the door, but stop to turn around and say, "He had great doctors. The cancer was just too aggressive and spread too fast. There wasn't anything that anyone would have been able to do."

A sob escapes from my mother, and she buries her face in her hands, no longer bothering to hold in her tears. I hesitate for a second, then walk over and put my arms around her. I can tell she's surprised, but she hugs me back. I can't remember the last time we hugged like this.

"I felt helpless too," I whisper, a few of my own tears falling into my mother's hair. "It was the worst feeling in the world."

I don't know how long we stand together like that, but eventually her crying subsides, and I pull away, give her a sad smile, and head up to my room feeling drained.

I must have fallen asleep because suddenly Charlie is shaking me awake. I whimper and cover my head with my pillow.

"Oh, no you don't," he says, snatching the pillow and tossing it onto the floor. It nearly hits Jim, who gives Charlie a cranky look.

"Wh–what time is it?" I say, stifling a yawn.

"Six o'clock," Charlie replies. "Mom said you were coming with us to Olive E Vino for dinner."

"Right," I say, sitting up. I almost start to make an excuse not to go, but my stomach gives a loud gurgle. Charlie, who must have anticipated what I was going to do, smirks at me.

"Need me to help you find something to wear?" he says smugly. He's already dressed in a pair of dark jeans, a navy shirt, and a khaki-colored jacket.

"Yeah." I grumpily throw my comforter to the side and stand up. "Let's do this."

Charlie ends up putting me in a simple pair of black pencil pants and a black blouse, murmuring the entire time about how if he keeps acting as my personal stylist, he's going to start expecting to be compensated.

"You keep insisting!" I object, but he conveniently ignores me.

My mother is downstairs waiting for us. She is perfectly made up and wearing a tight black dress, all evidence of her earlier distress totally gone as she smiles at us.

"This is exciting," she crows as she opens the front door to where Leo's car is already waiting for us. "The three of us didn't really get to spend any time together at the gala. And from what I hear, my friend Chiara hired an incredibly gifted chef."

From the car, I text Annie.

Me: guess who is on their way to a fancy new Italian restaurant?
Annie: ugghhhh so jealous
Me: i'm sure nothing will be as good as your lasagna
Annie: i mean, obvi. does this mean no phone date tonight?
Me: that's what i was texting to find out. will you be free later?
Annie: anything for you darling

I send a thumbs-up emoji and put my phone back into my purse. Annie and I had made a pact to talk on the phone every Sunday night, and I have too much to fill her in on between the gala and the earlier conversation with my mother to miss it.

We pull up to a brick building where a small crowd is gathered outside, including, much to my dismay, a few paparazzos.

"Great," I say crankily.

Charlie follows my gaze and says, "Yeah, I figured there might be a pap or two here. The restaurateur, Chiara, is on *The Real House Husbands of L.A.*"

I look at him blankly.

"It follows a group of stay-at-home husbands married to successful businesswomen," he clarifies.

I'm spared having to answer by Leo opening up the door to let me out. When I get to where my mother and Charlie are standing on the other side of the car, she says quietly, "Just follow me."

I reach out and grab onto the back of Charlie's jacket as we carefully make our way through the crowd of people to the front door. A man in a black dress shirt and headset rushes up to escort us inside, and I concentrate on not making any stupid faces as flash bulbs go off in rapid succession. I breathe a sigh of relief when we step through the door and into the welcome quiet. The restaurant is dimly lit by giant chandeliers hanging overhead from large wooden beams. The only decorations are the vines creeping up the walls and across the ceiling, creating a canopy effect.

"Wow," I say to Charlie as we are led to a booth tucked into the corner. "This place is really nice."

"I would expect nothing less," he says, settling into the booth and inspecting the copper-colored water glasses on the table.

"Are all of those people outside waiting to get in?" I ask, sliding in next to him as my mother demurely sits down across from us. The cushion is way more comfortable than I would have ever imagined, and I lean back against the soft pillows behind us.

"Some of them have reservations, some of them probably just heard about it and want to see if anyone famous shows up," he answers as we are handed menus.

A sophisticated-looking woman saunters over and says, "Jackie! I am so happy you could make it."

My mother stands up and the two of them give each other a quick hug and kiss on each cheek.

"I wouldn't have missed it!" my mother chirps, clutching the woman's hands. "Chiara, these are my children, Charlie and Cam."

We each reach out to shake her hand, then she and my mother start chattering away as someone comes to fill up our water glasses.

"How do she and Mother—I mean, Mom—know each other?" I ask Charlie curiously.

"Dear sister," Charlie says matter-of-factly, folding his hands in front of him on the table, "you will soon learn that this is a very small town with even smaller social circles. In this particular case, I believe she and Mom go to the same herbalist."

My mother finally sits back down, and a server comes over to take our drink order.

"Chiara insists we do the tasting menu and let the chef surprise us," my mother says. I'm a little disappointed to hear this considering I had my eye on a few pasta dishes, but I don't protest.

It turns out to be one of the best meals of my life. I have what Charlie once referred to as a "criminally pedestrian palette" because as a general rule I don't eat anything I can't pronounce. So I was pretty skeptical of this fancy food from the onset, convinced I would end up having to order a late-night pizza when we got home tonight. But, after a good deal of coaxing from my mother and Charlie, I agree to at least try everything. It turns out my palette isn't so pedestrian after all because there isn't one thing I don't like.

"I'm going to have to spend the next three days straight in the gym," my mother says dolefully as she daintily reapplies her lipstick.

"Worth it," Charlie says, scraping out the last of the salted caramel custard from its dish.

"Yeah, that was incredible," I sigh happily, closing my eyes as I settle back down against my pillow.

"You know, Cam," my mother says mildly, running a finger over the rim of her wine glass. "If you enjoyed it that much, this is the kind of thing you could be doing much more of if you wanted to."

I open my eyes to give her a skeptical look.

"I'm serious," she says earnestly. "If you just work on building up your web presence a little, you could be getting paid to go to restaurant openings and events every weekend."

"I already told you," I say, shaking my head, "I'm not interested in being a public figure or influencer or whatever. I just want normalcy."

I look to Charlie for back-up, but he shrugs a little. "I'm not going to lie, sis. The perks can be pretty nice sometimes."

When we're finished, Chiara leads us through a back door so we don't have to go through the crowded entryway again. As soon as we're in the car, my mother and Charlie start recounting the meal, comparing it to another restaurant opening they went to last month. I tune them out as I consider what Charlie said. I've never really thought about how much Charlie might have purposefully used being the kid of someone famous to further his career, but it makes sense. When he moved to L.A. to live with our mother, he almost immediately started a YouTube channel where he would review runway and red-carpet fashion and give his friends makeovers. My mother frequently made appearances in his videos, which I thought was something they did to spend time together. But I'm realizing it was probably by design, because the videos with my mother always had the most views. Now that Charlie has his own fashion line, I wonder how much of his success is because he's good and how much of it was because he had connections.

I change into my pajamas as soon as we get home and call Annie while I walk Jim around the yard. She makes me give her a detailed play-by-play of the entire meal.

"Amazing," she sighs wistfully after she determines that I've given her a satisfactory recap. "I mean, I do what I can from YouTube tutorials and cooking shows, but to be able to study under chefs of that caliber? I can't wait. Oh, and I almost forgot to tell you! My mom and I booked our trip to New York City next month to visit schools."

Annie and I decided when we were sophomores that after we graduated high school, we were going to move to New York so she could go to The Culinary Institute of America, and I could study art at the Pratt Institute. Over the last year I started leaning toward S.C.A.D. in Georgia, but Annie still has her heart set on New York.

"That's awesome," I tell her, forcing myself to sound enthusiastic.

"What about you? Do you have any college visits scheduled yet?"

"Nope," I admit, taking a seat in a wicker chair and petting Jim's head.

"Really?" Annie sounds suspicious. "I know there's still plenty of time, but I figured you would have gotten something lined up by now."

"I haven't really decided what I want to do next year," I say slowly.

"Are you serious?" Now Annie sounds mad. I wince, but Jim looks at me unsympathetically. I wrinkle my nose at him.

"In case you forgot, a lot has changed over the last couple of months," I say.

"But you have planned on going to art school for as long as I've known you," Annie counters.

"I don't know if that's what I even want to do anymore," I say wearily. "I just . . . don't know if I still have the passion for it."

"Cam." Annie's voice is gentler now. "It's totally fine if you need a break. But you can't just blow off college stuff."

"Okay, fine," I say, mostly to shut her up. "I'll look into it."

"That's my girl," she coos. We chat for a few more minutes about her plans for NYC, and I assure her again that I'll try to make some headway on the college front. I know she's right—my dad would be royally pissed if he knew I wasn't scheduling visits to the schools I've been saving brochures for over the last two years.

I walk back into my room with Jim and finish getting ready for bed. Just before I turn my bedside lamp off, I glance over at the box of my art supplies still sitting in the corner. If boxes could stare, this one would definitely be staring at me accusingly. My eyes fall on Jim, who is studying me from where he is curled up on the floor.

"Don't start with me," I chide him before plunging us both into darkness.

THIRTEEN

A few days later, Charlie persuades me to go out to lunch with him and his friend Alexis, who I met at the house party we went to the first weekend I was here. They take me to a little Mediterranean place and order several kebab dishes and different types of hummuses to share. I'm happy to sit back and listen to Charlie and Alexis gab about her awful summer internship. Charlie finished school last year, opting to do an accelerated two-year program, but Alexis is on the four-year track and doesn't graduate until next spring. From Alexis's stories, it sounds like her current internship at an up-and-coming eco-friendly clothing line is like *The Devil Wears Prada*, except instead of judging you for what kind of shoes you have on, they judge you for liking creamer in your coffee instead of soy milk.

As we pull out of the parking lot, Charlie peers at me in the rearview mirror. "I have a slight confession. We have a little pit stop to make before we go home."

"Charlie," Alexis says, giving him a wary sidelong look. "Did you not tell Cam what you're doing?"

"Why, what are you doing?" I ask suspiciously. When Charlie doesn't immediately answer, I say, "Oh my God, Charlie, you're making me nervous. What are you getting me involved in?"

"Okay, okay," he says hurriedly, as we pull into the parking lot of a plain-looking building. "Have you ever heard of leech therapy?"

"Leech therapy?"

Charlie parks the car and looks over at Alexis, but she just shakes her head as she plays with the end of one of her braids.

"You're on your own on this one," she says.

"Charlie," I say hesitantly, closing my eyes. "Please tell me leech therapy is not exactly what it sounds like."

"It is a practice that has existed for thousands of years," he says matter-of-factly, turning around in his seat. "It's supposed to be great for keeping the face looking fresh."

"You're going to let someone put leeches on your face?!" I say shrilly.

"Calm down," he hisses. "I'm already a little nervous, and you aren't helping."

"Oh, well, I am so sorry I'm not helping to ease your worry about someone sticking blood-sucking bugs on your body."

"Technically, they're worms."

I give him an incredulous look.

"Mom has done it before and said it did wonders for her skin," Charlie says defensively.

"Well, our mother is crazy."

"Are you going to come and give me moral support or not?"

"Fine," I snap, opening my car door. "But don't you dare come crying to me when you come to your senses about how completely unhinged this idea is."

The three of us make the short trek to the door bearing a small sign that says it is a "holistic medicine center."

"I just want to go on record that this is bananas," I say as Charlie pulls the door open. We're greeted by a little old woman who can't be more than five feet tall, and she ushers us into a room with a massage table in the center and several chairs over to one side. She has Charlie lay face-up, and Alexis and I each take a seat nearby. After disappearing for a few minutes, she returns carrying a jar of water filled with dark, squirming objects.

"Dear Lord," I whisper.

"Hold my hand," Charlie whimpers.

"I'm not getting anywhere near those things," I reply, scooting my chair as far into the corner as I can. Alexis, who is much braver than me, moves her chair close enough to reach out and take Charlie's hand as the old woman starts fishing the first leech out of the jar.

I watch in horrified fascination as she gingerly applies leeches onto Charlie's forehead, cheeks, nose, and chin. Other than wincing a little, he doesn't have much of a reaction, though his face is awfully pale. Once she's satisfied, she leaves the leeches to do their work, and we sit and try to make conversation as if this is totally normal. A while later, the little woman returns and starts carefully removing them and taping gauze to Charlie's face. He hands her a credit card, and we don't linger once she bustles back into the room with a receipt.

Since Charlie is still looking pretty peaked, I offer to drop Alexis off and drive us home. When we pile back into Charlie's car, we sit for a minute in dead silence. I start the car and turn to say something to Charlie, who is sitting in the front passenger seat, but the second I behold his bandaged face, I burst out laughing. After a pause, Alexis joins in, and eventually even Charlie is giggling weakly.

"You're a lunatic," I say when I've composed myself enough to start the car. "But I love you. I'm stopping for milkshakes."

The next morning, I wake up with a sense of determination. Today I'm going to draw something. Anything. Even if it's just a stick figure, it will be comprised of the best-drawn sticks this world has ever seen.

I decide to go to a yoga class first to clear my mind and realign my chakras and whatnot, and by the time I get home, shower, and get dressed, it's almost noon. Charlie pokes his head in and says he's taking Jim to the dog park, so I pack up a set of pens, pencils, and several sketch pads into my backpack, then throw in my latest unfinished graphic novel in case I feel extra inspired. There's a little park near the diner that I've been to a few times, so I figure it's as good a place as any to see if I can get past my mental block.

After scrounging around the kitchen for something I can make to bring with me for lunch, I throw together a turkey wrap and toss it into my backpack along with a bag of chips. On my way outside I cross paths with my mother, who is heading to lunch with a friend. She invites me to come along, but I tell her my plans, thankful to have a valid excuse for not being able to go.

"This may take a while," I say matter-of-factly to Leo as I get out of the car. "But I am not leaving until the Muses have spoken to me."

"Well," Leo says, closing the door behind me. "I hope your muses are feeling especially chatty today."

Even though the park is pretty crowded, I manage to find an unoccupied bench on a quieter corner of the main grassy area near where several older men have set up a few tables with chess boards. Blankets and chairs are scattered around where families are having a picnic lunch, and a group of guys and girls that look like they're a few years older than me are playing a game of ultimate frisbee. I'm struck by a sudden overwhelming feeling of loneliness. I used to be in both the jazz choir and the art club at my school in Arizona, and we would go out all the time to the movies or to dinner. I really miss being part of a group of friends.

I decide I'll probably be more receptive to the Muses on a full stomach, so I dig through my backpack and find my turkey wrap. Just as I'm taking a bite, a soft voice to my left says, "Yams."

I jump and turn to see Milo standing and holding a plastic bag of what looks to be takeout containers.

"Hey," I say after I manage to swallow my food without choking. "What are you doing here?"

"I come here sometimes in between shifts when I work a double at the diner since it's walkable," he explains. "Can I sit?"

Even though I'm still a little irritated from the other day, I'm also fully aware I have no justification for it. So I pick up my backpack to clear a space for him, failing to notice it's still unzipped. Sketchbooks and pencils come tumbling out and onto the ground.

"Shit," I hiss, scrambling to gather up everything. Milo stoops down, picking up and examining my unfinished comic book.

"Wow," he says, eyebrows raised as he flips through it. I toss everything else back into my bag and hold out my hand to him, but he doesn't immediately give it to me. "Did you draw this?"

"Yep," I say, feeling a flush creep up my cheeks. "It's not done though."

"It's really good," he declares when he finally gives it back to me. "You didn't tell me you could draw like this."

"It never came up," I shrug. "And I figured it would have been a weird conversational segue to be like, 'Hey, can I get some waffles? Also, I draw comics.'"

"Yeah, that transition could use some work," Milo says with a sly smile as he starts taking out his to-go containers. I try to be subtle as I glance sideways to see what he has, but he notices almost immediately. "It's Mongolian beef from my favorite Chinese place."

He takes the fork out of a set of plastic silverware. I look forlornly at the turkey wrap in my hand.

"Do you want to try it?" he asks.

"I couldn't possibly," I reply, but I'm already snatching the spoon out of his silverware set and reaching over to the container. I take a bite, closing my eyes to savor the sweet and tangy flavor. "Mmmmm, that's good."

Milo laughs, and I crack one eye open to look at him.

"What?" I ask.

"I've just never met anyone who has such a deeply emotional reaction to food."

"Is that a good or a bad thing?"

"It's definitely funny."

"That wasn't one of the answer choices."

The corner of his mouth ticks up into a smile. It's so easy to fall into this dynamic with him. I quickly steal another spoonful of beef before he can protest, watching the chess players as I eat it.

"You look sad," he says after a moment.

"What? Oh, no. That's just the way my face is. You know how some people have resting bitch face? I have resting sad face."

"I don't think there is such a thing," he says skeptically.

"Oh, there totally is," I correct him. "I've had random strangers come up and ask me if I'm okay. And that was before all of the sad stuff had even happened to me yet."

He doesn't respond, and I turn to see that he is studying me thoughtfully.

"Now what?" I ask, exasperated.

"Nothing," he says, looking away quickly and spearing a piece of broccoli onto his fork.

"Oh, no you don't," I protest, wagging a finger at him. "You don't get to look at me all contemplatively and not tell me what you were contemplating."

"Okay," he says slowly, glancing back over to me again. "I've noticed you do this thing where you make some throwaway comment in what I'm guessing is a reference to your dad that's kind of joking, but kind of not. I'm just curious why."

"Lunch and a psychotherapy session?" I answer crossly, feeling the anger in my gut perk its head up. "Lucky me."

"Don't do that," Milo says calmly.

"Do what?"

"Snap at me," he says. "You were the one who asked what I was thinking."

I take a deep breath and blow it out.

"You're right," I say. "I'm sorry." He continues to look at me expectantly, so I explain, "Making jokes has always been the way I deal with being uncomfortable. I think when it comes to the topic of my dad, sometimes it's easier to beat someone to the punch and bring it up first. Set the tone so they don't tiptoe around me, even though I know that's not the right way to handle it."

"I don't think there's really a right or wrong way to deal with losing someone."

"I'm pretty sure I'm handling everything the wrong way," I say, fishing out the bag of potato chips from my backpack.

"What was he like?" Milo asks quietly. "Your dad, I mean."

I go still, surprised by the directness of the question. I peer up at him and see him looking almost as surprised as I am that he asked it.

"I'm sorry," he says quickly. "You don't have to—"

"No, it's okay," I reply. "Um. Well, his name was Luke . . ."

I trail off as it occurs to me this might be the first time I've talked about my dad in the past tense with someone who didn't know him when he was alive. I watch the chess players for a moment as I decide whether or not I want to even have this conversation. Milo doesn't rush me, which I appreciate.

"He owned an auto repair shop," I say when I finally opt to keep talking. "You'd probably think that I would be one of those girls who knows all about cars since I grew up around them, but that isn't the case at all. Dad made fun of me about it all the time." I smile at the memory. "He loved doughnuts and watching Alfred Hitchcock movies and was an insanely good Scrabble player. Everyone who knew him loved him. You know over two hundred people came to his funeral? I counted the messages in this guest book thing my aunt got for it and there were two hundred and seven. I thought the idea of a guest book was stupid at first since it's not like it was a wedding or something happy like that, but after reading all of the nice things people said about him . . . I don't know. I'm kind of glad I have it now. Whenever I die, I hope I've made a difference to as many people as he did. I just . . . miss him."

I close my eyes and let out a shaky sigh, working furiously to hold back the wave of emotion that is threatening to drown me. I open my eyes back up and find Milo staring at me so intently that I almost recoil. But he just reaches a thumb up to brush away a tear that has escaped down my cheek. My breath catches for a split second as the wild thought runs through my head, *"He's going to kiss me, he's going to kiss me."* Instead, his hand drops back into his lap, and I silently admonish myself for even letting my mind go there.

"He sounds like an amazing person."

"He really was," I say, forcing a smile. "Okay, it's my turn to say something that makes you cry so we're even."

"I'm pretty sure it doesn't work like that," Milo says laughing.

"Oh, it definitely does," I object, the musical sound of his laughter so contagious that I can't help but join in. "A cry for a cry, as they say."

"Yeah, I think you already know the saying is "an eye for an eye.'" Milo continues to chuckle, then he glances down at his phone and swears. "I have to go. My shift starts in a few minutes."

He starts packing up his food, and suddenly I find myself saying, "Milo?"

"Yeah?" he says, not pausing as he shoves his now-empty take-out container back into the plastic bag.

"Why do you care?" I ask him quietly, echoing the same question he had asked me the night of the gala. He stills, looking over at me sideways.

"What do you mean?" he answers carefully. My initial inclination is to just say "never mind," but for some reason I persist.

"I've been asked a lot of questions over the last few months," I explain. "And I think I've gotten pretty good at interpreting them. For example, sometimes people feel obligated to ask you how you're doing, but they don't want to hear your real answer. They want you to say you're fine so no one has to be uncomfortable. And sometimes they're just nosey or have some kind of morbid curiosity about other people's tragedy because it isn't happening to them. And, of course, occasionally people actually care. It seems like you fall into that category. And I want to know why."

Milo considers this, giving me a searching look.

"I don't know," he says softly, and I get the sense he's telling the truth. "I just . . . want to know you better." When I don't say anything, he says in a lighter tone that sounds forced, "What kind of big brother would I be if I didn't vet my sister's new friend, right?"

This stings a little, but I try not to show it. He stands up to throw his trash away, then turns back around to me. He looks like he might say something but seems to think better of it. "I'm sure I'll see you soon," he offers instead, putting his hands into his pockets and rocking back on his heels.

"Have a good shift," I say. He lingers for a second longer before turning and walking toward the park entrance.

I sit for a while, absentmindedly watching the ultimate frisbee game. If Annie were here, she and I would probably make a game of counting how many times the players either high-fived or bumped fists, which seems to be roughly every ten seconds. I wonder if it would be the kind of game Milo would find entertaining, too. I let my mind wander through scenes of the two of us sharing lunch while we people-watch from our bench, or me sitting in the corner of the room sketching his band while they practice.

Enough, I chide myself. Deciding that the Muses apparently are going to continue to be stone cold bitches to me today and I'll try this again some other time, I text Leo to tell him I'm ready to go. He says he's about ten minutes away, so I pack my stuff up to go stand in the parking lot and wait. My phone vibrates, and I look down to see that Annie has texted me.

"Something you're not telling me?!" the message reads, followed by a website link. I click on it and nearly drop my phone when I see the *Chick About Town* story Annie has sent me. The story title reads, *"Cam Donovan Spotted with Mystery Man"* and is accompanied by a giant picture underneath of me and Milo sitting on the bench in the park not even thirty minutes ago. In the picture, it looks like he is lovingly touching my face, though I know it was just him wiping that stupid tear off my cheek. Feeling my heart sink to my stomach, I start scanning the story.

"Jackie Jenson's daughter, Cam Donovan, was spotted cozying up to an unidentified guy earlier this afternoon at the park. No word on who he is yet, but it certainly looks like she's enjoying the comfort of his arms!"

"Oh, no," I moan. "No, no, no."

I squint at the photo again and am relieved to see that from the angle it was taken, you really can't make out Milo's face. But by the time Leo's car arrives, I've decided I at least need to go and warn him.

We pull into the diner, and I tell Leo I'll only be a minute before dashing out of the car. Once I'm inside, I look around and spot Milo coming out of the kitchen holding a piece of pie. He gives me a startled look as I jog up to him.

"Hey," I say a little breathlessly. "Can I— Ooh, what kind is that? Peanut butter? Is it new? Sorry, not important right now. Can I talk to you for a second?"

"Yeah, let me drop this off really fast," he says, and I wistfully watch him deliver the pie to a table nearby.

"You want a piece?" Milo says when he walks back over to where I'm standing.

"Yes," I reply automatically. "I mean, no, not right now."

He leads me over to an empty booth, and I slide in across from him.

"Okay . . ." I'm suddenly feeling self-conscious about where to start. "Here's the thing. This online gossip blog has been a little weirdly obsessed with me ever since I moved here, even though I hardly do anything exciting enough to warrant this kind of attention. It's only because of who my mother is, but whatever."

Milo looks antsy, and I can tell he needs to go check on his tables.

"I'm sorry, I'll get to the point," I say. "I know you're busy. Somehow, they took and posted a picture from the park earlier. And it looks . . . well, it looks bad."

I take out my phone, which already has the *Chick About Town* article pulled up. I hand it to him and watch his eyes go wide. He scrolls through the story, then groans a little as he sits back against the booth.

"They might not ever even figure out it's you," I say apologetically. "I just wanted you to know in case you needed to give Leighton a heads-up."

"Yeah, thanks," Milo replies distractedly, massaging a spot on his temple. "I should probably get back."

"Of course," I say. The two of us stand up, and Milo starts to walk back to the kitchen.

"Milo?" I call after him. He pauses to look back at me. "I'm really sorry."

He just gives me a small nod and disappears into the kitchen. I can feel my face heat up a little as I turn and walk slowly back outside to where Leo is waiting. Even though I know this is in no way my fault, I still feel guilty.

FOURTEEN

I don't say much on the short ride home. After thanking Leo when he opens the car door to let me out, I go straight up to my room to call Annie.

"Wow," she says after I've caught her up on the events of the last few days.

"Right?!" I squawk loudly enough to startle Jim awake from where he's laid out on the floor in a patch of sunlight having a post dog-park nap. "Why does freaking *Chick About Town* even care what I do? I'm the non-famous kid of—let's call a spade a spade here—a D-list celebrity. Are they really so desperate for content they have to scrape the barrel for stories about me?"

"I don't know," Annie says sympathetically.

"Like, how did they find out I was at the park in the first place? I didn't even know I was going to go until this morning."

"I don't know," she says again.

"You should have seen the look on Milo's face," I say dejectedly. "Leighton already hates me. Or still doesn't know who I am. I can't really tell."

Annie spends the next ten minutes trying to cheer me up before she has to go. At first, she won't tell me why, but I needle her enough to the point she apologetically admits she is meeting some of our chorus friends for a bowling night.

"You don't have to feel bad that you have a social life without me," I assure her. "Really. Tell everyone I said hi."

I hang up and look down at my phone. It's not even five o'clock yet. I know I'm going to drive myself crazy if I sit around the house and wallow in self-pity for the rest of the night, so I decide to take Jim outside while I weigh my options. Charlie isn't in his room when I poke my head in on my way downstairs, so I text him. He responds almost immediately that he's about to go into some pitch meeting and won't be done until later tonight.

As I walk Jim around the yard, I start to type a message to Mei before remembering she mentioned she had a date with Eric tonight. I frown at my phone, then scroll through my contacts to Cassidy's number.

hey, it's cam. what are you up to?

I hesitate, my finger hovering over the send button.

"Oh, what the hell," I say out loud before mashing it unceremoniously and putting my phone in my back pocket. Jim finishes his business, and by the time I get back to my room I have a reply from Cassidy.

not a lot- u?

After debating for a second about whether I want to play it cool or just get to the point, I opt for the latter.

thinking about going out for tacos. care to join?

I get a reply almost immediately.

i know a great place- what's your address? i'll pick you up at 5:30.

"This is fine. It's totally fine. It's fine, right?"

Jim's droopy eyes follow me as I pace around my room.

I stop in front of the mirror to scrutinize my reflection. I've changed out of the t-shirt and jeans I was wearing earlier and into a top with black and white stripes and a pair of loose fitting black overalls.

"Does this outfit make me look like I think we're on a date?"

Jim starts licking his leg disinterestedly.

"I'm overthinking this," I say, running a brush through my hair, which I decide to wear down. "We are just two people casually grabbing some dinner."

I give Jim a treat as a thank you gift for being such a good listener, then head downstairs so I can let Cassidy in when he gets here. Almost as soon as I reach the bottom of the steps, I hear the sound of the call box for the gate. I punch the code in and stand at the window watching as a navy-blue BMW pulls around to the front of the house. When I see Cassidy start to get out of the car and walk to the front door, I hastily get my purse and walk outside before he can reach it.

"Hey," I wave as I close the door behind me.

"Hi." Cassidy flashes a smile as I approach him and leans in to give me a quick hug. "I was just coming to ring your doorbell."

"No need," I say, trying to sound light. "Nice ride."

I walk around to the passenger door, Cassidy following close behind to open it for me. I silently curse to myself. I'll bet he totally thinks this is a date. Which makes sense, because I definitely made it sound like I was asking him on a date. But considering there is no graceful way to say, "In case you are under the wrong impression, I'm really just in the market for some more friends right now because I get super sad and lonely when I'm by myself for long periods of time," I just thank him as he closes my door.

"Where are we headed?" I say as we pull out of the driveway.

"It's this place in West Hollywood called Taco House," Cassidy says, glancing over at me with a grin. "Best Mexican food in Los Angeles."

"My stomach is already grumbling," I reply. I feel my phone vibrate in my purse and pull it out to see my mother has texted to ask me what my plans are for later tonight. I send a quick reply letting her know I'm going out for dinner but won't be home too late.

"Sorry," I say, shoving my phone back into my purse. "It's my mother."

"I get the feeling you two aren't very close?"

I consider trying to steer the conversation to a different topic before deciding to answer honestly.

"Not really," I admit, watching the buildings fly past in a blur through the window. "She moved back to L.A. when I was really little, so I've never spent more than a few weeks at a time with her. It's hard to get close to someone like that."

"I get it," Cassidy volunteers. "I mean, kind of. My parents split when I was eight. They have joint custody of me and my little brother, so we spend time with both of them pretty evenly. But they both remarried and had kids, so sometimes it feels like my brother and I are only half a part of two families instead of fully part of one. Does that make any sense?"

"Yeah, it does," I say softly. "My dad never really dated anyone, and my mother had boyfriends off and on, but it wasn't ever that serious. I've never considered what it would have been like if either of them started a new family."

"It's not great," Cassidy says. Then he asks me about the art program at my old school, and pretty soon we're swapping stories about the weirdest art teachers we've each had. Before I know it, we are pulling into the parking lot of a bright green building with a giant sign on the front that says Taco House.

"Their guacamole is going to change your life," Cassidy informs me once we've been seated at a small outside table.

"That's perfect, because my life could use some changing. Though I didn't expect it to be guac-induced."

We peruse the menu for a few minutes before ordering a bunch of different tacos to try. The server brings out salsa and guacamole, and Cassidy wasn't lying—it's pretty amazing. I unabashedly stuff my face while Cassidy and I talk about school, movies, and music. We spend a while debating the strengths and weaknesses of the Marvel versus DC comic universes and where we see each franchise going next. I'm honestly surprised at how much I'm enjoying myself, and I keep wondering if it would be such a bad thing if this were a date. But then Milo's stupid eyes flash in my mind.

As Cassidy drives me home, I start completely panicking. I hadn't been able to stop him from paying for dinner, so now I'm trying to figure out how to gracefully end the evening without things getting awkward. Of course, all of this is assuming Cassidy even has any interest in me and would try some move that I would have to thwart in the first place. Maybe I just think way too highly of myself. Has Los Angeles made me some sort of egomaniac?

"Are you okay?"

My attention snaps back, and I realize we must have been sitting parked outside of the gate to my house for a minute now.

"I'm good," I say, clicking the opener in my purse and hoping Cassidy can't see my face flush in the darkness. I scan the windows as we pull up and see none of the lights are on.

"Guess no one is back yet," I say, more to myself than anything.

"Do you want me to come in with you?" Cassidy asks.

Shit.

"Screw it," I say, punching the overhead light on so we aren't sitting in the dark. Cassidy looks nonplussed. "Here's the thing. In the interest of complete honesty, I do think you are, like, stupidly attractive and, more importantly because I'm not shallow, pretty easy to talk to. But I texted you tonight because I was lonely and spiraling a little, I think, not because I was trying to ask you on a date. And I tried really hard to not flirt with you at dinner, but honestly, I'm bad at this kind of thing and don't really know what the difference is between what is considered flirting and just having an engaging conversation with someone of the opposite sex. Like, how stupid is it that guys think that a girl being friendly means she's ready to let you into her pants—"

"Wait, hold on—"

"What I'm trying to say is that I don't have a lot of friends here, and I would really like some. God, that sounds pathetic. Whatever. And I get that it's probably naive to think that guys and girls can just be friends, but you're a great artist and introduced me to juice, and I feel like we would make pretty good friends," I finish lamely.

Cassidy looks at me for a moment before bursting out laughing. As this was not the reaction I was expecting, I just sit in stunned silence and wait for him to compose himself.

"Cam," he chokes out once he is able to speak again. "Look, I like you. You're not stuck up like a lot of the girls around here. It's refreshing. But if you don't want anything more than friendship, that's fine. I'm not going to be a pushy asshole."

"Oh," I say, taken aback. "Well . . . okay then."

"You have to start giving me a little more credit if we're going to be friends," he points out.

"I can try," I say, then give him a skeptical look. "You really are cool with just being friends?"

"Sure," he says confidently. "It's actually kind of nice to have such a blunt conversation about it. It makes things less awkward."

"Oh yes, because this wasn't awkward at all."

He laughs again, and I begrudgingly smile.

"I'm going to go," I say, unbuckling my seatbelt. "Thank you for dinner. It really was some of the best tacos I have ever had."

"You're buying next time, pal," he retorts.

"You got it, buddy," I say, climbing out of the car. "Goodnight!"

Cassidy smiles and shakes his head a little before pulling away. I stand in the driveway watching him go, wondering if I have just unlocked the key to men and women finally being able to understand each other.

. . .

"Yeah, you haven't unlocked anything," Charlie tells me. It's the next morning, and we decided to have a lazy day bingeing movies on Netflix in his bed. The more I went over the events of last night in my head, the more I convinced myself that I truly had a breakthrough on behalf of all womankind. If more guys and girls had open and honest conversations with one another about their expectations instead of being vague and hoping for the best, navigating friendships and relationships would be so much easier. By this morning, I was fully ready to start writing my own self-help book.

"What do you mean?" I protest, popping a kernel of popcorn into my mouth.

"It's always way more complicated than you think it's going to be," Charlie says sagely. "Right now you two think you're fine with being friends. Hell, you probably believe that's possible. But someone always develops feelings."

"Maybe not," I say with a little less self-assurance. "Though he did say he likes me . . . but I think he just meant as a person."

Charlie gives me an incredulous look.

"Okay, fine," I huff. "It probably won't end well. But I'll take friends anywhere I can get them at this point. I'll have you know I had a thriving social life back in Preston. Yes, it included a lot of board game nights and book festivals, but it was still a social life."

"I'm sorry," Charlie says, his voice gentler. "I'm not trying to crap on your newfound friendship. I just want to make sure you're managing your expectations."

"You mean my expectations that everything is shit and nothing ever seems to go my way? Consider them managed."

"Am I invited to your pity party or should I let you have the room?"

I glower at him, then throw a piece of popcorn at his face. He quickly snaps it up and tosses it back at me.

"How did your meetings go yesterday?" I ask him, plucking the kernel off my t-shirt.

"It's too early to know yet, but it looks like I might be doing a winter line in collaboration with Coloro Cosmetics," he tells me excitedly. "It's this whole concept where they will create custom eyeshadow palettes and lipsticks based on my designs."

"That sounds amazing, Charlie," I say earnestly. "You really are an impressive person. I hope you know that."

"Oh, I do," he says, brushing his hair back dramatically.

"And so steadfastly humble, too." I nudge him with my shoulder. "Hey, I think I still have a stash of chocolate chip cookies in the kitchen. Are you in?"

"I swear I've gained ten pounds since you moved in," Charlie whines. "But yes, go get them."

I trot downstairs and start rifling through the kitchen cabinets until I find my package of cookies. It looks like my mother is starting to cook something, because a bunch of vegetables are piled up on the counter and the oven is preheating. Her laptop is sitting open next to the fridge, a recipe for veggie lo mein pulled up on the screen.

Deciding it would be a travesty to not have milk to go with my cookies, I nab two glasses and set them down. A little chirping noise sounds from my mother's computer, and I automatically glance over and see she has gotten a pop-up notification for a new email. Then I do a double-take at the snippet of text I can see from where I'm standing as an icy feeling washes over my body. The milk already forgotten, I step over to take a closer look.

At first, I think I must be hallucinating, but the email address on the notification plainly says "tips@chickabouttown.com." My heart starts thundering as I click to open the email.

Hey Jackie,

Just keep us posted if any good photo ops come up on Cam's schedule this week. It would be great to get another one of her with the guy she was out with yesterday—did you ever get any more info on him? Something with the two of you together would work, too.

Thanks,

Ashley

Chick About Town Contributor

I stand frozen, reading and re-reading the email. There are dozens of them in the thread, dating back to when I first got to L.A.

"Isn't it a little early for cookies? I was just about to make some lunch."

I turn around slowly to where my mother is standing in the entryway to the kitchen. My brain feels like it keeps alternating between slow motion and fast-forward as it tries to process what is happening.

"What's wrong?" she says, moving toward me. I jerkily take a step backwards, my back hitting the counter painfully.

"You got an email," I say, and my voice is eerily calm despite the heat starting to crawl through my veins.

"Okay . . ." my mother trails off, cocking her head to the side a little with confusion. Suddenly I feel a surge of hatred toward everything about her, from her perfectly curled blonde hair down to the leopard print pumps she's wearing.

"It's from *Chick About Town*," I continue robotically. "Wanting to know what chances they'll have to get pictures of me this week."

My mother's face goes white, and she opens and closes her mouth a few times looking for all the world like a beautiful blonde fish.

"Cam—"

"HOW COULD YOU DO THIS?" I explode with a yell that rips painfully through my throat.

"I can explain—" my mother says, holding both of her hands out placatingly.

"You can *EXPLAIN?!*" I scream, pointing angrily at the laptop. "What is there to explain, Mother? What possible justification could you have for selling me out to a FUCKING GOSSIP BLOG?!"

"I'm sor-sorry," my mother sputters, and I can see tears starting to form in her eyes. Good. "When you first got here and they posted about you . . . Vic thought it might be a good idea to keep them interested until you decide what you want to do."

"'What I want to do?'" I fume. "I have made it perfectly clear to you over and over again that I don't want the attention, but you listen to your stupid agent who I've barely ever talked to instead of me?"

"We just thought you might change your mind," my mother whispers. "I didn't want you to regret not taking the opportunity—"

"Opportunity?!" I ask incredulously. "What opportunity? I'm not like you, Mother. I'm not interested in whoring my life out to the whole world. The only reason I'm here is because Dad is gone and for whatever reason you insisted that I come here. I would *never* choose this. I would *never* choose you."

My mother makes a noise halfway between a gasp and a sob, and I can tell my blow has landed. Feeling like I can't stand to look at her for one more moment, I storm past her. Charlie is standing at the top of the stairs open-mouthed, but I ignore him. I turn the corner of the hallway intending to go to my bedroom, but the door to the billiards room is open and I find myself going in.

Jackie Jenson has done some pretty desperate things to stay relevant over the years, but to exploit her own daughter like this? How low can a person get? The photos from *Chick About Town* keep cycling through my head like a slideshow. Was this why she wanted to do all of that stuff with me? Not because she actually wanted to spend time with her own daughter, but because she knew she was guaranteed to have a picture if she arranged a public outing herself?

Slowly, I walk up to the rack of pool cues on the wall, take one down, and drag it behind me, the rubber bumper skittering slightly on the hardwood floors as I pace the room. Stopping at one of the giant windows overlooking the Los Angeles skyline, I feel the anger in the pit of my stomach that I've been working so hard to keep at bay start to bubble over.

I loathe this city and this enormous house and how quickly my life got turned upside down. It's not fair. It's just not fucking fair.

Before I fully grasp what I'm doing, I lift the pool cue over my shoulder like a baseball bat...

...and start swinging.

Listen to Track Six: "Out of My Head"

FIFTEEN

"**O**h my God, Cam!"

I come back to myself at the sound of Charlie's panicked voice and look around. I'm still standing in the billiards room holding my pool cue, but now the floor is covered in shattered glass. A gentle breeze is coming in through the empty windowpanes.

"You're bleeding," Charlie chokes out, his eyes brimming with tears as he stands in the doorway. I look down with mild interest to see blood dripping from a long gash on my right forearm. "Don't move—there's too much glass on the floor. I'll be right back."

Charlie rushes out of the room, and I peer down at the house slippers I'm wearing, which seem to have protected my feet from getting cut up. I gaze dazedly around at the damage I've done. The entire room looks like it is buried underneath a blanket of glass.

My mother comes running in but stops short at the sight of me bleeding all over her ruined room. Realizing I'm still clutching the pool cue at my side, I hastily drop it. My mother winces at the cracking noise it makes as it hits the floor. Charlie flies in behind her holding a broom.

"I'm just going to clear a path for you," he says as he starts carefully pushing glass shards off to the side. "Then I need to take you to a hospital to have that looked at."

"I'm fine," I say quietly, but Charlie shakes his head.

"You need stitches."

"I can take her," my mother volunteers. I meet her eye for just a second and see she is looking at me as if I'm a complete stranger. I quickly look away.

"No," Charlie says firmly. "I can do it. You should call and see if someone can come out to clean this up today and board up the windows."

By now Charlie has swept enough glass to the side that there's a path for me to get to the door. He grabs my left wrist, and we carefully pick our way out of the room. I can feel my mother watching us, but I don't look at her again.

"Come on," Charlie says, ushering me into the bathroom. "We need to wrap your arm in something."

We find an old bath towel, and Charlie helps me create a makeshift cover for my arm after we rinse it off. I still have drops of blood staining my pajamas. The adrenaline or shock or whatever it was I was running on right after I smashed the windows is wearing off now, and my cut has really started to hurt.

"Thank God I have leather seats," Charlie grumbles as he peels out of the driveway. When I don't reply, he bangs a hand angrily on the steering wheel making me jump and says, "What the hell happened, Cam? One minute you're going down to get cookies and the next all hell is breaking loose."

"I forgot about the cookies. I could totally go for some cookies right now."

Charlie just glares daggers at me.

"Our mother has been telling *Chick About Town* where and when I'll be out so they can take pictures for their blog," I sigh, suddenly feeling drained. "I saw the emails with my own eyes. She's been doing it ever since I got here. When I saw that I just sort of . . . lost it."

"What did she say about it?"

"That it was Vic's idea, and she was only trying to do me a favor in case I changed my mind about wanting to be a public figure or whatever."

"I'm sure she really believes she was trying to help," Charlie says tentatively.

"Are you *serious* right now?" I screech. "You're actually going to defend her?"

"No, no," he counters quickly. "I just mean I know Mom. She wasn't doing it to be malicious. Somehow in her mind she thought she was doing the right thing."

"That's the problem, Char," I practically wail. "If she knew me at all she would know that I don't want the same things the two of you do."

We pull into the parking lot of the hospital and follow the signs to the emergency room entrance. When we get inside, Charlie helps me fill out the check-in forms since my arm is now throbbing with pain. It doesn't take too long before an attractive male nurse (seriously, does everyone in this stupid town have to be so good-looking?) is taking me back into a room.

Forty-five minutes and eight stitches later, I'm told I am free to go. Charlie and I follow the nurse around a few corners toward the exit, but just as we reach the automatic doors, they open and we almost smack into someone hurrying inside.

"Sorry—" I start to apologize before seeing who it is and jumping back with a yelp.

"Cam?" Milo says, eyebrows flying up. He's holding a grease-stained bag from the diner.

"Charlie?" I whisper sideways through my mouth, not taking my eyes off of Milo. "How much blood did I lose? I think I'm hallucinating."

"You aren't," Charlie hisses. "Stop acting so weird."

I close my eyes for a second, suddenly very aware of my messy hair and bloodstained pajamas and the bad karma that is at work here. Much to my dismay, when I open them back up Milo is still standing there looking confused.

"Hello there," I say lamely.

"What are you doing here?" Milo says before spotting my bandaged arm. "Holy . . . are you okay?"

"Oh, this?" I ask, trying to sound casual as I hold my arm up. "Just a flesh wound. You should see the other guy. What are *you* doing here?"

Milo holds the sack of food up.

"Just bringing Dad some lunch after my shift."

In all of the commotion, I had completely forgotten we were at St. Agnes where Dr. Chen works in the E.R.

"That's nice of you," Charlie supplies when I just keep repeatedly nodding like a bobblehead doll that came to life. Milo gives me another worried look.

"We should go," I blurt, yanking on Charlie's arm. "See you later, alligator!"

Charlie gives Milo an apologetic wave over his shoulder as I drag him through the doors. When we get in the car, instead of putting the keys in the ignition he just folds his hands on his lap and stares at me expectantly. I avert my gaze and fiddle with a loose string on my bandage until I can't stand it anymore.

"What?" I say tersely.

"What is the matter with you?" Charlie says plaintively. The worry in his voice evaporates my instinct to get defensive. "Will you please talk to me?"

"I just wasn't expecting to see Milo of all people. It caught me off guard."

"Not just that," Charlie reaches over and clasps my hand. "Though I hope you don't act that weird with people all of the time."

I roll my eyes, my mouth twitching into a small smile. But Charlie gives me another beseeching look.

"I know I haven't been around as much as I should. Or checked in with you enough to see how you're doing."

"I'm fine," I say automatically.

Charlie looks pointedly at my arm.

"Okay," I hedge. "Maybe I'm not great, but I'm dealing."

"You know I'm here for you no matter what, right?" Charlie gives my hand a little squeeze. "You can talk to me about anything."

"I know," I say, squeezing back. "So do you think I'm grounded?"

Charlie thinks this over for a minute as he starts the car and pulls out of the hospital.

"I think Mom knows she messed up," he acknowledges. "But it's not going to be cheap to fix those windows. It could go either way."

I rest my head against the back of the seat as I contemplate this. Is this who I am now? Someone with such a volatile temper that they become destructive? My entire life, I've always been so laid back, the first one to play peacekeeper when any of my friends had a disagreement. Dad and I hardly ever fought, either. My heart sinks just thinking about what he would say if he could see what I did today. He probably wouldn't even recognize me anymore, and the thought twists something in my stomach so painfully that I almost double over.

The car comes to a stop, and I find we're sitting in the drive-thru of In-N-Out Burger.

"I figure it's better to go into battle on a full stomach," Charlie explains.

"I love you so much right now it hurts," I lean over to give him a quick side hug. "Oh wait . . . nope, that's the pain of eight stitches."

We order our food and pull into a parking spot to eat. Thankfully, Charlie doesn't bring anything else up about our mother or *Chick About Town*.

There are several work trucks parked outside the house when we get back. As I have done for the past few hours, I alternate between feeling an odd sense of justice and immense guilt. All I want to do is take a shower and curl up in bed for the rest of the day.

I dash upstairs, glancing in the billiards room as I walk past. It looks like all of the glass has been cleaned up, and now a handful of guys are nailing plywood boards onto the windows. I wince a little but continue on to my room. Jim perks his head up from where he's sprawled out on my bed.

"I'll take him out for you," Charlie says from my doorway.

"Oh, my God, could you?" I sigh in relief. "I just want to get cleaned up and take a nap. These pain meds are making me sleepy."

"You're going to have to face Mom eventually," Charlie warns me, getting Jim's leash from where it's draped over the couch.

"I know, but 'eventually' doesn't need to be right now," I say. Charlie walks over and wraps his arms around me in a tight hug before leading Jim out of my room. The door shuts with a soft click, and I'm left trying to figure out how in the world I'm going to take a shower while not getting my bandage wet per my doctor's instructions. I end up using a trash bag and tape to make a protective barrier and settle for drawing up a bath instead of my usual shower. I stretch out in the tub, letting my right arm dangle over the edge.

The reality of what happened today settles over me, and before I know it a steady stream of tears is running down my cheeks. I passively let them mingle in with the water dripping down from my wet hair. It feels almost cathartic to not try and fight it for once.

If I'm being honest with myself, the thing that stings the most is how betrayed I feel that my mother would exploit me to *Chick About Town* knowing how I felt about it. She's the reason they speculated about my supposed "partying" and if I'm having some sort of breakdown (which I'm starting to think they might not be too far off about), and they are the ones who posted that stupid picture of me with Milo in the park. I wasn't under any delusion that my mother and I have some great relationship, but I at least trusted that she had listened to me when I said I wasn't comfortable being in her spotlight.

The bathwater has started to get cold, so I carefully get out, dry off, and put on a clean pair of sweatpants and a t-shirt. Jim is sitting outside of the bathroom when I open the door, and I make a mental note to get Charlie something really nice to thank him for everything he's done today.

I check my phone and see I have several new text messages. The first is from Mei wanting to know what happened because Milo told her he saw me at the hospital. I text her back to let her know I'm okay and ask if she wants to meet at the diner for breakfast tomorrow so I can fill her in. I haven't quite decided if I want to actually tell her the truth or make up a less psychotic-sounding version of events. The other message is from a number I don't recognize.

Hey- it's Milo. Got your # from Mei. I just wanted to check on you to see if you're okay.

My heart flips over in my chest. I stare at my phone for a minute before typing my reply.

hi... I'm good. cut myself on some glass, but it was nothing a half-dozen stitches couldn't fix. eight to be precise, but i don't want to be a braggart.

His response comes through almost right away.

Ouch, that sucks. I'm glad to hear you're on the mend.

I reread his message a few times trying to decide if it means anything significant that he texted me. The obvious answer is no, he: 1) has a girlfriend; and, 2) isn't trying to open up further conversation beyond just making sure I'm not dying or anything.

thanks, I end up replying. *and sorry about how weird I was when I saw you earlier. just chalk it up to painkillers.*

I hit send, assuming I won't hear anything back from him. But then my phone chimes.

How do you explain all the rest of the time? :P

I smile to myself.

HILARIOUS. good to know you have a back-up career as a comedian if the whole music thing doesn't work out.

It takes a few minutes for him to respond.

I'm multi-talented. What can I say?

and so very modest, I type back.

He replies with a shrugging emoji, and I decide to leave it at that. I can really feel the grogginess from the pain medication kicking in, so I bury myself in my comforter and fall asleep almost right away.

A soft knock at my door stirs me awake. I crack an eye open to see my mother peeking her head in. The memory of today's events comes rushing back and an instant dread hits me.

"We need to talk," she says, and there's a firmness to her voice I haven't heard before. Knowing there is no getting out of this, I sit up and watch as she situates herself at the foot of the bed. She crosses her legs daintily, wrapping her hands around her knee. Not wanting to be the first to speak, I try to keep a neutral expression as I wait for her to say something. She just sighs and shakes her head a little, sweeping away a loose strand of blonde hair that catches on her lip gloss.

"How is your arm?" she asks, eying the bandage. I shrug.

"It hurts a little," I admit. "They said it would for a few days."

"Listen, I owe you an apology," she says in a way that makes me suspect she has rehearsed this. "It was completely out of line for me to be in contact with *Chick About Town* about you. I realize that now. I'm truly sorry, and I hope you will forgive me."

I try not to show my surprise. So far, this conversation is going far better than I expected.

"But what you did today is unacceptable."

Here it comes.

"Ever since you've been here, you have been temperamental and angry. I know this transition has been . . . difficult. I thought maybe it would get better over time, but what happened today proves to me that you need some professional help."

My jaw drops open. My mother's eyes are fixed on me, and I can tell she's bracing for my reaction while trying to maintain her resolve.

"I've made an appointment for tomorrow afternoon with a therapist that comes highly recommended, Dr. James Landry," she continues resolutely, ignoring me as I gape at her. "I think it will be good for you."

"You have no right to make me go see a shrink," I say through gritted teeth.

"I'm your mother," she says calmly. "So I do, actually. And my mind is made up."

She stands up, smoothes down her black pencil pants, and walks out without so much as another word. I continue staring at my closed door, caught between a mixture of shock and irritation. The rational part of me knows that she's letting me off easy for practically destroying an entire room of her house. But the irrational part of me is seething at the idea of having to go talk to a stranger about my feelings.

There's another tap on the door.

"I really don't want to talk about this anymore," I yell crossly. The door opens anyway, and Charlie is standing there holding a plate with a sandwich and some chips.

"Oh," I say sheepishly. "It's you."

Charlie crosses the room to me and sets the plate on my bedside table.

"How are you holding up?" he asks, crouching down to pet Jim where he is laying on the floor at the foot of my bed.

"I'm guessing Mother told you," I answer grumpily, folding

my arms across my chest. I probably look like a petulant child, but I don't really care.

"She did," Charlie acknowledges. He straightens back up and gestures for me to scoot over, then crawls into bed next to me, careful to not jostle my injured arm. "I know you probably aren't happy—"

"Oh, I'm not—"

"Let me finish." He puts his index finger to my lips to silence me. "You can't tell me you've been totally yourself since you lost your dad. No one expects you to be, but you've been through a lot, and it isn't such a bad idea to talk to someone who's better equipped than we are to help you through it."

Angry tears start to prick the back of my eyes.

"I just want to be strong enough to handle it on my own," I whisper fiercely. Charlie wraps an arm around me and pulls me in, letting me rest my head on his shoulder.

"I know," he says soothingly. "That's what makes you such a stubborn asshole."

Despite everything, a laugh escapes me.

"Really," Charlie reassures me. "Therapy isn't so bad. Hell, I've been going for years."

I don't bother arguing with him, recognizing a losing battle when I see one. I eat my sandwich, and we spend the next few hours watching mindless television in my bed until I can't keep my eyes open anymore. Charlie tucks me in and kisses me on the forehead before turning off my lamp and whispering, "It's going to be okay, sis."

I nod, resolving to figure out tomorrow the best way to get through this therapy business without delving into all of the stuff I don't think I'm ready to face yet.

SIXTEEN

I text Mei the next morning to let her know I'm not going to make it to breakfast, though I don't tell her why. She asks if I want to come over for dinner and spend the night at her house instead.

"Am I grounded?" I inquire as my mother and I sit in the car on the way to my appointment.

"Oh," she says, as if this is the first time the thought is occurring to her that what I did is probably punishable by more than just a string of therapy sessions. "Um . . . I guess I hadn't really planned on grounding you—"

"So it's okay if I spend the night at Mei's tonight then?"

My mother looks flustered as she pulls out a sparkly compact and checks her reflection in what I assume is a way to stall for time while she thinks this over.

"I'm fine with that," she finally says. "But when you get home, we really should sit down and have a discussion about some changes we need to make going forward."

"Sure," I say, scrolling through my phone to avoid having to talk anymore.

A few minutes later, we're walking into a sleek medical office building, my mother's Jimmy Choo stilettos clacking loudly on the marble floor as we step into the elevator. She presses the button to the fourth floor as I stare down at my feet with my arms crossed, trying not to sneeze from the gardenia scent from her perfume.

"Dr. Landry is the best there is. His podcast is always trending on Spotify." My mother says this as if it's all the evidence I would need that his credentials are legit.

"Impressive," I say flatly.

"Just try to keep an open mind," my mother implores as a beep sounds and the elevator doors open onto a posh waiting room.

I throw myself into a plush leather armchair and watch several fish dart around in a giant tank that sits along one wall while my mother checks me in at the front desk.

"Leo will bring the car around to pick you up at four o'clock," she says a minute later, coming over to perch on the edge of a chair next to me.

I nod, not taking my eyes off the bright orange fish.

"Chamomile?" A beanpole of a man in his early forties with salt-and-pepper hair stands in the doorway to the waiting room, looking over a pair of silver reading glasses. I wince before I grab my backpack from where I'd slung it on the floor next to me and stalk over to him.

"It's Cam," I say pleadingly. "Please just call me Cam."

"And I'm Jackie," my mother says, coming up behind me. "Jackie Jenson."

"Ah, yes," the man extends a hand toward her. "Dr. James Landry. Very nice to meet you. I look forward to speaking with you and your daughter today."

"Oh . . . I wasn't aware that I was expected to go in with her," my mother says, trying to look concerned but not able to fully furrow her brow thanks to her most recent round of Botox. "I have a prior commitment."

Dr. Landry frowns. "Generally I like for the parent to sit in on the first session so they can voice their concerns and be part of the goal-setting process."

"There's really no way out of my obligation." My mother looks uncomfortable, which brings me a small sense of satisfaction. "I'm under contract."

"Very well," Dr. Landry replies, looking nonplussed.

As my mother sweeps from the room, I give Dr. Landry my best do-you-see-what-I'm-dealing-with look before letting him lead me down the hallway.

"What, no couch?" I ask when we reach his office and he gestures to a chair. I slump into it as he takes up the chair opposite me. I look around, squinting slightly from the sun streaming through floor-to-ceiling windows on the far side of the room. The office is decorated with abstract paintings. I make a vow to myself that if he makes me look at them and tell him what I see and how they make me feel, I'm never stepping foot in here again.

"Do you want there to be a couch?" he replies, scribbling in a yellow legal pad.

I narrow my eyes at him. "Is this going to be the kind of thing where you answer all of my questions with a question?"

"Is that what you think therapy is?"

"I am so not doing this bit with you," I mutter, shaking my head.

Dr. Landry looks up at me placidly.

"This is your time," he says, sitting back in his chair and crossing his legs. "You can choose to spend it however you like."

"What if I choose to spend it in complete silence?"

"You are free to do so."

"That's what I want to do."

"If that's the case, you aren't off to a promising start with it."

My mouth drops open slightly in surprise, but I recover quickly. Point to Landry. If we were different circumstances, he doesn't seem like he would be so bad. But we aren't under different circumstances.

Dr. Landry and I have now been staring at each other in this weird standoff I accidentally initiated for thirty-seven minutes. I know this because I've checked the clock at least twice during every single one of those minutes. I'm starting to regret the stubborn stoicism route I chose, but I feel obligated to see it through because I'm no quitter, dammit.

"That's our time for today," Dr. Landry says mildly after what feels like an eternity. If he's irked that I have just taken up an entire hour of his life refusing to speak to him, he doesn't let on.

After he leads me back out to the waiting room, he flips through his notes and says, "It looks like we have a standing weekly appointment for a while, so I will look forward to seeing you next week."

"Can't wait," I say and make a beeline out the door.

"I'm sorry again about having to flake on breakfast this morning," I say to Mei. We're sitting in her family's bonus room playing MarioKart on an old Nintendo 64. It turns out her family has a whole working collection of old gaming systems, and upon finding this out I insisted she teach me how to play something. She selected MarioKart and is currently doing literal laps around me as I crash into flying shells and walls every few seconds.

"No worries," she says, sticking her tongue out in concentration as her Princess Peach avatar slams into Donkey Kong. "Was it something to do with your arm? What happened?"

"Yeah, kind of," I reply. "I cut myself on some glass and had to get stitches."

"Ouch," Mei says, wincing.

Somehow my Wario is just doing circles in place. The game ends with me so far behind everyone else it doesn't even let me finish the race.

"That was hard to watch," Milo says from behind me. He's leaning against the door frame with his arms folded across his chest, his full attention on the T.V.

"She's a first-timer," Mei explains.

"No way," he says sarcastically, walking over to sit next to me on the couch.

"Hey now," I wrinkle my nose at him. "I'm also playing injured, so I'm not able to live up to my full potential here."

"Why did you choose Wario?" he asks curiously.

"Because he told me 'Imma gonna win,'" I confess. "His confidence was seductive."

Milo snorts.

"If you're so great, why don't you show me how it's done?" I offer the controller to him with a flourishing gesture.

"Don't mind if I do."

Milo handily wins the next race despite my taunting and jeering. He then fishes out a third controller so the three of us can all play together. The next hour is filled with a lot of trash-talking and false bravado on my part, though I do manage to get third place in one of the races. By the time Mrs. Chen is calling us in to dinner, my cheeks hurt from smiling so much.

"Are you joining us?" Dr. Chen asks Milo when we walk in. "I thought you had plans with Leighton tonight."

"Nope," Milo says lightly, getting himself a plate and silverware to add an extra place setting at the kitchen table. I see Dr. and Mrs. Chen exchange a look and make a mental note to ask Mei about it later tonight.

"This looks amazing," I say earnestly when we're all seated at the table. Mrs. Chen has made a traditional Chinese meal with steamed dumplings, Peking roasted duck, and several vegetable dishes.

"I love when we have company for dinner," Mei beams. "That's when she makes all the best stuff."

Mrs. Chen acts like she's offended, but there is a smile playing at her lips.

"Shall we?" Dr. Chen says, offering me the plate of dumplings.

"Mmmmm," I moan as I take my first bite.

"I forgot to warn you about how intense Cam can be with food," Milo says, smirking at me.

"Excuse you," I point my chopsticks at him accusingly. "I've eaten with your parents before, and they still invited me back. So there."

Milo just raises his eyebrows up at me.

"I will not apologize for having an honest, though I'll admit sometimes visceral, reaction to good food," I say haughtily, scooping another helping of vegetables onto my plate.

"Nor should you," Dr. Chen says with a laugh.

For dessert, Mrs. Chen produces several cartons of ice cream from the freezer along with chocolate and caramel sauces so we can each make our own sundae. Mei suggests we get out a board game, so we end up deciding to play a round of Clue while we eat our dessert. Fortunately, I'm much better at Clue than I am at Mario-Kart, and it doesn't take me too long to figure out it was Professor Plum in the ballroom with the rope.

"We should go out to the hot tub," Mei suggests a few minutes after Dr. and Mrs. Chen have gone up to their bedroom for the night.

"I didn't bring a swimsuit," I frown.

"That's okay. We keep extras for guests just in case."

"Okay, sure," I say, standing up and stretching.

"Oh, I suppose you think you're joining us?" Mei jokes as Milo follows suit.

"Aw, come on," I chime in. "We should let him. He has been a pretty integral part of our girl's night so far."

"Just for that I think I will," he says with a wink, heading outside toward the pool house. Mei and I make our way up to her bedroom to change.

When I emerge from the bathroom wearing the brand-new one-piece swimsuit that fits me far better than I would have anticipated, I try to act casual as I ask, "So was it just me or did Milo get a little weird when your parents brought up Leighton?"

"Yeah, I guess he did a little," she says as she ties her hair up in a ponytail with a scrunchie.

"Wonder what that was about," I prod.

"I promise I would tell you if I knew anything," Mei says. "I'm not exactly the first one he comes running to when he has relationship problems."

"I know," I say quickly. "I'm sorry."

"There's no need to apologize." Mei hands me a towel, which I wrap around myself. "I just don't want you to get your hopes up. Besides, I heard from Eric who heard from Cassidy that you two had dinner the other night. I can't believe you didn't tell me."

"Oh, crap," I say. "I totally forgot."

As we walk down to the hot tub, I recount my conversation with Cassidy where we agreed to just be friends.

"Yeah, that's never going to happen," Mei says when I finish.

"You sound like Charlie."

"Charlie knows what he's talking about."

"Shit," I say as we reach the edge of the hot tub.

"What?"

"I forgot about this," I say, waving my bandaged arm.

The door to the pool house opens and Milo comes out in his swim trunks, a towel draped around his neck. I glance away quickly, but not before seeing the toned muscles of his abs and chest. He always struck me as being pretty slender, so I'm a little dumbfounded to see how fit he is.

"What's wrong?" he asks as he approaches us.

I point to my arm and say, "It's fine. I'll just pull up a pool chair and hang out while you guys go in."

"Cam isn't supposed to get her bandage wet," Mei clarifies. Milo narrows his eyes as he looks at my arm thoughtfully.

"Hold on," he says suddenly, then jogs toward the house. He disappears for a minute, leaving me and Mei to look at each other questioningly. When he reappears, he's holding a small package.

"Here," he says, thrusting it toward me proudly.

"Here . . . what?" I turn the box over in my hand to examine it more closely. The label reads Cast and Wound Protector with a picture of a man in what looks like a clear glove so long that it almost reaches his armpit.

"There are certain perks when your dad works in a hospital," he says. "Mainly, the quality of your home medicine cabinet."

I open the package and pull out the protector, which is basically a big plastic bag with a band at the end to keep it suctioned to the skin. Indeed, when I put it on, it goes practically all the way up my entire arm. Mei and Milo erupt into laughter.

"It's like my arm is wearing a giant condom," I say crossly as I hold it up. Mei tries to answer but can't speak because she is giggling too hard.

"It's definitely a look," Milo chuckles, laying his towel down and stepping into the hot tub.

"This is absurd. Aren't hot tubs supposed to be all sexy and stuff?"

"Not anymore," Mei wheezes as she eases herself into the water.

I consider taking it off and insisting that it's worth sitting out just to reclaim a little of my self-respect. But the water looks so nice, and I'm not too proud to admit that the idea of having an excuse to be this close to a half-naked Milo has its appeal.

So I put my chin up in the air and, with as much dignity as I can muster, saunter over to the hot tub and settle in. The water is the perfect temperature. I lean my head back and close my eyes, letting the jets hit the spot between my shoulder blades.

Mei starts chattering away about the final showcase she's

working on for her drama class, and I'm happy to just sit and listen for a while. I don't know if it's my full stomach or the low rumble of the hot tub jets, but the weight of the last few days feels particularly heavy. I keep spacing out as Mei and Milo talk, thinking about how the last 48 hours seem like they happened to someone else.

"Earth to Cam," Mei says, waving a hand in front of my face.

"Huh?" I say a little dazedly.

"I was asking if you want a soda," Mei repeats, standing up and stepping out onto the tile. "I'm going inside to get one for myself."

"Yeah, sure," I say. "Thanks."

I watch her trot off toward the house, and when I turn back around, I find Milo looking at me intently.

"What?" I ask, suddenly feeling self-conscious.

"Are you okay?" he asks, his eyebrows drawn together with concern.

"Oh, yeah. I think it's just the heat. And this giant arm balloon I'm sporting."

"No, I mean overall. You had me a little worried when I saw you at the hospital."

I start to reach up to tuck some loose strands of hair back into the bun on top of my head before remembering my arm is covered in plastic. I sigh, using my left hand instead to try and do it one-handed. After a few fumbling tries, Milo moves closer to me.

"Here," he says, gingerly reaching his fingers up to thread a few locks of my hair into my hair tie. His face is inches from mine, and I watch the corners of his mouth turn down in concentration as he gently adjusts my top knot. His eyes meet mine, and his hands linger for a moment near my face. I idly wonder if he can hear how rapidly my heart is beating over the sound of the hot tub jets as I swallow hard.

He clears his throat and he drifts back to where he was sitting across from me.

"There," he says, his voice breaking a little. "Good as new."

"Thanks," I say, hardly about to get out more than a whisper.

"Who's thirsty?" Mei chimes, trotting out holding three cans of soda. She glances back and forth between me and Milo a few times. "Did I miss something?"

We stay in the hot tub until we are all sufficiently wrinkled, then Mei and I head up to her room to dry off and change. We decide to finish the night with a romantic comedy marathon, though we fall asleep after only a movie and a half.

I'm standing in the sand. I look around and recognize the small beach house Dad and I used to rent every spring when we went out to Georgia to visit Aunt Margaret. Squinting against the sunlight, I scan the shore and see a silhouette standing at the edge of the water I instantly recognize as my dad. I start to walk but break into a run as I draw nearer.

"Daddy?" I say breathlessly when I reach him. He turns to look at me, a broad smile on his stubbled face.

"Hey, kiddo," he says warmly. I want to throw my arms around him, but I'm afraid if I touch him, he might disappear.

"I miss you so much," I say, the words filled with every ounce of emotion I've been trying not to feel lately.

"I know," he says, looking back out at the ocean. "I miss you, too."

"I don't think I can do this without you."

Tears are streaming down my cheeks. Dad faces me again, reaching over to take my hand.

"Don't look so sad," he says. "Everything is going to be okay."

I wake with a jolt, still feeling the ghost of Dad's hand in mine. My pillow is wet with tears, and I lay there for a minute paralyzed by my grief. I can tell by Mei's even breathing that she's fast asleep. The clock by her bed says it is 2:37 a.m. Feeling like it will be a while before sleep finds me again, I get up, put on a sweatshirt, grab the book I brought with me, and quietly tiptoe downstairs.

SEVENTEEN

Using the flashlight on my phone, I stop in the kitchen first to get myself a glass of water. As I start to walk toward the living room, I spot a bag of M&Ms sitting on the counter. There's a magnetic notepad on the fridge, so I rip a page off and scribble a note that says "*I.O.U. one bag of M&Ms. With my deepest gratitude, Cam.*" I leave the note in place of the candy and walk into the living room.

I curl up in the giant two-person armchair and flip on the little table lamp next to it. I'm just getting settled back into the chapter I was on when I hear a soft rustling behind me.

"Yams."

I jump so violently that my book goes flying across the room, and I tumble out of my chair. Milo's dark figure puts his hands up in a pacifying gesture.

"Sorry," he whispers, taking a few steps into the soft glow of the lamp light to extend a hand and help me up. I glare up at him from where I'm sprawled out on the floor.

"Haven't you figured out by now that doesn't work?" I ask crankily, letting him pull me back up to my feet.

"Yeah, we don't have the best track record with it, do we?"

I walk over to pick my book up, and when I turn around, Milo is sitting on the couch with my bag of M&Ms. His hair is especially tousled-looking, and there is something about that and his red plaid pajama pants that makes him look younger.

"Hey!" I hiss, reaching to snatch the M&Ms from him. He dangles them just out of my grasp, smirking.

"I know for a fact these are not yours," he points out. I abandon my efforts and flop back down on the chair.

He pours himself a handful and offers them to me.

"What are you doing in here?" I ask, cupping my hand that isn't bandaged up so he can give me some.

"I saw the light on and was curious," he explains, tossing an M&M in the air and catching it in his mouth. He gives me a self-satisfied look, so I tilt my head back dramatically and pour my entire handful of M&Ms into my mouth. I give a little bow as he claps softly, his eyes crinkling with laughter.

"So," he says as I try to chew as gracefully as I'm able to with a mouth full of chocolate. "What are you doing up at this hour?"

I swallow with a gulp.

"Oh . . . uh," I stammer, running my tongue over my teeth. "I . . . well, I had a bad dream. Except it wasn't bad, really."

Milo tilts his head quizzically.

"It was about my dad," I say after taking a sip of my water. "We were just . . . talking."

Milo nods slowly.

"You never answered my question from earlier," he points out.

"What question was that?"

"If you're okay."

"You know," I remark. "In the interest of balance and fairness, you already just asked a question. It should be my turn to ask you one."

"Okay, fine."

"What are *you* doing up at this hour?"

He scratches the back of his neck, looking uncomfortable.

"I couldn't sleep," he finally says. "I . . . broke up with Leighton today."

I pause just as I'm about to eat some more M&Ms, my hand suspended in midair halfway to my mouth. I can feel my pulse quicken at this unexpected piece of news.

"Oh, God," I gasp a little as something dawns on me. "Please tell me it didn't have anything to do with that stupid picture of us in *Chick About Town*."

"No, no," Milo says quickly. "It wasn't that."

"So then what happened?"

I can't believe how ballsy I'm being right now.

"Nope," Milo chides. "We're taking turns, remember?"

"Fine," I say.

"So, *are* you doing okay?"

"You are unrelenting. Fine. Not really, no." He waits for me to continue, but I just smile sweetly bat my eyelashes at him.

"What, that's all you're going to say?" he says, sounding exasperating.

"It was a complete answer. Apparently them's the rules."

"Okay, new rules," he says, popping a few M&Ms in his mouth. "I'll talk if you will."

I mull this over, weighing the pros and cons. On the one hand, he's definitely going to think I'm crazy if I tell him about everything that has transpired over the last few days. But I'm dying to know what happened between him and Leighton.

"Deal," I consent. "But you have to start."

"You drive a hard bargain," Milo chuckles.

"It's worth it," I say mysteriously. "Because boy, do I have some stories to tell you."

"Now I'm hooked," he jokes, but then his smile fades. "When Leighton and I first started dating three years ago, things were different. We were different. For one thing, we were still in high school and had all these plans to go to college together. But then I joined up with the band, and her Instagram started gaining traction and she wasn't interested in college anymore, so neither of us wound up where we thought we would be."

I pull my legs in, hugging them to my chest and wrapping my arms around them as I listen. I've always gotten cold when I get nervous, and suddenly the room feels like it's freezing.

"I think I've just been stubbornly holding on to what we used to be," Milo continues. "But she's changed a lot since her career started. And it's not just her—I've changed, too. It was time to stop trying to force it to work."

"How did she take it?"

"Not great," Milo says with a wry smile. "She's convinced I'm going to change my mind."

"Do you think you will?"

"I don't think so," he says quietly, but the way he says it makes it sound like he isn't so sure. He stares off at nothing for a moment, then looks at me. "You're up."

"Oh, boy," I exhale slowly. "Where to even begin."

Surprising myself, I actually find it pretty easy to recount the roller coaster that has been the last few days. When I finish, Milo has an inscrutable expression on his face. I immediately start wondering if I have just made a horrible mistake by telling him all of this.

"So . . . thoughts? Comments? Observations?" I prompt lamely. Milo nods a few times.

"Yeah," he begins. "I think therapy will probably be good for you."

"You . . . what?" I say incredulously. "Didn't you hear the part about how invasive it feels to be forced to talk to a stranger about the most intimate details of my life?"

"How do you ever expect him to not be a stranger anymore if you don't actually talk to him?" Milo says reasonably.

"How . . . I . . ." I splutter. "But—"

"Cam, you're an intelligent person. If someone else told you all of the things you just told me, what would you say to them?"

I pretend to ponder this, though I already know the answer.

"I would tell them that they are the least qualified person to know how to deal with all of this because they've never experienced it before," I say dully. "And that they obviously aren't doing so great with it, so they should probably get professional advice from someone who has been trained on how to help people who have lost someone."

Milo nods, tossing me the bag of M&Ms, which I catch one-handed.

"I think you've earned the rest of those," he says.

"I'm not an angry person," I feel the need to say, setting the bag on the table next to me. "At least, I never used to be. I don't really know what I am now."

Milo gets up and comes over to sit next to me on the chair, angling to face me. I unfold my legs to make room for him. His knee brushes up against mine, but neither of us pulls away.

"I'd say you're a pretty awesome person who is going through some shit," he says gently. I look sideways at him and smile. "And I also think you should try and get some sleep."

He stands up, and I try to not look too disappointed as I do the same. I turn the lamp off, and it's completely dark save for a small nightlight by the stairs. We each turn on the flashlight on our phones and take a second to let our eyes adjust, then walk the few steps toward the living room door in silence.

"Well, goodnight," I whisper.

"Goodnight, Cam."

I can feel Milo watching me as I carefully pick my way up the stairs, but when I turn back around, he's already walking out the door back to the pool house.

I don't wake up the next morning until after 10:00. It only took a matter of seconds for me to fall asleep once I got back up to Mei's room and tucked myself into my little cot, not giving myself the chance to dissect my conversation with Milo.

"Morning, sleepyhead," Mei says in a sing-song voice when I walk into the kitchen.

"I am so sorry," I apologize, plucking a muffin out of a basket sitting on the table. "I never sleep this late. You should have woken me up!"

"You just look like such an angelic little cherub when you sleep," Mei jokes. "Plus, I heard you get up in the middle of the night, so I figured you needed it."

"I'm sorry," I say again, taking the seat across from her at the kitchen table. "I tried really hard to be quiet."

"Oh, I fell back asleep almost immediately," she says.

My phone chimes, and I look to see a text message from my mother asking when I'll be home. I must have an irritated look on my face because Mei asks, "Is everything alright?"

"Yeah," I say, placing my phone face-down on the kitchen table. "But I should probably head home soon."

"I was going to kick you out anyway," Mei says, snatching a muffin for herself. "I have to get ready. I'm going to a movie with Eric."

"Who am I to get in the way of true love?" I reply.

"You know," she croons. "Cassidy does keep asking about you. Are you sure you can't just give things a shot with him? It would be so much fun for all of us to go out together."

"I'm sure," I laugh. "I have way too much going on right now to worry about dating."

I don't know why I'm not telling Mei the truth about the windows and Dr. Landry when it was so easy to talk to Milo about it last night. Maybe I just don't want to have to go over all of the details again so soon. It really is pretty embarrassing.

We finish our breakfast and make plans to have lunch and do some shopping together later this week. I text Leo and run upstairs to pack my bag. As I'm walking out of the Chens' house, I see Milo coming out of the pool house. He gives me a little two-finger salute, and I smile back before getting into Leo's waiting car.

When I get home, my mother is waiting for me on the living room couch, typing away on her laptop. She looks up and closes it when I walk in.

"Oh good, you're home," she says.

"I was just headed to the kitchen for something to drink," I say, speeding up to try and avoid a prolonged conversation.

"We should talk," my mother says. I stop in my tracks and give the kitchen a longing look before setting my bag down and taking a seat on the arm of the couch.

When it becomes clear that there is no way in hell I'm going to be the one to start this conversation, my mother says, "How was your session yesterday with Dr. Landry?"

"It was fine," I say vaguely, examining my nails so I don't have to meet her eyes. My mother gives me an exasperated look.

"Now you listen to me, Chamomile," she admonishes. I cringe at the use of my full name. "I can be just as stubborn as you are. You are sorely mistaken if you think I'm going to back down just because you won't engage in therapy." At my look of indignation, she adds, "Oh, yes, I got an email from Dr. Landry letting me know you refused to speak to him yesterday."

"What about doctor-patient confidentiality?" I say, feeling utterly betrayed.

"There is nothing for him to keep confidential if you don't say anything," my mother points out sensibly. I just throw my hands in the air.

"Fine!" I shout, my voice full of venom. "You can just add therapy to the list of ways you're trying to commandeer my life without even asking me."

"As I already explained to you," my mother says in a forced

calm tone. "I know that I shouldn't have been in touch with *Chick About Town*. I simply wanted you to have options—"

"What about what *I* want?" I snap. "Though how could I expect you to know what I want when you've never cared enough to know even the most basic things about me?"

My mother flinches. She's quiet for a second then stands up, readjusting the blouse she has tucked into her wide-legged trousers.

"Follow me," she says, turning to walk toward the stairs. Baffled, I hesitate before getting up and trailing behind her. She walks into her bedroom, then leads me through a door to what I had assumed to be a closet but turns out to be a small office. She stands in front of a wall of picture frames. Annoyed, I come up beside her, wondering what in the world the purpose of this could be.

I glance at the wall, then do a double-take as I comprehend what I'm looking at.

The entire wall is covered in pieces of my artwork, dating all the way back to the little handprint pictures I made in preschool. Some of them are ones I made her during the summers I spent here when I was younger, most of which have some form of "I love my mommy" scribbled in the shaky handwriting of a child. Others are from middle and high school that dad must have mailed her. All of them look like they have been professionally framed, even the ones from when I was little that are just a bunch of squiggly lines.

My throat tightens as I continue to scan the dozens of drawings and paintings. When I steal a look at my mother, she has silent tears rolling down her face as she looks fondly at the wall.

"I . . ." I start, not knowing what to say.

"Cam, I know I've made a lot of mistakes," my mother says softly, grabbing my hand. "But all I want is for you to be happy. If you want a life out of the spotlight, if you still want to go to art school—you have my blessing. I just . . . knew that with losing your father, some of the things you wanted might be different now.

When something terrible happened to me, this life—this career— saved me. It gave me choices. I was only trying to make sure you had choices, but I went about it all wrong. I'm so sorry."

Her voice breaks on the last word, and I can tell she wants to hug me but is holding back. Not able to say anything around the giant lump in my throat, I give her a little nod of permission. She sweeps me into a hug, and we just stand there like that, holding each other and crying in front of a wall full of art that I'm secretly terrified I will never be able to add anything to again.

After we're finally able to recompose ourselves, my mother timidly asks if I would want to watch a movie or something. I reluctantly agree on the condition we order pizza, mostly because the idea of seeing my mother eating something with that many carbs is oddly thrilling. She clears her schedule for the rest of the day, and we both change into sweatpants and settle in on the couch.

Charlie eventually joins us, and the three of us stay up late watching classic eighties movies and making fun of all of the big hair and bright clothes. My mother even lets Jim climb up on the couch and lay next to her with his head on her lap. Throughout the night, I keep stealing little glances at her, wrestling with the idea that as much as I have accused her of not knowing me, I may know even less about her.

EIGHTEEN

The next few weeks seem to fly by. My mother has kept her word, and there hasn't been a single new post about me on *Chick About Town*. We've started going to Tuesday and Thursday morning yoga classes together, and she, Charlie, and I now have weekly Sunday night dinners at home. She even offered to come with me to the east coast to visit some colleges, but I've been avoiding giving her a definitive answer. She doesn't know that I still haven't been able to bring myself to draw anything since Dad died, though I'm proud to say I did bring it up in my session with Dr. Landry last week. Taking Milo's advice, I decided to at least make a little bit of an effort in therapy. So far, we haven't delved too deeply into anything, but it's starting to get easier to talk to him.

For as smoothly as things have been going with my mother, it has been the exact opposite with Milo. Things aren't bad or anything, but I think a part of me was expecting him to make a move after he broke up with Leighton. Even though the two of them haven't gotten back together, nothing has changed between us. I still go to the diner a few times a week, and Mei still just rolls her eyes every time the two of us start going back and forth about something. But he hasn't texted me since he saw me at the hospital, and even though I've started typing a dozen messages to him, I always end up deleting them.

"It would be pretty skeezy of him to start dating someone immediately after getting out of a long-term relationship," Charlie points out one Thursday afternoon as he, Alexis, and I are all sitting around the living room painting our toenails.

"But couldn't he at least, like, declare his intentions or something?" I reply, wiggling my toes and admiring my handiwork as I wait for my first coat to dry.

Charlie snorts. "'Intentions?' My dear sister, how can he possibly declare his intentions for courtship when you haven't even made your societal debut yet? It would be most improper. Imagine what the *ton* would say."

I just scowl at him.

"Don't let him give you a hard time," Alexis says, brow furrowed in concentration as she applies the topcoat to her neon green polish. "He's in no place to be dispensing relationship advice when he can't even work up the nerve to ask out—"

"That is completely off-topic," Charlie interrupts, glaring daggers at Alexis. But I'm already crab walking over to where she's sitting with her back against the couch.

"Hey," I say sweetly, giving her my most saccharine smile. "You know, of all of Charlie's friends I've met, you're my favorite. And the hottest. Now what is it you were saying?"

Alexis looks back and forth between me and Charlie a few times before shrugging a little and saying, "Charlie met a guy at the dog park, but he's decided to play hard to get and won't just ask him out."

"Judas!" Charlie gasps.

"Excuse me very much," I say, barely containing my delight. "Did you say at the dog park?"

Charlie sighs dramatically, screwing the lid back onto his nail polish before crossing his arms.

"It's just a guy I run into there sometimes when I take Jim," he says haughtily.

"Who you are low-key obsessed with," supplies Alexis.

"And you didn't tell me?!" I practically shriek. "What's his name? What does he look like? What kind of dog does he have?"

"Ugh, fine," Charlie says, rolling his eyes. "His name is Aidan, he looks like a Calvin Klein model, and he has a labradoodle whose name is Daisy, if you must know."

"Wait, wait, wait," I say, clapping my hands together with glee. "Does this mean that Jim is your wingman? Right before you go in do the two of you fist bump each other and then Jim says, 'go get 'em, bro?'"

"Okay, we're done here," Charlie says, throwing his hands up in exasperation. He stands up and starts heading toward the kitchen. "You need to reconsider where your loyalties lie," he says to Alexis as he passes her. He takes a few more steps before turning back around to point at me. "And it will be a cold day in hell before you catch me fist-bumping anyone."

I dissolve into a fit of giggles as Charlie lifts his chin and strides out of the room. Alexis just shakes her head, looking amused.

"You have given me such a gift today," I tell her after I catch my breath. "I don't know how I'll ever repay you."

The next afternoon, I'm sitting on the floor of my room when Charlie pops his head in.

"What are you doing?" he asks, surveying the art supplies strewn all around me.

"Mei has her final showcase tonight for the drama class she's been taking," I explain. "I'm making her a sign."

I hold up the piece of poster board on which I've written "MEI DAY, MEI DAY" in big, glittery letters.

"Love," Charlie says approvingly. "Listen . . . I don't want you to even start with me, but I actually was planning on taking Jim to the dog park today."

Jim, who has been lying on my bed and watching me work, tilts his head to the side looking hopeful. I hop up off the floor, brushing glitter off my t-shirt.

"I said don't start," Charlie holds a hand up as I open my mouth to say something.

"I was just going to say that sounds like a great idea." I walk over to where I have Jim's leash draped over my footboard, hook it onto his collar, and lead him over to where Charlie is still standing in the doorway. "Here you go," I say cheerily, handing it over to him. "Have fun!"

"Thank you," Charlie says, looking at me suspiciously. "You have fun tonight, too."

I wait until Charlie has nearly reached the stairs before I run after him.

"Hey, I almost forgot!" I say coming to a stop right in front of him. As he turns to face me, I lift a fist up to him. "Go get 'em, bro."

Charlie just gives me a death stare before turning his back on me and marching down the stairs with Jim happily trotting beside him.

As I watch Leo pull away from the entrance of the community theatre in Santa Monica where Mei's showcase is, I'm starting to regret not having Charlie or Cassidy come with me.

No, I tell myself. *You are fully capable of attending something by yourself because you're a strong and confident woman. Or at least, you're a strong woman. Well, you're a woman. Or a girl I guess, technically. Not a girl but not yet a woman?*

I pull myself out of my feeble attempt at a pep talk before it can go any further off the rails and balance the poster I brought for Mei under one arm while I fish around in my purse for my ticket.

After locating it, I fall into the line of people steadily moving towards the doors.

There aren't any assigned seats, so as soon as I step into the black box theatre space, I stop and awkwardly stand there trying to figure out where to sit.

"Psst," a voice says from somewhere over to my right. I turn and see Milo sitting by himself towards the middle of the very last row.

"Hey," I say, moving out of the aisle so people can get past me. "Are your parents not here? Why aren't you sitting with them?"

"They are," he replies, gesturing towards the front of the theatre where, upon looking closer, I can see Dr. and Mrs. Chen sitting in the third row. "But you're going to want to sit back here."

"Oh?" I say, crooking an eyebrow.

"Trust me." Milo beckons for me to come sit next to him, so I carefully make my way to where he is as he moves the bouquet of flowers that had been occupying the seat to his other side.

"Aw, you shouldn't have," I exclaim, putting a hand over my heart.

"Oh, no you don't," he says, pretending to use his body to shield the flowers from me. "Mei would kill me. She has some kind of rivalry with another girl in the class, and if she doesn't end up with the most flowers at the end of the night, I'll never hear the end of it."

"Oh, you mean Katie?" I say, recalling the name of the girl Mei has been complaining about regularly at our post-theatre class dinners. "Well, yeah. She's constantly stepping on everyone's lines and has a terrible habit of acting with the voice and not the body."

Milo blinks at me a few times.

"What?" I say, carefully propping the poster I made up on the armrests of the chair next to me so it's facing out. "I pay attention."

The lights flicker a few times, signaling for everyone to be seated. I settle back into my own seat and look sidelong at Milo.

"So explain to me why we're sitting all the way back here?" I ask him.

"You'll see."

A few minutes later, the theatre fades to black save for the emergency lighting along the aisles. In the dim glow, I can see Milo looking at me intently.

"Why are you staring at me?" I whisper out of the corner of my mouth.

"I'm just looking forward to watching you watch this."

A few moments later, I understand why.

A single spotlight hits the stage, illuminating a guy that is wearing nothing but a black leotard and a pair of steampunk goggles.

"I am a fly," he says, spreading his arms out and flapping them like wings. "Today, I die."

My jaw drops open as the full stage lights come on and I see more people in leotards flittering onstage and surrounding him. Milo is sinking down into his seat, hands covering his mouth as he shakes with barely suppressed laughter.

"Your face," he manages to hiss at me. "It's priceless."

"I am a father," the guy onstage says in a booming voice. Several other "flies" run up to hug him. "I am a friend," he continues, going down a line of leotard-clad people and shaking each of their hands in turn. "I am the casualty of your road trip weekend."

Two people in red leotards, one of which I recognize as Mei, enter the scene, each holding half of what looks like the front of a car constructed out of cardboard. They both run up behind the main guy and collide with him as he spreads his arms and legs wide, clearly simulating being splattered across a windshield.

"Cruel Subaru," he wails, as the rest of his fellow flies fall to the floor, crying out and banging their fists on the floor. "What did I ever do to you?"

The scene freezes, and the lights go dark again. I turn to gape at Milo, who has composed himself enough to sit back up in his seat and is watching me with a look of childlike joy on his face. The lights come back up before I can say anything, though that's fine with me, because for one of only a few times in my life, I'm speechless.

The following hour and a half is comprised of vignettes and tableaus that all seem to be competing to be the most abstract or make the deepest observation about the folly of man or whatever. In addition to being in the background of several other students' pieces, Mei has a scene where she's featured as a puppet of a teenage girl, with a boy dressed as a cellphone acting as her puppeteer. People come out on stage each wearing a sign around their neck with a different social media app, and she proceeds to hug them all one by one until they form a circle around her. When she realizes she's trapped, she tries to break out, but they slowly descend upon her until she gets swallowed up. Then she re-emerges a minute later dressed as a cavewoman.

Out of respect, Milo and I don't say anything out loud to each other, but there is no shortage of meaningful looks and arm pokes exchanged between us in reaction to what we are witnessing. I'm so taken aback by it all I don't even realize at one point that our knees are touching until he shifts away to fish some chapstick out of his pocket.

"So do you see now why I sit in the back at these things?" he mutters afterwards as we watch people slowly file out of the theatre.

"There are parts of that I can never unsee," I reply, shaking my head a little. "Like, that last one. I get that the guy in the suit made out of monopoly money was supposed to represent late-stage capitalism or something, but there was so much more gyrating than I would have ever expected. Which, to be fair, was no gyrating."

Milo laughs, standing up and stretching as he scans the theatre. I follow his gaze and spot his parents making their way towards us.

I grab my purse and my sign for Mei, and we join them as they head outside with the rest of the attendees to wait for the performers.

"What did you think?" Dr. Chen asks me as we wait.

"Oh," I say, quickly trying to think of a response. "I mean, wow. It was definitely...impactful."

Milo snorts, which he impressively manages to turn into a believable cough. Dr. Chen just gives me a meaningful look and says, "Indeed."

My phone buzzes, and I look to see I have a text message from Mei.

"We need move about six feet to my left," I relay to the Chens as I scan the message. "Apparently we aren't quite in Katie's sightline and Mei wants to have maximum visibility when we give her all of the flowers and stuff."

After we shuffle over to where Mei directed us, she appears, and we all make sure to shower her with compliments a little louder than we normally would.

"Well done, everyone," Mei says, sneaking a glance over to where the girl I presume is Katie is standing with her parents, looking sulkily at the single red rose they brought her. "Maybe next time she'll think twice before calling my performance 'inauthentic and unfocused' during critiques."

The Chens offer to take me to dinner and drive me home afterward, so I text Leo and my mother and pile into the car with Dr. and Mrs. Chen and Mei. Milo drove separately, but says he'll meet us at the pizza place for dinner.

"Why wasn't Eric there tonight?" I ask her, realizing for the first time I hadn't seen him in the audience.

"He had something to do with his family tonight," Mei answers. "Though I would have asked Cassidy if I had thought about it."

"Still trying to make fetch happen, eh?" I tease her.

"I just think you should spend a little more time with him," she says airily. "You know, so you can have some more friends here besides just me."

"Ouch," I say with an exaggerated wince.

"You know what I mean."

When we get to the pizzeria, Milo already has a table. We all decide to split a few pizzas while we give Mei a full review of the showcase, going act by act. To my relief, she also thought most of it was bizarre.

"I would so much rather just be in a traditional play," she says as she grabs another slice of pepperoni. "But any experience is good to add to my resume."

Pretty soon we're all stuffed and trying to stifle yawns as we wait for the server to bring back Dr. Chen's credit card.

"I can take Cam home if you want," Milo says nonchalantly after the server returns. My eyes snap to him, but he's looking at his dad. So I try to be subtle as I turn to Mei and raise my eyebrows at her. She gives an almost imperceptible shrug.

"Sure," Dr. Chen says, not looking up from the receipt he's signing. We head out to the parking lot, where I give Mei a hug and tell her for the hundredth time today that her talent is unmatched, then thank Dr. and Mrs. Chen for dinner.

"You ready?" Milo says, spinning his keys on one finger.

"Ready as I'll ever be," I say, trying to not sound as nervous as I feel. He walks me to his car, a pretty nondescript blue sedan, and opens the door for me on the passenger side.

"What the shit," I whisper to myself after he closes the door and walks around to the driver's side. When he gets in, I give him my address to put into his phone, and we set off back to Beverly Hills.

"I can't tell if I'm craving pie," I break the silence. "Or if wanting pie is just my Pavlovian response now when I'm in your presence."

"I guess there are worse things I could be associated with," he laughs, glancing at the clock. "The diner is closed already, but I do know a place that serves warm cookies that stays open late."

I consider this. "I think cookies are a worthy substitute for pie. Let's do it."

About ten minutes later, we're ordering a variety box of six cookies from a place called The Cookie Jar. We bring them out to his car and sit there as we sample each of them and debate which ones are the best.

"Respectfully, you are out of your mind," I say through a mouthful of snickerdoodle.

"Agree to disagree," Milo counters, examining his half of an oatmeal raisin cookie. "But I stand by the fact that the oatmeal raisin is better than the peanut butter."

We finish the rest of the cookies, though with vastly different opinions on which ones were the best, and drive the rest of the way to my house. Conversation between us feels so easy and natural, though the closer we get to my house, the more my stomach feels like there are tiny circus performers doing backflips in it.

As I'm pressing the button on my gate opener, I'm legitimately worried I might hurl cookies all over Milo's car. He comes to a stop in front of my house, puts the car in park, and opens the door to get out. By the time I follow suit, he's come around to my side and is waiting for me.

"Thanks for being my back row buddy," he says as I shut the car door behind me. "It definitely made the evening more entertaining."

"Any time, though it may take me a while to recover from that. Plus I need time to really contemplate and internalize the messages. Like, how am I supposed to avoid hitting bugs with my car? That's the biggest issue here— they were so quick to tell me all the problems but I certainly didn't see them offering up any solutions."

I know I'm babbling, so I force myself to shut my mouth. Milo just laughs a little.

"Goodnight, Cam."

He starts to lean into me, and for a moment all I can think is *he's finally going kiss me*. But he just gives me a quick hug, which I reciprocate only after a fraction of a pause I hope he doesn't notice.

NINETEEN

Mei ends up getting her wish, because I do find myself hanging out with her, Eric, and Cassidy more often. One Sunday afternoon after the four of us spend a few hours wandering around a flea market, Mei is insistent she has a craving for chili cheese fries that only Joe's can satisfy.

"Cass, I can't believe you haven't eaten here before," Mei says as she whips her little Beetle into a parking space. "It's delicious, plus my brother totally hooks it up."

Mei and Eric tell us to go ahead and get a table while they go to the restroom, so Cassidy and I slide into a booth. He reaches past me to grab a few menus from the stand on the table, but I shake my head when he tries to hand one to me.

"I practically have it memorized by now," I brag.

"Impressive," he says with a laugh. "So tell me what's good."

Just as I'm hitting my stride enthusiastically describing the delicate nuances of flavor in the bacon cheeseburger, I hear someone clear their throat. I look up to see Milo standing next to the table holding his notepad.

"Hey," I say in greeting.

"Hey," he replies, not looking me in the eye. "What would you like to drink?"

"Diet Coke for me," Mei chirps as she and Eric walk up and sit across from us. Milo starts a little in surprise, then glances at me and Cassidy with what I swear looks like . . . relief? Did he think we were on a date? Even if he did, what right does he have to get all weird about it? It's not like he hasn't had plenty of opportunities to tell me he sees me as anything other than a friend, even though there are moments when I could swear he's about to and stops himself. I don't know how many times a girl is expected to get friendzoned before it's officially pathetic, but I've got to be getting close at this point.

"Milo, you've met Eric," Mei says. "And Cassidy was with us at your show last month, but I don't think you got a chance to talk to him."

"Nice to meet you," Milo says a little stiffly.

"You too, man," Cassidy replies cordially. Milo gives him a curt nod before getting the rest of our drink orders and walking away. I try to pay attention to the conversation, but when I steal a glance toward the server station, I find Milo is watching me. We both look away quickly.

We get several plates of chili cheese fries for the table and each order a milkshake. When Cassidy catches me looking longingly at a patty melt Milo is bringing to another table, he says, "You should get one."

"Oh, I would," I explain. "But I've started doing this weekly dinner thing with my mom and brother and they would be pissed if I spoiled my appetite."

Cassidy just surveys the chili cheese fries and my milkshake and gives me a pointed look.

"Trust me," I say, using my fork to snag another fry from the plate. "This is nothing."

"How do you want to split the checks?" Milo says in a tight voice. I hadn't heard him walk up.

"The two of us," Eric says, gesturing toward Mei.

"And you can put us on one check," Cassidy points at me.

"Oh, no," I say quickly. "I can cover mine—"

"Don't worry about it," Cassidy waves me off as he pulls his wallet from his pocket. I sink down in my seat a little, not daring to look up at Milo as Cassidy hands him a credit card.

"You really didn't have to do that," I hiss after Milo walks away.

"I owe you, remember?" he asks, giving me a perplexed look. "From the other day when we all went to that Jamaican place that was cash only?"

He's totally right. We had already gone through the buffet-style line and loaded up our plates before getting to the cash register and seeing they didn't take cards. Cassidy didn't have cash on him, so I told him I would cover him. He had insisted he would make sure to pay me back to keep everything fair.

"Of course," I say. There's a beat of silence before Mei starts asking Cassidy about what colleges he is applying to. I throw her an appreciative look.

Milo comes over and puts the checks down on the table.

"Have a good one," he says, then heads to check on another table without so much as looking at me.

As we gather our stuff and head out the door, I look over my shoulder to see Milo leaning against the counter, arms folded while he watches us leave.

"I don't know what crawled up his butt today," Mei says, following my gaze.

We've barely stepped outside when I find myself saying, "I think I left my, uh, pen inside. My favorite pen. I'll be right back."

I dash back through the door, leaving my friends standing looking puzzled. I march up to Milo where he's still standing at the counter.

"Can I speak with you?" I say in a haughty voice. He nods and leads me over to an area of the diner where the tables are empty.

"What is your deal?" I demand.

"What do you mean?" he asks evasively.

"Oh, don't act like you don't know what I'm talking about."

"I don't."

"You were . . . well, you were being kind of an ass."

"How?"

I feel a prickle of annoyance climb up my spine.

"You were being all weird and formal," I say accusingly.

"I was doing my job," Milo says, starting to look annoyed himself.

"Bullshit."

We just stand there glaring at each other for a moment.

"Forget it." I whirl on my heel and storm away.

"Whoa," Cassidy says after I slam the car door shut behind me and thrust my seatbelt into its holder. "I guess you didn't find your favorite pen?"

"Oh, I found it," I say irritably. "But then I was like, why do I even like this stupid pen? What has this pen ever done for me? This pen doesn't deserve to be my favorite pen. There are plenty of other pens. Perfectly nice pens."

I look around to see Mei, Eric, and Cassidy all staring blankly at me.

"I . . . feel very passionately about pens," I say lamely. "So what is everyone up to this week?"

Mei starts describing the new drama workshop she's thinking about signing up for, and I listen to her chatter away until we pull up to the front of my house. I give them one last wave as they drive away, then head inside.

I can smell whatever my mother is cooking as soon as I walk through the front door. As my stomach rumbles in response, I make a mental note to send Cassidy a picture with my plate of dinner and an "I told you so" text later.

I wander into the kitchen and set my purse down on the counter. My mother is gingerly lifting a casserole dish out of the oven.

"Hey, Mom," I say, making a point to use the familiar term. "That smells amazing. What is it?"

She turns and gives me a smile, peeling off her pink oven mitts.

"Zucchini lasagna roll-ups," she says proudly. "And don't worry, I made you some garlic bread, too."

"That's what I like to hear," I say happily. Charlie's footsteps thunder down the stairs, and he jogs into the kitchen.

"Am I late?" he says breathlessly. I lovingly poke him in the side when he comes to stand next to me.

"Not at all," my mother says. "I just pulled dinner from the oven."

"I had a FaceTime meeting that ran long," he says, giving me a retaliatory pinch on the arm.

"Making big business moves?" I ask.

"Actually, yes," he brags as the three of us take our seats at the table and my mother dishes out the lasagna roll-ups onto our plates. "I was invited to show at Paris Fashion Week in the fall."

"Char, that is incredible!" I cry as my mother squeals with joy.

Charlie beams as he reaches for the garlic bread. When he sees me giving him a smug look, he says, "Shut up. I've earned this."

We spend most of dinner letting Charlie fill us in on all of the details surrounding Fashion Week.

"Enough about me," he finally says, though I know he would be happy to prattle on about his designs and plans for Paris for the rest of the night. "What did you do today?"

"I went to a flea market with some friends," I say through a mouthful of zucchini. "Nothing too exciting."

"I had my first vaginal steam," my mother chimes in as casually as if she were telling us she had been to the grocery store. I practically spit my food out in shock. Eyes watering, I reach for my glass of water and swallow a few gulps to keep myself from choking.

"You . . . what?"

"I had a vaginal steam," she repeats mildly before taking a sip from her wine glass.

"I know I'm going to regret this," I begin, ignoring Charlie snickering behind his hand. "But what the hell is a vaginal steam?"

"It's an herbal cleansing of the vagina," my mother explains. "It was very refreshing. I feel very mellow down there now."

"My GOD," I screech, absolutely horrified.

"Oh, don't look so scandalized," she says dismissively.

"Mom, really, I'm glad we are working on our relationship," I say, closing my eyes and massaging my forehead. "But let's never talk about your vagina again."

"And here I thought your generation was supposed to be sexually liberated," she observes. "A woman's body is her sanctuary, you know."

"Well, I for one am very happy for you and your mellow sanctuary," Charlie says, folding up his napkin, setting it on the table, and standing up. "Hey, do you have today's mail? I'm expecting something."

"It's on the kitchen island, but I haven't had a chance to go through it yet," my mother replies. Charlie grabs the stack of envelopes and brings them over, setting them down in the center of the table as he sits back down. I glance at the letter on top and freeze.

It's addressed to my dad.

I must make some kind of noise because Charlie and my mother look at me, then follow my line of sight to the envelope.

"Oh, Cam," my mother says, quickly snatching up the stack of envelopes and hugging them to her chest. "I'm so sorry. I've been making sure to go through the mail and pull out anything with your father's name on it . . ."

"Why is he getting mail here?" I manage to say.

"This is the forwarding address for anything sent to you at your old house in Arizona," my mother explains as Charlie looks at me sympathetically. "Anything addressed to your father is supposed to go to your Aunt Margaret, but there have been a few things that have mistakenly come here. Sometimes it takes a while for mail to stop for someone that has—"

"I need to go feed Jim," I interrupt, hurriedly getting up from the table and taking my plate to the sink. From the corner of my eye, I can see my mother and Charlie exchange a look. I ignore them and bound up the stairs to my room, trying to remember how to breathe.

At our Thursday evening dinner at Joe's, Mei declares that her parents are out of town this weekend at a conference, so she has decided she's having a party tomorrow night.

"I've never thrown a party before," she discloses as she dips one of her chicken tenders into a little container of honey mustard on her plate. "I mean, obviously I had birthday parties when I was a kid. But the most recent was a *High School Musical*-themed one when I was twelve, and the most scandalous thing that happened was that Rosie McGregor got her first period. I'm actually kind of nervous."

My eyes unwittingly seek out Milo, though I know he isn't here tonight. According to Mei, Discount Curses has a showcase for a record label coming up, and Milo has only been working breakfast and lunch shifts so the band can get in some extra evening practices. It's probably for the best. I haven't seen him since he acted so weird about Cassidy, so I don't really know if we're on good terms or not.

However, curiosity gets the best of me, and I do ask, "Does your brother know about it?"

"He does, but he isn't thrilled about it," Mei confesses. "He says he won't tell Mom and Dad though."

"Who all is coming?" I ask, trying to keep the apprehension out of my voice. On the one hand, I know it will probably be beneficial to go to a social event where I can meet some more of the kids I'll be going to school with. But I also thought I had a little more prep time to really fine tune the details in cultivating my Mysterious New Girl persona.

"Mostly theatre people," she says, starting to tick off names on her fingers. "Toby and Aaron. And Claire—you met all of them at that art showcase. Eric and Cassidy, of course. And then probably another twenty or thirty people from the drama program and a handful of the chorus kids I'm friends with." I must look slightly alarmed because she quickly follows with, "I promise you'll like them. And it's not like it's going to be a drunken rager or anything. Usually at these things people just get a little tipsy and end up performing numbers from musicals all night. I went to a party last year where they did the entire scene of "Empty Chairs and Empty Tables" from *Les Misérables* and can't remember the last time I wept so hard."

I reassure her that it will be fun and I'm excited to meet more of her friends, then mostly opt to let her chatter on about what kind of food she wants to get and what she's thinking about wearing while I finish eating my patty melt. As we leave, I promise to get to her house early to help her set up before I slide into the backseat of Leo's car and head home.

The next afternoon, Charlie walks into my room to find me on my hands and knees donning yellow elbow-length cleaning gloves and furiously scrubbing the baseboards in my room.

"This is new," he says from the doorway where he's standing, head tilted slightly to the side and eyes narrowed.

"I'm going to a party tonight," I offer up as an explanation.

"Mmm, okay. Put down the bristle brush and let's unpack that."

I huff a sigh but do as he says, wiping my forehead with the back of my arm and taking up the seat next to him on my couch.

He just crosses one leg over the other, folds his arms, and stares at me.

"Ugh, fine," I say. "Mei is having a party tonight and she's really looking forward to it but I'm . . . nervous."

"Why?"

"I don't know." My gloves make a squelching noise as I peel them off my hands and set them on the coffee table. "I wasn't that nervous when I went to that party with you, but for some reason my anxiety is, like, really high for this. And when I get anxious, I tend to fixate on projects to keep myself busy."

"Like manically cleaning your baseboards?"

"Exactly."

"Well, it makes sense that this party would make you feel different," Charlie says knowingly. "These are the people you're going to be going to school with for the next year. There are stakes."

"Gee, thanks," I say sullenly. "That makes me feel so much better."

"Chamomile. You are one of the most unhinged people I have ever met, but it's mostly in a fun way. Just be yourself and you'll be fine."

"Aw, Charlie," I croon in my most syrupy voice. "Did you make that up just now? Hallmark has nothing on you, you wise old hoot owl."

"Okay, smartass," Charlie retorts, hitting me lightly on the leg.

"Seriously, Char," I say, scooting over so I can lay my head against his shoulder. "Thank you."

"Would it make you feel better if I drove you to the party? I'm not going to stay though, that would be weird."

"Well, you weren't technically invited, so . . ." Charlie smacks my leg again so I rush to say, "I'm kidding! I would very much appreciate it if you took me."

. . .

As I get out of the car and readjust the simple dark green sundress I chose for tonight, Charlie says, "Make good choices!" and gives me a finger gun. I roll my eyes and shut the door, watching him as he backs out of the driveway. I'm here early as promised, and the only other car I see in the driveway is Eric's. Mei is already at the gate to greet me as I approach the side of the house.

"Oh, thank God," she says, pulling me through and leading me by the wrist into the kitchen. "I'm having a salsa emergency of epic proportions."

The salsa emergency turns out to be Cassidy and Eric, both looking sheepish, sopping up the contents of what must have been a gallon-sized container of it off of the floor using an entire roll of paper towels.

"I have no salsa," Mei says, throwing her hands up in the air in defeat. "Should I just call the whole thing off?"

I don't answer right away, as I am too busy gawking at the kitchen table, which has been buried underneath a pile of full-sized bags of various chips that stacks up practically as high as the overhead chandelier.

"Mei," I say, biting my lip to keep from laughing. "How many bags of chips is that?"

"Fifty-two," she says distractedly, her eyes still on Eric as he dumps a wad of paper towels into the garbage can.

"Yeah, I think you'll be fine without the salsa."

"Are you sure? Because five of those bags are tortilla chips—"

"I'm sure," I say firmly, stepping forward to examine the pile more closely. "You seem to have all of your bases covered. I'm seeing every member of the 'itos' family, all the different pretzel shapes, tortilla chips both in scoop and triangle form. You did good work here, kid."

"Okay . . ." Mei replies without much conviction. "If you say so. I guess we can go ahead and preheat the oven for the pizza rolls."

As she opens the freezer door to reveal boxes of pizza rolls stuffed into every possible square inch of space, all Eric, Cassidy, and I can do is exchange wide-eyed looks and start hunting around the kitchen in search of baking sheets.

By the time people start arriving, bags of chips and coolers of beer and hard seltzer have been strategically set around every flat surface in the house and pool area, and the entire kitchen island is covered in rows of pizza rolls. Mei seems satisfied, clearly in her element as she flits around greeting everyone as they come in. I hang back in the kitchen with Eric and Cassidy, plucking a hard seltzer out of the cooler. As I pop the lid, take a sip, and examine the can, I catch Cassidy watching me with an amused look on his face.

"First time drinking?"

"No," I counter defensively. "My friends back in Arizona and I got our hands on a bottle of peach schnapps once and not to brag, but things got pret-ty wild."

He just laughs and takes a sip of the beer he's holding. "Honestly I don't drink that much either," he confesses. "I try to be pretty strict on myself once pre-season football workouts start."

"Someone with quite the zeal for juice did tell me once that the human body is a temple," I say with a grin.

"I'll cheers to that," he says, clinking his can against mine.

I spend the next few hours doing all of the stereotypical Teen Party activities. I play beer pong, though I do insist on filling my cups with hard seltzer because I would rather have Sprite that tastes like it's mad about something than the liquid equivalent of water-soaked crackers. I let Mei introduce me to what feels like an endless string of people, then proceed to make the requisite small talk about the upcoming school year. I somehow successfully avoid having to talk too much about my mother. And once someone busts out the Karaoke machine, I even take Cassidy up on his request to be the Annie Oakley to his Frank Butler for a fumbling rendition of "Anything You Can Do." We take several exaggerated bows, and as the intro to "La Vie Bohème" from *Rent* starts up, Cassidy leans over and says, "Do you want to go outside for some fresh air?"

I nod, still a little breathless and now slightly sweaty, and grab another cold seltzer from a cooler before following him outside to the pool. He has already kicked off his shoes and is sitting at the edge with his feet dangling in the water. I peel off my sandals and take up the spot next to him, carefully arranging my dress around my knees. Gingerly, I dip my toes in while holding my can up against my neck.

"Ahhhhh," I sigh, closing my eyes and enjoying the jolt of icy coldness.

"So what's the verdict?" Cassidy asks. I look sideways at him questioningly. "Can you do anything I can do better?"

"Truthfully, it felt pretty evenly-matched to me. You were a worthy adversary." I set the seltzer can down so I can lean forward and brush my fingertips against the water.

"I like you, Cam," Cassidy says softly.

My back straightens in surprise, and I sit up so I can face him.

"I know we talked about just keeping it friendly, and I totally respect it if you still feel that way," he says, his offensively good-looking eyes searching mine as his offensively good-looking mouth turns up in a rueful smile. "But I at least have to shoot my shot, right?"

My head is swimming, and I know it isn't from the couple of drinks I've had tonight. My logical side is telling me this boy is nice and easy to talk to and fun to hang out with. It would be so easy to slip into this. The rest of my summer, maybe even my school year, could be filled with double dates with Mei and Eric and cheering Cassidy on at football games and not feeling so alone anymore.

But he isn't Milo.

So? a voice in my mind argues. *Screw it. This is what people are supposed to do in high school.*

Cassidy is still watching me patiently, and I find myself nodding. The next thing I know he has one hand cupping my neck and his lips are pressing into mine. I force my brain to turn off and lean into him, parting my own lips to intensify the kiss, letting physical instinct take over.

We both jump at the sound of the gate slamming shut behind us. I spin around to see Milo, holding a keyboard case as he looks between me and Cassidy.

"Sorry to interrupt," he says slowly. "Cam, is he bothering you?"

I scramble to my feet, but I must stand up too fast because a wave of dizziness hits me, and I feel myself start to wobble. In an instant, Cassidy jumps up and puts a supportive hand on my back to keep me upright. The lightheadedness passes quickly, and I realize Milo has dropped his case in order to grasp my arm to steady me, too.

"I've got it," Cassidy throws him an appreciative look. "Thanks, man."

"I'm good," I say, wiggling out of both of their grips and turning to Milo irritably. "What do you mean, 'is he bothering me?' Did it look like he was bothering me?"

Milo's jaw tenses as we stare each other down. Finally, he snatches up his keyboard case and starts to walk past me, muttering "never mind."

"What is your problem lately?" I practically growl at him.

"That just seemed out of character for you is all," he says, not breaking his stride as he stalks toward the pool house. "I wanted to make sure he wasn't taking advantage of you if you had been drinking."

"I can handle myself," I say through gritted teeth, following him as he reaches the door. "I already have an older brother, you know. I don't need another one."

Milo sets his keyboard case down on the stairs of the pool house before spinning around to face me again. "That's not—" he says haltingly. "I mean, I wasn't—"

"Enough!" I cut him off as I pivot on my heel to storm off. "And love triangles are my least favorite book trope, I'll have you know!" I shout over my shoulder as an afterthought. When I reach Cassidy and see the grim look on his face, my anger falls away, and I'm left feeling like a deflated balloon.

"I'm going to grab my purse and text my brother to come pick me up," I tell him. "Will you wait outside with me?"

He nods, so I hurriedly put my shoes back on, run in to say a quick goodbye to Mei, and text Charlie to come get me as I jog out to where Cassidy is sitting on the front steps. I plop down next to him, and we sit in silence for a moment before I say, "I am so sorry, Cassidy."

"You don't have anything to be sorry for," he objects, shaking his head.

"No, I do," I say, wrapping my arms around my knees. "I shouldn't have kissed you like that. Not that it wasn't great, because it was. You're *really* good at it, by the way. Top notch. But the thing is, I am like the emotional equivalent of that jar of salsa that you dropped—"

"Eric dropped it."

"That Eric dropped earlier. And my metaphorical floor salsa is really messy right now, and I don't want you using up all of your psychological paper towels trying to clean it up."

"You're losing me a little here."

"Copy that. What I'm trying to say is that I really, *really* like having you as my friend, and I hope you still want to be after tonight."

Cassidy exhales deeply, and I brace myself for him to tell me how much of an asshole and a tease I am, but he just says, "I understand. Plus, I kind of get the sense you have a thing for Mei's brother."

I wince.

"Really, Cam. We're good."

Headlights flash as Charlie's car pulls into the driveway. Cassidy and I stand up, obviously unsure of how we should end this conversation. I decide to take the proverbial bullet and say, "Just so you know, I concede."

"Concede?" he asks, looking confused.

"When it comes to being one classy sonofabitch, anything I can do, you *can*, in fact, do better."

This elicits a bona fide laugh from Cassidy, and he leans in to give me a quick hug.

"Get home safe," he calls after me as I climb into Charlie's car. Once I'm inside, Charlie opens his mouth to say something, but I cut him off.

"I swear to you, Char, if you say you told me so, I am going to commit fratricide right here in this car. And yes, I do want you to feel uncomfy at the fact that I looked up the official term for killing one's own brother."

TWENTY

A few days after the party, I decide to take Jim for a mid-morning walk in the park. Charlie is in meetings most of the day and my mother has a podcast interview this morning, so I woke up with grand plans to set up an easel outside on the patio and try to draw the L.A. skyline. After sitting and staring at it for over an hour, I abandoned my efforts, feeling a need to get out of the house.

Leo, who was kind enough to get a seat cover for his car for whenever Jim was going to be riding with us, drops the two of us off at the park. I figure I'll just follow the walking path and let Jim set the pace, which I know will be slow with his propensity to stop and smell anything we pass by.

We're just starting to make our second lap when I spot a familiar figure sitting on one of the benches, eating a bagel and tapping a foot rhythmically to whatever he's listening to in his earbuds. I groan, but before I can map out an exit strategy, he looks up and sees me.

"Shit," I hiss through my teeth, causing Jim to look up from the rock he's sniffing to cock his head to one side at me. I walk Jim up to where Milo is now removing his earbuds and putting them in a case. He raises an eyebrow as Jim trots right up to him to try and sniff his food.

"Hello to you, too," Milo says, keeping the bagel out of Jim's reach.

"Jim, that's not for you," I say sternly. "Park it."

Jim immediately sits right by my feet, his attention now on a father and son playing catch nearby.

"'Park it?'" Milo asks, popping the last bite of his bagel into his mouth.

I quickly explain my unconventional list of commands Dad and I taught Jim. Milo laughs, though it sounds a little forced, and gestures to the empty space on the bench next to him, crumpling up his bagel wrapper and tossing it into the trash can nearby.

I root around for something to say and land on, "Are you working today?" as I sit down, and Jim settles in at my feet.

"No," Milo says. "We actually have a follow-up meeting with the label that is interested in signing Discount Curses."

"Wow. So I take it the showcase went well. Does that mean no USC next year?"

Milo takes a sip from his coffee before answering. "Nothing's a done deal yet. But if we do end up recording an album, I think I'll at least try to take a few classes part-time."

"That makes sense," I agree. "Hey, listen . . . about the other night—"

"I acted like an ass," Milo says simply, reaching down to pat Jim on the head. "I was having a weird day, but I shouldn't have taken it out on you. I'm sorry."

"Oh," I say, not really knowing what to make of that. "Do you want to talk about it, or . . ."

I let the unfinished question hang in the air. Milo just shrugs a shoulder.

"It's nothing."

I bristle a little at his vague answer and decide to press the issue. "Does it have something to do with Leighton?"

"I mean, yeah. We talked for the first time since we broke up and she really wants to get back together."

"What do *you* want?"

"I'm not sure," he confesses.

I try not to let the sting of his answer show on my face. What hold does this girl have on him? I can feel my temper start to rise, and I stand up, desperate to leave before it can take over. Jim looks at me expectantly.

"Well, I hope you figure it out," I say more icily than I intended. "I should go."

Milo sets his cup down on the bench and stands, his brow knitted together in confusion. "Did I say something wrong?"

I feel my face flush. *Walk away, walk away, walk away.*

"You are unbelievable, you know that?" I demand instead. "It's still Leighton? Really? What about me?"

My voice cracks on the last word. Milo gawks at me but doesn't say anything.

"I don't have a lot of dating experience," I barrel on. "But I know when I have a connection with someone. There is something here, and I am so sick of feeling like I'm alone in this when I'm pretty sure you feel it too, especially after the other day when you were so clearly jealous of Cassidy at the diner, not to mention at the party. I know I'm kind of a mess, but at least I'm not completely clueless. Because in case you haven't noticed, I'm crazy about you, you absolute fucking ignoramus."

I can feel the people around us staring, but I don't care. The only two people in the world right now are me and Milo. He looks pained as he shoves his hands into his jeans pockets. The seconds tick by, but he still doesn't say anything. I can feel my heart sinking, and I know I have to get out of here before I start crying.

I turn to leave, but Jim remains stubbornly planted where he is sitting.

"Come *on*, Jim," I say, but he still doesn't budge. I let out a frustrated noise. "Jim, chop chop."

He instantly responds, and I stride toward the parking lot as fast as I'm able to without breaking into a run. Milo doesn't come after me, and I try to keep my shoulders from shaking as I cry just in case he's still watching.

Listen to Track Seven: "Wish I Could (But I Can't)"

Fortunately, Leo is still nearby, so I don't have to wait very long for him to come pick me and Jim up. He doesn't say anything when he sees my tear-streaked face—just pulls out a travel pack of Kleenex from his glovebox and hands it to me.

"You just let me know if you ever need me to give someone a piece of my mind for you," he says after we pull up to the house and he opens my car door.

"Thanks," I laugh in spite of myself and head inside. It feels so shallow to be this much of a weepy mess over a boy, though a part of me knows deep down that it probably isn't just about Milo. I make a stop in the kitchen to pluck a pint of ice cream from the freezer and grab a spoon before trudging upstairs and sitting on my bedroom floor, Jim nestled next to me. For a while I just pet him and let the tears soak into my t-shirt, feeling sorry for myself. After a while, I crawl into bed and turn on one of my favorite 90s rom-coms. Eventually Charlie appears with a takeout bag of In-N-Out in hand.

When he sees my face, he says, "Do you want to talk about it?"

"Not really," I say moving over on my bed to make room for him. "But I'd love to eat some fries about it."

After watching another movie together, Charlie invites me out to the hot tub with him, but I decline.

"Hey," he says, turning back around at the doorway. "I was going take Jim to the dog park tomorrow morning, and before you give me any shit about it, I've already asked Aidan to get coffee afterward."

"Oooooh," I croon, hopping off the bed.

"Oh, my god, stop," Charlie says as I throw my arms around him.

"You're right," I say seriously, stepping back. "This is exciting and I'm incredibly happy for you, but that doesn't mean I can't be mature about it."

"Thank you," Charlie says primly. Slowly, I raise my right fist up in front of me.

"Go get 'em, bro."

The next morning, I've just finished putting my wet hair into a braid when the sound of the doorbell pierces through the silence, making me jump. Warily, I peer around the stairwell and see an impatient-looking woman with a severe black bob standing outside on the landing. She looks vaguely familiar, but I can't quite place her.

"Mom?" I shout. "Charlie?"

Mom doesn't seem to be home, and Charlie must have left with Jim already, so I go downstairs and open the door a crack.

"Hello, Cam," she says without any preamble, not looking up from her phone.

"Um," I respond. "Sorry, who are you?"

"I'm Vic," she replies impatiently. "Your mother's agent."

"Ah," I say, instantly recognizing her from the handful of times

I've met her over the years. So this is the woman that convinced my mother to get in league with *Chick About Town.*

"Well?" she says expectantly. "Can I come in?" She doesn't wait for me to answer before pushing past me and walking into the living room. Stunned, I close the door and chase after her.

"My mom isn't going to be back for a few hours," I say, watching helplessly as Vic starts wandering around the room and taking pictures on her phone.

"Oh, I won't be long," she says indifferently, picking up and examining a statue on the mantel.

"Whaaaaat is happening?" I say on an exhale. I can see how my mom could be so easily railroaded by this woman. She's a hurricane in a power suit.

"I'm just getting specs on the house for the show," Vic says before briskly walking into the kitchen.

"Show? What show? Does my mother know you're here?"

"*The* show," Vic says as if this explains everything. When I continue to look at her blankly, she purses her lips and says, "I can't believe she hasn't mentioned it. Hulu wants to give your mother her own reality show. You know, following her life and Charlie's rise in the fashion industry. And your transition to L.A., of course."

"She . . . she . . . what?" I stammer, dumbfounded. Vic doesn't even look at me as she starts snapping more photos of the kitchen.

"You all are going to be the next Kardashians," she says definitively. "Everyone is going to know your names."

I stumble backwards, a sharp pain shooting into my side as I hit the corner of the kitchen counter. My entire body has gone as cold as if I just drank a pitcher of ice water. There's a ringing in my ears, and if Vic says something else, I don't hear her. I turn and sprint up the stairs to my room, in too much shock to even shut the door behind me. I stare unseeing at the floor as I stand there gasping for breath and trying to make sense of this information.

We're going to be on a reality show. Hell, we *are* the reality show. That means cameras are going to be here at our house, following us around constantly. Our lives will be cut up into 22-minute segments edited for maximum entertainment value for the whole world to judge.

I can't believe I actually trusted my mother when she said she was done trying to force this kind of life on me. She took the first opportunity she got to further her own career, even if it was at my expense yet again.

I won't do it.

I rummage around my closet until I find a duffel bag, then start blindly shoving things into it. I sling it over my shoulder, grab my backpack, and look around before remembering Jim is at the dog park with Charlie. My heart sinks a little, but I silently vow to Jim that I'll be back for him.

With an almost crazed resolve, I go downstairs to the drawer in the kitchen where my mother keeps cash for emergencies and the spare car keys. Through the glass doors I can see Vic on the patio, obliviously taking pictures of the pool and the lawn. I have a sudden urge to go outside and hurl her phone off the side of the hill, but I resist.

Instead, I open the drawer, snatch up the envelope of cash and stuff it into my backpack, then stare at the four sets of keys. Feeling like the Goldilocks of automobiles, I assess my options. One of them is for Charlie's BMW. Too obvious. The second set is for my mother's custom pink Range Rover. Too identifiable. The third is for her bright blue Mercedes convertible. Too showy. But the fourth set is for the black Audi Charlie had as his first car and still uses sometimes for road trips when he doesn't want to put miles on the BMW. And it is just right.

I punch the button to the garage door and hop into the Audi, tossing both my backpack and duffel bag onto the passenger seat beside me. Blowing out a breath, I start the car up and carefully maneuver out of the garage. I pause in the driveway, the fact that I have no real plan beginning to settle in. But after a few moments' contemplation, I program my Aunt Margaret's address into the navigation system. How I'll make it all the way from California to Georgia on what little I brought with me is a problem for future me.

"Fuck it," I say out loud, and hit the gas.

I turn the radio on to avoid having to think about anything. I'll have more than enough time on the road to examine every angle of my current situation. For now, I just want to lose myself in some cheesy Top 40 music and pretend like I'm out for a casual drive.

Listen to Track Eight: "Drive"

After about an hour, I decide to stop for gas and to stock up on snacks. I check my phone, but I don't have any new calls or text messages. I idly wonder how long it will take for anyone to realize I'm gone. A little voice in my head says I probably should have left a note, but I push it away. I'm now fully equipped with chips, candy, soda, and a tank of gas, so I head back on the road.

By the time the sun starts sinking and turning the sky a burnt shade of orange, I'm exhausted. I pull off at an exit near Flagstaff that looks like it has a lot of restaurants and hotels, park in a space at the first shopping center I see, and fish out the cash envelope from my backpack. I carefully count it out, coming to a total of just over $2500. Shaking my head in disbelief that my mother considers this much money to be her little stash of emergency cash,

I do a quick search on my phone for nearby hotels, ignoring the text message and missed call notifications that are now starting to pile up. I bookmark a few that look like they might just be sketchy enough to not ask for an I.D.

The first hotel I try insists on putting my driver's license on file, but at the second, the front desk guy looks at the several hundred dollar bills I slide across the counter to him and hands me a room key without asking any more questions. I try not to show how shocked I am that this actually worked as I take the key and head back outside to find the corresponding numbered door.

The room is simple—a little outdated, but much better than attempting to sleep in my car. There's a little laminated sheet on the nightstand with a list of nearby food options, so I call the number for a pizza place and put in a delivery order. I flip on the television and try to concentrate on the episode of *Parks and Recreation* I find, but everything I have successfully been barricading from my mind up until this point is starting to seep through.

Did Charlie know? A stab of hurt goes through me at the notion he would hide something this big from me. And what about my mother? I actually believed her when she said she was going to respect what I wanted. If it was all a lie, I didn't think she was capable of such quality acting. I've seen the only movie she's ever been in, a horror film called *Beets Me* where a vegan woman (played by my mother) is stalked and killed by her own vegetables. She was, and I cannot emphasize this enough, terrible. So I never dreamed she could bullshit me so convincingly.

There's a knock at the door, and a quick glance through the peephole shows me a sullen-looking girl holding a pizza box. I give her a twenty-dollar bill and take the pizza straight to the bed, where I sit under the covers and eat my feelings while I watch Ron Swanson try to navigate handling 94 meetings in one day.

Four episodes and five pieces of pizza later, I know I've stalled long enough and brace myself to finally look at the bottom of my phone, where it tells me I have 17 missed calls and 27 new text messages. I scan through the texts, most of which are increasingly worried-sounding messages from my mother. There are several calls and texts from Charlie, a few from Mei, two from Aunt Margaret, and . . . one from Milo.

Hey, Milo's message reads. *Your brother texted Mei and she told me your mom can't find you? Are you okay?*

I stare at the screen for a moment, then plug my phone back into the charger sitting on the nightstand next to me. I know I'm being such a dick by not checking in with anyone, and part of me doesn't care. Surely someone would have to be gone longer than this to be considered a missing person. Or am I a runaway? Could I get arrested for this? Have I technically stolen Charlie's car? Intent on not delving too deeply into that line of thinking, I put on the pair of sweatpants and t-shirt I packed, wash my face, brush my teeth, and tuck myself into bed.

After a night of restless sleep, I don't even bother getting out of bed until an hour before I have to check out. Part of me is tempted to book a second night with how much I'm dreading what is waiting for me on both ends of this little impromptu road trip. I've come too far to turn around and go back to Los Angeles, where my mother and her television show are waiting to turn the little bit of a life I've been able to rebuild completely upside down again.

But I also know that escaping like this is the equivalent of putting a band-aid on a bullet hole. My feeble hope is that by the time I make it to Aunt Margaret's, maybe everyone will think it's too much of a hassle to send me back and I can just stay there.

I have another several dozen texts and missed calls from my mother and Charlie, the most recent from him saying that if they don't hear from me by noon today they're going to the police. I mull this over, then ultimately opt to send Charlie a message that says, *"i'm safe. just needed to get away. i love you."*

As I take a quick shower and get dressed, my mind starts replaying my last conversation with Milo. The image of him just standing there not saying anything when I told him how I felt about him still stings like a fresh wound. Brushing the thought away, I collect my things and head down to the lobby. After returning my key at the front desk and grabbing a banana and granola bar from the free continental breakfast, I'm in the car again.

A few hours into my drive, I see a sign that makes my whole body go rigid: I'm half a mile away from the exit that will take me to Preston. My heart squeezes in my chest as I approach the split in the highway, and at the last possible moment I veer right, an invisible string pulling me towards my hometown.

Like much of Arizona, the drive is pretty much just desert, and there are very few cars on the road. I'm left with little distraction from the thoughts swirling inside my brain. The closer I get to Preston, the more it feels like some kind of emotional dam has broken, and the rage and grief that have been churning inside of me for the last few months become unbearable. At one point, I pull off onto the shoulder of the road and let out a bloodcurdling scream, not stopping until my throat is raw and my body is shaking with uncontrollable sobs. I open the car door, lean out, and vomit my measly breakfast up onto the dirt. Closing the door again and wiping my mouth with the back of my hand, I look at myself in the rearview mirror. My face is red and puffy, with tears still steadily streaming down my cheeks. My eyes look hollow and sunken in, and half of my hair has come out of its bun, limp strands matted up all around my face.

"Great," I say hoarsely to my reflection. "I look exactly the same way I feel."

I fix my hair and pop a piece of gum in my mouth before putting the car in drive and easing back onto the highway. I feel delirious, but the adrenaline starts to kick in once I begin to recognize familiar roads and landmarks. It is so surreal to be back here that I want to cry, but I'm pretty sure my tear ducts are too exhausted to work. As I drive down the streets I called home for so long, I half-expect to see my dad coming out of our favorite doughnut place or standing outside of the hardware store chatting with the owner. I slow down as I drive past his auto repair shop. It looks exactly the same, though I wouldn't have expected it to change that much in the short time I've been away. Dad ended up selling it to one of his long-time mechanics once we realized he probably wasn't going to get better. I would stop in and say hi, but I just . . . can't.

My breath catches when I see the cemetery. Dad and I were never really churchgoers, but he insisted on being buried at the Methodist church right down the street from his shop. He joked that it was so he could keep an eye on the shop from beyond the grave, but I think it gave him some peace to feel like he was doing things the traditional way at the end.

A car honks behind me, and I become aware that I've stopped in the middle of the road. I wave an apology and turn the GPS off as I pull into the cemetery. I remember exactly where my dad is buried and find myself putting the car in park a short walking distance from his headstone. For a moment, I can't move. I should have brought flowers or something. But if I leave now to go get some, I don't think I'll be able to come back.

Slowly, I open the car door, slinging my backpack onto my shoulder as I step out onto the gravel road. I swallow hard and focus on putting one foot in front of the other until I reach the spot where my dad is. The grass has started to grow back, but I can still see the outline of where the earth was dug up. I don't know how long I stand there just staring at his name, engraved so precisely into the sleek black stone with his "born" and "died" dates and "Loving Father, Scrabble Aficionado" carved underneath. He had insisted on that one.

I drop my backpack on the ground and, after double-checking that no one else is around, curl up on my side right there on the dirt, putting my palm onto the cool earth.

I search for the right thing to say, and my voice cracks a little as I utter the only thing I can think of.

"Hey."

Listen to Track Nine: "Hey."

Minutes, or maybe hours, go by as I tell my dad everything that has happened since I moved to L.A. I'm sure I look insane to anyone walking by, prostrated on the ground talking to no one, but it doesn't matter. And it would make for a great story to say that there was some gust of wind or something that made me feel like Dad's presence was here with me, but I don't, and that's okay. It's enough to just be able to be near him again.

"I'm so angry now, Dad," I find myself saying as I push myself up and sit cross-legged on the ground, leaning the side of my head on the gravestone and rubbing my eyes. "I knew I was going to be sad, but I didn't know I would be so angry. And I never thought I would be angry with you, but I am. I'm so mad at you for leaving me, and I don't know how to make it stop."

Suddenly, I don't feel like talking anymore. I pull my backpack toward me and unzip it. As I rifle around in the pockets for my chapstick, I'm surprised to discover a sketchpad. I take it out and gingerly set it on my lap, bending my knees to use my thighs as a surface to bear down on. I dig through the bottom of the bag and find a pencil. I close my eyes for a moment, letting out a shaky breath. Then, for the first time in months, I draw.

My dad's face is staring up at me. There are several smudges from where I wasn't able to catch a teardrop in time before it fell onto the page, but for the most part, it's good. I was scared I wouldn't remember the subtle nuances of how to shade around the nose or get the eyelashes just right, but muscle memory kicked in, and I am now looking at a full sketch of my smiling father. I trace his jaw with my finger, unable to keep from laughing a little. Shaking my head, I wonder what time it is. I must have left my phone back in the car. My stomach rumbles loudly, and a wave of hunger hits me. I stand up, my legs a little wobbly from sitting for so long.

An older-looking man is laying a wreath down on a grave nearby, and a family is gathered around another one a few rows of headstones away from me. I try to be as quiet as I can while I gather my stuff and put it into my backpack. I've made it halfway to my car when I pass a woman in a pair of yoga pants and a pink tank top sitting on a nearby bench, holding a bouquet of flowers. I have to do a double take, but there is no mistaking her.

It's my mother.

TWENTY-ONE

I look at her blankly, my mind trying to make sense of seeing her here in my town, near my dad's grave. She catches me looking at her and stands up shyly, setting the flowers down on the bench. I've never seen her looking so disheveled. She doesn't seem to have any makeup on. Her eyes are rimmed with red where she clearly has been crying, and her hair hangs in a limp ponytail. I watch warily as she walks toward me, taking the last few feet at a run as she throws her arms around my shoulders.

"Oh my God," she says into my neck. "I was so worried."

"What are you doing here?" I say coldly, my arms still hanging at my sides. She pulls away, sniffling a little.

"I just had a feeling this is where you would be," she says, her eyes searching my face as if to check me for cuts or bruises. "I can't explain it. So I chartered a plane and flew out here. You were already here when I arrived. When I saw . . . Well, I didn't want to bother you."

"How long have you been sitting there?"

"I don't know," she says, shrinking back a little in reaction to the ice in my voice. "Forty-five minutes maybe?"

"What the hell, Mother?" I snarl.

"What do you mean?" she says, looking both taken aback and slightly angry. "I should be asking you that. You take off without any warning, without letting anyone know, and in your brother's car, no less. What were you thinking?"

I pretend to look around dramatically.

"Should we do that again?" I ask venomously. "I want to make sure we get some good stuff for the cameras."

"What on earth are you talking about?" my mother asks, looking genuinely baffled.

"For your show, of course," I clarify. "Or should I say *our* show?"

For a moment my mother continues to give me a bewildered look. Then understanding dawns on her face and her hand flies to her mouth.

"Cam," she says in a muffled voice. "Oh no, Cam. You have it all wrong."

"I had a little chat with Vic," I say coolly. "Pretty insulting way to find out that I'm going to be a television star, but then I guess I should expect nothing less from you."

"Vic was at the house?"

"Oh, yes," I divulge. "She was, oh how did she put it . . . ah, right. 'Getting specs.'"

"That *bitch*," my mother says savagely as she shakes her head.

"Whatever," I sneer. "I was going to find out about the show eventually, you know."

"There is no show!" she says vehemently. "I turned it down weeks ago when Vic first approached me with the offer."

"You . . . what?"

"She came to me about it right around the time of your . . . well, what happened in the billiards room," she explains desperately, a pleading look in her eyes. "It was going to follow both me and Charlie, but there was really no way around involving you as well."

"So Charlie knew about it?" I cut in.

"Yes," my mother says simply. "He and I discussed it and immediately agreed to decline the offer."

"I don't understand," I say slowly. "Why would Vic come to the house and tell me the show was happening if you turned it down?"

My mother sighs dejectedly. "Because she is still pushing for us to change our minds. But it doesn't matter what she wants from now on because she is so fired."

I gawk at her, feeling too worn out to stand anymore. I walk over to the bench my mother vacated and move the flowers aside so I can plop down, leaning over and putting my head in my hands. After a moment, I sense my mother sit down next to me. Neither of us says anything for a while. When I finally sit up, she's looking across the gravel pathway at my dad's headstone, tears falling steadily down her face.

"I didn't think I would ever come back here after the funeral," she says softly. "I honestly didn't even think I'd be able to bring myself to come to the funeral at all."

"Well, you did," I say bitterly. "And you brought the paparazzi with you."

"For the last time, I didn't!" my mother bursts out angrily.

"But don't you get it?" I ask scathingly. "Whether or not you were aware ahead of time that they would be there doesn't matter. If you hadn't come, they wouldn't have had a reason to either. So you're still responsible for it, whether you liked it or not. Which I'm sure at least some part of you did."

"Why do you always assume the worst of me?" she accuses.

"How could I not assume the worst of the person who left me when I was a baby?" My mother gapes at me in stunned silence. I'm equally as surprised, though I try not to show it. I've never examined my feelings about my mother's early departure from our lives too closely, but as soon as the words fly out of my mouth, I'm certain they're true. I know I should stop, but there's something oddly satisfying about seeing the pain I'm feeling reflected in her eyes, and I say, "Really, Mother, didn't you figure out after you had Charlie how to prevent having another kid you weren't going to take care of?"

My mother makes a noise somewhere between a gasp and a sob, and I know I've gone too far.

"You," she chokes out. "Have no idea what you're talking about."

"It seems pretty straightforward to me," I say tightly, the irrational part of my brain refusing to back down. "You didn't want to give up the spotlight, and a baby wouldn't have fit into your fabulous lifestyle, so you left Dad to do it on his own."

"THAT'S NOT TRUE!" my mother cries shrilly. A woman standing at a nearby grave gives us a stern look, but I barely notice as I look skeptically at my mother.

"And what exactly about that isn't true?"

There's a defeated look on her face, and she swallows hard a few times before she continues. "When I met your father, I fell so hard so fast. He was unlike any man I had dated before, but that's what I loved about him. The men I had been with in L.A. always seemed to have an angle. They always wanted something from me. But not your father. He didn't care about the money or the fame —hell, he didn't even seem to care about my past. He saw me in a way that made me feel more like me than I had in a long time. And when I found out I was pregnant, I truly felt like I was ready to leave L.A. and live a normal, simple life in Preston.

"But after you were born, I panicked." My mother rubs a spot on her temple. "Cam, you have to understand. Back when I dropped out of college, I was so young and had no plan for my life when all of the sudden this charming, famous football player walks into the bar I was working at and starts paying attention to me. Me. I was a nobody. And then I wasn't, and it felt nice.

"When the tape leaked, I couldn't get out of bed for days. I was completely humiliated. And the media was so vicious. He and I were both on that tape, but I was the one being called a slut and a whore and a gold digger. But then Vic contacted me and said she could turn what happened to me into an opportunity to make some money. 'Build my own empire,' as she put it. If it was between that and going back to bartending with a ruined reputation . . . well, it was a no-brainer.

"I made a point to say yes to everything: brand deals, fragrance lines, television shows. I did it all, and to my shock, the offers just kept coming in. I know to you it probably seems like what I do is superficial and unimportant, but the only thing I have ever been good at is being a brand. It's my entire identity, my entire life. When it really hit me after you were born that I would have to give up everything I had worked so hard for if I moved to Preston, the idea of being a nobody again was devastating.

"So I begged your father to move to L.A. with me so that the three of us could be a family and I could continue to work, but he refused. He said his life was here. Deep down I already knew this place was too much a part of *his* identity for him to leave. He would have been absolutely miserable in L.A. But I also knew that as much as I loved him and as much as I loved you, I would have been equally as miserable here. Either path would lead to one of us resenting the other, and we didn't want that. And then there was you . . .

"There was no way we could have equal custody of you without constantly disrupting your life. So your father asked me for full custody with the plan of you coming to stay with me in L.A. during the summers and alternating holidays. He said he respected my decision about the type of life I wanted, but that you should be able to make your own choices someday when you were old enough about whether or not you wanted your life to be public. It killed me, but I knew he was right, so I did the hardest thing I have ever had to do. I agreed to let him raise you so that you could have a normal life."

My head has started to ache, almost like it's refusing to process this information. All I want is to crawl into my own bed and sleep so that maybe with some rest I can reconcile what my mother is telling me with the assumptions I've been making about her my whole life.

My mother takes a shuddering breath, closing her eyes as fresh tears trail down her cheeks. "When he called to tell me how sick he was, he made me promise that you would come and live with me after he . . . I know you think that I was the one who forced you to come to L.A., and of course that was what I wanted, but ultimately your dad was the one who insisted on it."

"Why did you never tell me any of this?" I manage to croak out. "If it was so hard for you to be away from me, why were you always too busy to spend time with me when I was in L.A.?"

"Because I was ashamed," my mother answers quietly, looking down at her hands. "Not a single day has gone by where I haven't questioned if I did the right thing by not moving here. It was easier to justify to myself when you were with your father and I knew you were doing so well, but when you were with me it was a constant reminder of the fact that I wasn't brave enough to give up my life in L.A. for the two of you. Plus you look so much like him. . . I loved your father, Cam. I have never loved anyone else the way I loved him."

My mother's voice breaks on the last word, and she looks away as she sobs pitifully. Slowly, I slide over and put an arm around her, dissolving into my own fresh tears.

We sit there for a while like that in silence, each lost in our own thoughts.

"Did you want to lay the flowers down?" I finally ask. My mother nods. She stands up and looks expectantly at me, but I shake my head. "You go."

She gives me a sad little smile before picking up the bouquet and making her way carefully over to Dad's gravestone. I watch as she gently places the flowers on the ground, her shoulders shaking as she cries. She kneels down and runs a hand over his name, tracing the letters with her fingers.

I scan my memories as I sit there, looking for any hints that she harbored feelings for my father all those years, but I don't find any. She kept that part of herself well hidden from me. I wonder what my life would have been like if we had gotten to be a family—me, my mother, my father, and Charlie. But thinking about the "what-ifs" just makes me too sad right now.

I stand up as she walks back toward me.

"So . . . what now?" I ask her.

My mother had taken a cab from the airport to the cemetery, so thankfully she's able to drive us in Charlie's car to get some dinner because I'm practically a zombie by the time we sit and order. I suggest we go somewhere slightly out of town as opposed to some of my old favorite spots. I'm not ready to run into anyone I know and have to explain why I'm here out of the blue looking like such a train wreck.

We book a hotel room in Preston for the night and an afternoon flight back to Los Angeles tomorrow. She's arranged for Charlie's car to be transported back to L.A., which I know must be expensive, but I'm selfishly relieved to not have to turn around and drive all the way back. I text Annie and tell her my mother and I are in town and to not ask me any questions about it right now, but I would love to meet up with her for breakfast. She messages back insisting we come over to her house so she can cook all of my favorites for us and that she won't take no for an answer.

My mother and I drive the short way to the hotel, and as soon as we walk into the room, I immediately drop my things on the floor and practically collapse into the nearest bed. I'm asleep almost as soon as my head hits the pillow.

When I open my eyes the next morning, I'm completely disoriented. I look over to see my mother sitting in the other bed, a cup of coffee in hand as she reads something on her laptop. She looks over and sees me.

"Good, you're awake," she says as she closes her computer. "How are you feeling?" She gets up and opens the door of the mini-fridge, pulling out two bottles of water. She offers one to me.

"Better," I answer, opening it and taking a sip.

"I brought you some fresh clothes," my mother goes on. I notice that it looks like she has already showered and is now back to looking like her usual perfectly put-together self, her hair in bouncing blonde curls and her makeup more minimal than usual but still flawless.

"You did?"

"I didn't know what you had with you," she explains as she rummages around in her suitcase. She pulls out one of my t-shirts and a pair of leggings.

"Perfect," I say in relief. After taking a shower myself, I quickly blow-dry my hair and put it into a ponytail, then change into the clothes my mother brought for me.

We travel the short distance to Annie's house, pulling into the driveway right on time. She flies out the front door and runs up to fling her arms around me.

"You have SO much explaining to do," she hisses into my ear. I just laugh and squeeze her tighter.

"You've met my mother before," I say when I finally pull away.

"It's good to see you again, Ms. Jenson," Annie says, giving my mother a friendly wave. "Come on in. I've got cinnamon rolls in the oven and the griddle is heating up for bacon."

"Oh, hell yes," I moan, letting Annie lead me and my mother into the house. Annie's mom is in the kitchen and gives me a big hug before pouring glasses of orange juice for us. She and my mom go and sit in the living room, giving me a chance to fill Annie in on the events of the past few days while she finishes cooking.

"Wow," she says, staring at me with wide eyes when I finish.

"Yeah."

"I mean, wow."

"I know."

"I can't believe you stole a car."

"Really?" I ask in disbelief. "That's your biggest takeaway from all of this?"

"I don't even know how to start unpacking the rest of it, love," she says, pulling the cinnamon rolls out of the oven. "I'm just glad you're in therapy now because you two have A LOT to work through. But for now, let's eat!"

After taking the last bite of my slice of bacon, I sit back in my chair and place a hand happily on my stomach.

"God, I miss you," I sigh, closing my eyes.

"I miss you too, Cam," Annie replies tenderly.

"I was actually talking to the cinnamon rolls," I say with a wink. Annie sticks her tongue out at me.

"Girls, I hate to cut the visit short but we have to be at the airport in an hour," my mother reminds me. I offer to help Annie with the dishes, trying to buy a little extra time.

"Maybe the next time you visit it could be for longer than twelve hours," Annie proposes. "And maybe you could give me a heads-up first. Oh, and maybe don't steal a car to do it."

"Still on that, huh?"

"Oh, I'll be on that forever," Annie says plainly. "It's funny now that I know that no one is pressing charges against you."

"Don't speak too soon," I groan. "I still haven't talked to Charlie. He is going to kill me."

"Yeah . . . probably," she agrees.

"Thanks for the support," I joke. She sets her dish towel down and turns to me, a serious look falling over her features.

"You know I support you no matter what, right?" she says solemnly. "I mean it. You can talk to me about anything. It sucks to know you didn't come to me when things have been so bad lately."

"It's not that I didn't want to talk to you about it," I tell her, my voice tight. "I just . . . couldn't. And lately it feels like I've mostly been reacting first, thinking later. Which I know is not good. I'm going to work on it, I promise."

Annie leans over to give me a quick side hug.

"It's going to be okay," she whispers. I don't answer for fear that if I do, I'll start crying again. When we finish, my mother waits in the car while we say our goodbyes.

"Well, this sucks," Annie says shakily. "I feel like I just said bye to you, and now I have to do it all over again."

"I know," I say glumly. "I'll be back soon, though."

"And I need to come visit you in L.A.," Annie replies. "I want to meet this Mei and make sure she's good enough to be your California best friend."

We give each other one more hug, then I get into the car quickly before I change my mind and petition my mother to just let me live with Annie and finish out my senior year here.

Up until the moment my mother and I board the plane, I brace myself for the crushing sense of emptiness that I felt the last time I was leaving Preston knowing it wasn't my home anymore. To my relief, it doesn't come. Maybe it's progress, or healing, or just knowing I have a lot of catching up to do when it comes to the years I've spent being unfairly resentful toward my mother. But as I look out the plane window and watch my hometown grow smaller and smaller below me, it feels way more like the start of something rather than the end.

TWENTY-TWO

The second we walk in the front door Jim bounds over to me like he hasn't seen me in weeks.

"Hey, buddy!" I coo, reaching down and wrapping my arms around him. Jim immediately wriggles out so he can nuzzle me in the face. He even manages to lick my mother's hand when she isn't looking.

"I've got to get ready for a dinner meeting," she says, patting Jim on the top of the head. "I can cancel it though, if you want me to."

"No, that's okay," I answer. "Do you want to have lunch together tomorrow?"

"I would love that," she says, smiling at me before starting up the stairs.

"Hey, Mom?" I call after her. She turns back to look at me. "I'm really sorry. For disappearing and scaring you, I mean. I'm sorry about everything."

She walks back down to me and gives me a hug. "I love you."

"I love you, too."

I follow her up the stairs so I can put my bag down in my room, then set off to look for Charlie. I spot him lounging in a pool chair in the backyard. I take a moment to steel myself before walking outside. He's got earbuds in and sunglasses on, and I'm tempted to say 'yams' as I try to approach without startling him. Instead, I plant myself in the lounge chair next to his, stretching my legs out and looking at the water. Slowly, Charlie turns his head to look at me, removing his headphones and shades. I can feel his eyes boring into me and I wince.

"Hello," I say lamely.

"Seriously?" Charlie retorts. "Is that all you have to say for yourself?"

"Look, I know you're pissed at me," I say, turning to face him. "But I promise there isn't a scratch on your car, and I'll make sure the tank is filled up whenever the tow truck brings it—"

"Cam," Charlie says, shaking his head. "Do you really think I care about the car?"

I gape at him for a moment.

"Uhhh . . . yes?"

"I don't give a shit about the car," Charlie says heatedly, coming over to sit on the end of my chair. "Do you have any idea how terrifying it was to get that call from Mom telling me you were missing? For all we knew, you could have been kidnapped by some crazy stalker or had been in an accident and were lying in a ditch somewhere."

I had been so ready for Charlie to be angry about his car that I hadn't even considered this is what he would be upset about. I lower my eyes, feeling like the biggest jerk in the entire world.

"I'm sorry," I mumble. Charlie puts his hands on my shoulders, forcing me to look back up at him.

"Mom said you found out about the show and that's why you left," he says, his eyes serious. "I understand why you were upset, but you can't just fly off the handle every time you get angry. You didn't even ask me or Mom about it."

"I know," I say a little defensively. "But after what happened with *Chick About Town* you have to see why it was pretty believable that Mom would have done something like this."

"I get it," Charlie says. "But that still isn't an excuse to take it as far as you did."

"I'm sorry," I say. "I really am. But I think . . . maybe things are going to be better now. I have a lot to tell you."

"I'm all ears," Charlie says as he returns to his own chair. "Though I will say, you better be glad you took the Audi instead of my BMW. I would have disowned the half of you that is related to me if you had."

I snort. "Come on, Char. I may be a petty criminal now, but I'm not stupid."

I try not to leave the house much over the next few days. At the emergency therapy session my mother scheduled for me the day after we got back, you would have thought patients came in all the time and told Dr. Landry that they hijacked their brother's car and drove to a different state without telling anyone because they thought their mother was going to force them to be on a reality show. He just listened and nodded, occasionally asking me a question, but for the most part he was pretty unruffled by the whole thing. I almost wanted to start adding in crazy fake details just to see if I could get more of a reaction out of him, but I resisted the temptation.

At Dr. Landry's behest, my mother and I sat down and had probably the most productive conversation we've ever had with each other. I can tell that me knowing about how things actually ended between her and Dad is a weight off her shoulders. She seems lighter now, like she doesn't have to try so hard to be perky all the time. We spent hours laughing and crying as we swapped stories about Dad, like we're both finally able to talk about and remember him instead of constantly avoiding the topic.

To my surprise, I got a text from Milo saying he heard I was back, and he was glad I was okay. He must have gotten the information from Mei, who I messaged after our flight landed to say that I was fine and that I promised to fill her in on everything.

For lack of being able to think of the right thing to respond, I sent Milo a thumbs-up emoji, which is definitely *not* the right thing to respond. I've been trying not to think about how I left things with him, what with professing my unrequited love and all.

I've also been drawing almost nonstop the last few days. Something that was dormant inside of me has reawakened, and all I've wanted to do is work on my comic book series. I even finally scheduled a few college tours, though I'm not sold on the idea of going to school on the east coast anymore. It's a weird feeling—I'm finding my way back to some of the parts of me I lost when Dad got sick, but they're slightly different than before. I think I'm okay with that. It's like painting a picture, then throwing it away and trying to recreate it again. Even if you use all the same colors and paint the same subject, it's not going to be an exact replica of the first one. But that doesn't mean it won't still be good.

One morning a few days after returning to L.A., I feel up to the task of catching Mei up not only about my little road trip but about what happened with Milo, so I text her to see if she wants to meet up. She replies almost immediately.

Mei: *omg yessssss, but come over! we have doughnuts.*

I hesitate for a moment before replying.

Me: *will your brother be there? i kind of don't want to run into him. long story.*

Mei: *you're safe, he has a double today*

Me: *then I'll see you in 15 minutes*

"I'm going to Mei's for a bit," I say, popping my head into Charlie's studio. "Do you want me to bring you back some lunch?"

"Oooh, yes," he says from his design table. "I'm craving sushi."

"I can make that happen," I say obligingly. "Mind if I borrow the car?"

I had concluded after getting back that it was time to find a happy medium between being chauffeured everywhere and attempting to drive myself across the country, but seeing as how I don't have my own car, currently my only option is to borrow one.

"I knew there was going to be a catch," Charlie says, putting a hand over his heart and shooting me a look of feigned indignation.

"But I'm asking permission," I point out. "Personally, I think that shows real character growth."

"You are the worst," he retorts. "Fine. But I want lobster rolls."

The doorbell hasn't even finished ringing before Mei is ushering me into her house. I barely manage to grab a few doughnuts from a box in the kitchen as she hurries me up to her room and shuts the door.

"Tell. Me. Everything," she says as we both sit on her bed. "And no, you can't eat your doughnuts first. Multi-task."

So, as I eat, I do tell her everything, starting with my last conversation with Milo.

"And he didn't say anything?" she says, eyes narrowing behind her red glasses.

"Nothing," I confirm, picking sprinkles off my doughnut dejectedly.

"Ugh, my brother can be such an idiot sometimes. I don't know what the hell that was about, but he's been super on edge lately, especially the days when you were missing."

I look up at her. "Really?"

"Oh yeah," she nods eagerly. "I think he was really worried about you."

I don't really know what to say to this, so I forge ahead with my story about my encounter with Vic and taking off for Georgia. When I get to the revelations about my mother, Mei actually has tears in her eyes. By the time I'm done, we're both dabbing our eyes with Kleenex and poking fun at each other for being so sensitive.

"Wow," Mei says once we have composed ourselves. "Just, wow."

"I know," I agree. Then I turn to fully face her. "Mei, I owe you an apology."

"Me?" she replies, looking confused.

"Yes. I know we haven't known each other that long, but if I hadn't had you as a friend since moving here, I think I would have lost my mind. Well, lost it more." I grin at her sheepishly. "But I've been so caught up in my own stuff lately that I haven't been a good friend and spent enough time asking about you and your life."

"Oh," Mei says, looking startled. "I mean, there's not that much to tell."

"What about Eric? Anything new there?"

"Well, he did ask me to officially be his girlfriend the other night," she says, her eyes lighting up.

"And you didn't text me?" I ask incredulously.

"I just knew you had a lot going on," she says with a little shrug.

"You better give me every single detail."

We spend the next few hours talking about Eric, then about the productions Winston Academy's theatre department just announced it will be putting on next year. When Mrs. Chen knocks lightly on the door and tells Mei they need to leave for a dentist appointment, we all head downstairs together.

"I'm really glad you're okay," Mei says after walking me to my car. "But next time you impulsively decide to do something so dramatic, you better include me. That's the kind of life experience I need in order to become a better actor."

I laugh. "Deal."

. . .

Not quite ready to go home yet, I decide to go sit in the park for a while and draw. As I'm pulling in, I see a food truck has set up in the parking lot. I purchase an ambitious number of street tacos, then start wandering around looking for a place to sit and eat. One of my usual benches is unoccupied, so I set my backpack on it and begin pulling out all of the to-go boxes and sauces. Just as I'm about to start on my first taco, a soft voice interrupts me.

"Yams."

I freeze, then look up. Milo is standing a few feet away, hands in his pockets as usual as he gives me an assessing look.

"Hey," I say, hastily setting my to-go box down and standing up.

"Mei told me you were here." He regards me for a second, then closes the distance between us to pull me into a hug. For a second I don't respond, caught completely off-guard. Then I slowly wrap my arms around him in return as he says roughly, "I thought it was my fault."

"Thought what was your fault?" I ask, my voice muffled against his chest.

Milo backs away looking flustered.

"When we were here and you . . . you said you have feelings for me," Milo exhales, eyes wild as he searches my face. "And I froze and couldn't say anything back. Then the next thing I know Mei is telling me you're missing and I . . . thought it was my fault."

"Well, that was awfully presumptuous of you."

"I can't tell if that's a joke."

"I think it was one of those jokes where the thing that the person says is true but they deliver it in a way that adds levity to the situation." Milo's eyes continue to bore into mine. "Or not. But really, you don't have to feel guilty. I had a breakdown for entirely different reasons than you. Mostly."

"Oh," Milo shakes his head a little, his hair flopping over one eye. My hand twitches a little, wanting to push it out of the way.

"We're good," I assure him, trying to keep my voice light. "I'm

good. It's nice of you to worry about your sister's friends like that."
Milo continues to stare fixedly at me. Growing irritated, I roll my
eyes as I say, "Dude, whaaaaat?"

The next thing I know Milo's hands are on my face and he's
kissing me. Before I can comprehend what is happening, my lips
automatically part in response. Then my brain catches up and I
step back quickly.

"Wait," I say, narrowing my eyes at Milo, who looks just as
stunned as I feel. "What are you doing?"

"I'm kissing you," Milo says roughly.

"And what about Leighton?" I ask, my heart thundering. "I
thought you were still hung up on her."

"I thought I was for a bit," Milo says impatiently. "But I'm not
anymore."

"What changed?"

A little voice in my head is screaming at me to stop being an
idiot and asking questions and just kiss him again, but I hold
myself back. Milo takes a step toward me.

"You were right," he says quietly. "There is something here.
I've felt it since the first day you came into the diner if I'm being
honest with myself. But I couldn't just end a three-year relationship unless I was really sure. Plus, with everything you were going
through, I thought you needed the space."

"And now?"

"And now if you want space, or time, or if you've changed your
mind, I'll respect that," he says firmly, then his lips curl up in a
small smile. "But I'm crazy about you too, you absolute fucking
ignoramus."

He has barely gotten the last word out before I grab his shirt
and pull him toward me, kissing him desperately the way I have
wanted to for so long now. He reaches up to cup my face in his
hands, his gentle touch a contrast to the urgency of his lips.
When we finally pull away, his face is flushed, and he's grinning
broadly.

"My tacos are getting cold," I say breathlessly. Milo's eyebrows shoot up, but I point at my to-go box still sitting on the bench.

"How are you thinking about food right now?" he asks, shaking his head at me as we sit down on the bench.

"You've met me, right?" I joke, offering the box to him. He smiles and leans over to quickly brush his lips over mine before picking up a taco. I'm positively beaming as I get one for myself.

"This is perfect," I inform him happily as I take a bite.

"I assume you're referring to the taco?"

"Obviously."

That night, Charlie and I are sitting on the couch sharing a bag of pretzels and watching some British reality show he has gotten hooked on.

"Okay, what is up with you?" he says, pausing the television.

"What do you mean?"

"You keep randomly smiling. It's weird."

"Milo and I kissed."

"What?!" Charlie cries, reaching for a pillow and smacking me in the face with it.

"Hey!" I exclaim as my eyes water. "What was that for?"

"That was for letting me watch three episodes of this beautiful dumpster fire before bringing it up."

"Geez," I say, rubbing my stinging nose.

"I want to know everything."

Just as I open my mouth to reply, my mother comes in from the kitchen.

"Hi," she says cheerily, her blonde hair bouncing a little as she sits down next to Charlie. "What are you two up to?"

I debate waiting until Charlie and I are alone before telling him about my afternoon with Milo. But whereas a few months ago I would have clammed up immediately and retreated to my room, now the idea of letting my mother into my personal life a little doesn't bother me.

"Hey, Mom," I say. "The guy I like finally made a move today. Let me tell you about him."

Listen to Track Ten: "Cautiously Optimistic"

Acknowledgments

First and foremost, thank you to every single one of you that streamed my songs, added them to your playlists, mailed me the most heartfelt and beautiful letters and drawings, bought a piece of my merch, left a sweet comment on one of my videos, got a tattoo of my lyrics, came to see me on one of the rare occasions I play live, and, of course, decided to pick up this book and take a chance that I can write more than just song lyrics. Whether you've been with me on this ride for ten minutes or ten years, you are the reason I get to do what I love.

To Mark: It is so fun doing life with you. I couldn't imagine having a more supportive husband, whether it's wanting to hear my new songs when I come home from recording sessions, forcing your students to listen to my music, reading and rereading this book over the last seven years, or simply never discouraging me from executing any of the ambitious plans and ideas I've had for my career. I love you.

To my family: Mom and Dad, thank you for encouraging our creativity and never putting any limitations on what the possibilities could be for our careers. The only reason I've been able to do this for a living is because you never pigeonholed us into majors or jobs just because they were more practical, and I don't thank you for that enough. Kate, you are more delectable than a million Crumbl cookies. Aunt Bee and Kelly, thank you for coming to all of our plays and performances through the years and for sharing my music with your friends.

To my friends: I don't want to brag, but there are just too many of you to name :). But you know who you are. A special thank you to Megan Duke for being my book buddy all of these years.

To Daniel: As with everything we have created together, I'm so proud of the album we made for this book. Thank you for being such an incredible collaborator and friend.

To Casey Bond and Quinn Loftis: It is so inspirational the way you each have created such a beautiful community of your readers and how generous you are with your time and knowledge. Thank you for the incredibly kind endorsement quotes for *The Have Not* and being the kind of authors and people that any new writer should aspire to emulate.

Thank you to Jennifer Rees for editing this story and giving me such positive and encouraging feedback.

And finally, thank you to each person who read some iteration of this book over the years and gave me your thoughts and feedback so that I could feel confident enough to put this out into the world. It's a way bigger ask than just listening to a four-minute song, and I'm so appreciative that you took the time to do it.

I don't really know how to wrap these kinds of things up gracefully, so I'll just borrow what I say at the end of my YouTube videos: I love you guys, and I'll see you next time!

About the Author

Beth Crowley first began sharing her original music on YouTube in 2011 and has since released more than 100 songs and garnered hundreds of millions of streams, with listeners describing her as knowing "how to put a finger on the pulse of pain" and "having a way of singing what is hard to say." Drawing inspiration for more than thirty of her songs from novels, Beth always knew that when she inevitably wrote a book of her own, she would want to write music to go with it. Her debut novel The Have Not includes an accompanying soundtrack of original songs written to provide the reader/listener with a unique experience combining Beth's two passions: music and storytelling.

facebook.com/bethcrowleymusic

x.com/bethjcrowley

instagram.com/bethjcrowley